Jordan moved over to the sink, turned on the hot tap and ran her fingers under the water, testing the temperature.

He watched her carefully, and knew without a doubt she would. "Let it run for a minute. Don't give up yet."

Her eyes met his. "There you go, reading my mind again. I wasn't giving up."

How many times had he said that to her as a kid? At some point, someone had convinced her quitting was the only option when things didn't work, but Clay had never gotten that message. Whatever was broken could be made right with enough time and attention, even the hot water and the cranky old marina cash register.

The words were achingly familiar.

Her cheer when the water turned hot made him laugh. "I guess it really is the little things, isn't it?"

She enthusiastically scrubbed her hands, even though there was no soap, but he decided to follow her lead.

Dear Reader,

Most of us understand the bittersweet emotions that accompany going home again after time away. Maybe your favorite restaurant has closed or new owners painted the prettiest house in the old neighborhood the wrong color. Everything seems smaller because you've grown.

In *Her Cowboy's Promise*, Clay Armstrong and Jordan Hearst are returning to Prospect, the small town located high in the Colorado Rockies where they spent one summer vacation working together. Clay is struggling under the demands of his growing business, his partnership and his family. He just wants some peace. Finding Jordan right next door again is an unexpected opportunity to get answers about that summer. At sixteen, misfit Jordan swore she would never return to Prospect, but it may be the place she'd been searching for her whole life, with the cowboy who feels like home.

Thank you for joining me on my return to Prospect, Colorado. To find out more about my books and what's coming next, visit me at CherylHarperBooks.com.

Cheryl

HEARTWARMING

Her Cowboy's Promise

Cheryl Harper

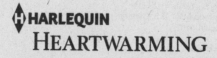

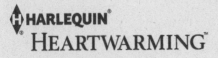

ISBN-13: 978-1-335-47548-0

Her Cowboy's Promise

Copyright © 2023 by Cheryl Harper

Recycling programs
for this product may
not exist in your area.

For questions and comments about the quality of this book,
please contact us at CustomerService@Harlequin.com.

Harlequin Enterprises ULC
22 Adelaide St. West, 41st Floor
Toronto, Ontario M5H 4E3, Canada
www.Harlequin.com

Printed in U.S.A.

Cheryl Harper discovered her love for books and words as a little girl, thanks to a mother who made countless library trips and an introduction to Laura Ingalls Wilder's Little House books. Whether the stories she reads are set in the prairie, the American West, Regency England or earth a hundred years in the future, Cheryl enjoys strong characters who make her laugh. Now, Cheryl spends her days searching for the right words while she stares out the window and her dog, Jack, snoozes beside her. And she considers herself very lucky to do so.

For more information about Cheryl's books, visit her online at cherylharperbooks.com or follow her on Twitter, @cherylharperbks.

Visit the Author Profile page at Harlequin.com for more titles.

CHAPTER ONE

THE LAST TIME Jordan Hearst had flopped down on the bed in this small room, she'd been sixteen going on thirty and angry enough to vow that she'd never return to the Majestic Prospect Lodge again. After losing her mother and being forced to move away to California from Denver, her summer exile here at the "rustic" fishing lodge had seemed the final straw. The one she'd never recover from.

Her father's insistence that she cut all ties with the "wild" friends she'd managed to make in the midst of that was completely unfair. Skipping class to head to the beach with the kids who had cars and access to unlocked liquor cabinets had saved her sanity even if it destroyed her GPA. His plan to "protect" her and her college hopes had required cutting all ties with those friends and spending the summer safe in far away small-town Colorado under the positive influence of her great-aunt Sadie.

Everything that summer made Jordan angry, but her older and younger sisters, Sarah and Brooke, had been surviving the move without making any waves. Everything Jordan did caused ripples, so her "summer vacation" in Prospect, Colorado, meant a healthy distance from bad influences, a guaranteed job at the Majestic's lakeside marina, and plenty of fresh air and open space to cool her temper.

It was also one more decision someone had taken from Jordan.

That day, when her father deposited her at the lodge, the unfairness had burned hot and sure, so Jordan had ignored her father's goodbye. Instead, she'd glared at the glossy poster for the Colorado Cookie Christmas Television Special until he'd given up on getting a goodbye and left.

Jordan smiled wryly now, and smoothed the poster she'd taken down from the wall. Sadie Hearst, the Colorado Cookie Queen of television and cookbook fame, flashed a brilliant smile. She was wearing the red gingham apron as always, but a Santa hat had replaced her usual white Stetson. Sadie had always been ageless, so it was hard to guess how old she would have been in the photo.

How could she be gone?

Jordan rolled the poster carefully and put it on top of the box she'd finished packing.

Thank goodness for Jordan's Summer of Exile and especially for Sadie.

As soon as the door closed behind Patrick Hearst, Sadie had made some things very clear to Jordan. First, being mad was one thing, and no one could tell her to feel differently, but kicking the furniture and crumpling the Lady of the Lake quilt her mother had made to show how angry she was? That would end there and then. They, like her, deserved better treatment. Jordan's glare had accomplished exactly nothing against Sadie's skill and experience with a snarl of her own. She and Sadie had squared off more than once that summer, but it was easy to look back and see how the visit had changed her forever.

Her great-aunt's overwhelming love for both Jordan and what life had to offer had been exactly what she'd needed then.

Still, Jordan had managed to keep her promise to herself not to return to the Majestic until this moment.

Sadie had packed up and moved to LA

after that summer, and the lodge had been closed, boarded up for almost fifteen years since the last manager had quit. Much of the place had been frozen in time, like this small bedroom in Sadie's apartment on the back of the lodge, where that poster had been hanging all this time. A souvenir of the amazing career Sadie had built.

Jordan waved away the dust motes floating in front of her face, doing her best to ignore the heartache—the reminder that Sadie was no longer going to be near to set Jordan straight when she needed it.

That loss was scary.

Especially facing it as an unemployed thirty-something who should be a lot further along in her career—that is, as soon as she chose one.

At least Sadie had left the Majestic Prospect Lodge to Jordan *and* her sisters. Her great-aunt had done so, though, without any direction as to what she wanted done with the place. Typical Sadie, wily as ever. She might have been raised here on the shores of Key Lake outside a tiny old mining town, but their great-aunt had built her Cookie Queen Corporation through charm, sharp business intuition and following her heart. Baking and the ability to entertain crowds had taken her from a public access show filmed in her Rocky Mountain hometown into the big leagues of food television, with homes in LA and New York.

Jordan had chosen her latest job with a tech company providing project and security testing because the salary was fine. Spending days staring at a computer screen from her spot in the middle of a cube farm was neither interesting nor fine. However, it had paid the bills comfortably, leaving plenty for good restaurants and the attractions of Southern California with the group of friends she'd collected.

Quitting because her sister needed help in Prospect had been impulsive, but no one who knew her was shocked. Jordan had learned her lesson about making her own choices early on, so when her boss told her no and she knew the answer had to be yes, Jordan had followed her gut.

Unfortunately, the rent on Jordan's apartment was due soon. And while the inheritance from Sadie would include funds after her homes and other assets were sold and divided among her seventeen nieces and nephews—her favorite "do-gooders, no-gooders and rapscallions"—it wouldn't be available to Jordan for some time.

Leaving the Majestic to Sarah, Jordan and Brooke, instead of any of their other cousins, had been a valuable gift and Sadie's last shot at guiding them...somewhere.

It was beautiful acreage on the shores of hidden, pristine, shining Key Lake.

Selling it for vacation home development would make all three of them wealthy enough to follow their own dreams.

But it would also destroy this piece of their history and Sadie's legacy.

Right now, the sisters were in limbo, neither planning a future for the once-cozy lodge, nor selling it. Instead, they were giving the real estate agent time to find the nearly impossible: a buyer who wanted to run the Majestic as it was. That buyer would need funds to renovate and an affinity for small-town life.

It had been weeks since they'd given the agent the go-ahead to list the lodge.

So far, Erin Chang hadn't had a single showing.

The waiting was getting to Jordan. Prospect didn't offer much in the way of distraction.

But this place needed enough work to keep

them all busy. Jordan inhaled deeply, immediately experienced the tickle of decades of dust and sneezed loudly enough to shake the rafters twice in a row.

"Dramatic much?" Sarah drawled from the hallway.

"Did you know if you don't shut your eyes when you sneeze, your eyeballs might pop out?" Jordan nodded. "It's true. I read it on the internet, so you can trust that information." The broken fingernail on her ring finger scraped denim as she wiped her hands on her jeans. She chose to view the nail as a badge of honor, proof of her dedication and effort. "Ready to load up boxes?"

"Yes, let's see how many we can get in the SUV." Sarah rubbed her forehead, leaving behind a smudge of dust. "I'm not going to test your sneezing theory. I want my eyes to stay where they are."

So far, Sarah had negotiated a sale of Sadie's undeveloped pastureland to the ranch owners next door; the buildings, prime lakeshore access, marina and land behind the lodge going up into the foothills of the mountains remained. If Erin Chang failed to find the buyer they dreamed of, they'd have to sell to someone who'd tear the lodge down to build a luxury home or…

That was the problem, finding any other option that fit their lives.

Brooke's frequent requests for updates on whether any new buyers had contacted the agent suggested she was ready to sell as soon as possible. It was worth a lot of money, and life in New York was expensive, even without her husband's political aspirations to finance. Brooke's interest made perfect sense.

Selling the lodge meant clearing out all of Sadie's remaining memorabilia. Jordan and her sister Sarah had been working to inventory and box up anything of value.

Sarah had matched every one of Jordan's hours, and together, they'd made progress clearing the Majestic of Sadie's things, but it was an exhausting job. They were both excited about returning to the bed-and-breakfast in town, Bell House, for hot showers and cold drinks. Jordan picked up a stack of two boxes and followed Sarah through the short hallway to where Sarah's SUV was parked behind the lodge.

At one time, the vacation spot had been no-frills—clean but simple rooms for people and families who'd spend all their time out on the lake. Now? The bare bones were still there and mostly solid, but the rest of the place needed a lot of TLC.

Siding repairs.

A new roof.

Landscaping.

A critter catcher.

Possibly a paranormal expert to remove whatever had made crashing noises in the restaurant's commercial kitchen and occasionally wafted the smell of sugar cookies through the air.

If they sold the lodge, all of that would be someone else's problem. Jordan had made the decision the day she'd returned to the lodge that she would do everything she could to make the Majestic shine, so that if they managed to get an interested buyer to Prospect, they would understand it needed renovation, not demolition.

As long as the new Majestic was improved, not razed and rebuilt, erasing all of their history and Sadie Hearst, she and her sisters would be content.

"I can't get used to how beautiful these trees are right now," Sarah murmured as soon as they stepped outside. "Have you ever seen colors like this?"

"Only in pictures. Movies." Jordan studied the golds and reds that formed a backdrop for the lodge. If the dry wood siding could be revived and the bare flower beds restored, this sunny day would be perfect for promotional shots, advertising the Majestic as the perfect autumn getaway.

After they'd settled the boxes in the back of the SUV, Jordan threw her arm over Sarah's shoulder. "How're the ideas for museum displays coming along?" Sadie's larger-than-life personality and career that included TV shows and appearances, bestselling cookbooks, name-brand appliances and a women's Western-wear line meant there were pieces of history here that no one wanted to lose, no matter what they decided to do with the lodge. Sarah's newest position for the Cookie Queen Corporation was cataloging and curating the collection for a to-be-determined museum location. Luckily, Prospect had plenty of storefronts available in the historic, Old West downtown that drew tourists.

"Well, I know cousin-slash-Cookie Queen executive Michael is going to want a full accounting of what we found here, in case any of it works for the displays in the headquarters' lobby. I'm doing my best to make an inventory of what we've packed up, so that when I get back to LA, I can find things and organize quickly." Sarah shut the car door. "I'll email him this inventory. If all goes to plan, he'll have identified specific pieces he wants to see, streamlining the entire process. That may free up some time to figure out what to do with my condo." Sarah tapped the clipboard she'd discovered in their great-aunt's desk the week before. "This has been helpful."

"Since you shouted 'eureka' as if you'd struck a vein of silver when you uncovered that," Jordan said, "I believe you." Her older sister hadn't had her normal time for strategizing and planning, so finding a usable organizational tool had seemed like a gift from above, no doubt.

Sarah laughed. "Sadie would say I'm 'micromanaging' again. Are you getting tired of my micromanaging, Jordie?"

Actually, she was filled with compassion for her frequently annoying older cousin, Michael. He'd better get on board with Sarah's program if he knew what was good for him.

In her mind, Jordan referred to this as Sarah's

"bustling mode." Where she bustled from one location to another, each step determined, and all her decisions were forceful and final.

If Sadie were still around, Jordan would make sure to tell her that Sarah had learned to manage by watching her. Their great-aunt had been filled with the same energy and determination, as well as a bubbling optimism.

All three of the Hearst sisters had inherited that determination, or what Sadie called "cussed stubbornness," but they showed it differently. Sarah assessed carefully. Sarah planned. Sarah executed.

Like a victorious general conquering enemy territory.

Jordan? She had two speeds: stop and go. That's it. Proceeding carefully made her itchy, and waiting was the worst. Sometimes, being unpredictable worked out to her benefit, too. Unfortunately, she tended to run away from things as fast as she ran toward them.

"I'm taking your extended silence as confirmation that you're ready for me to leave town. I'm coming back, you know. You're going to be bored without me." Sarah moved around her to toss the clipboard onto the passenger seat that would hold her sister's suitcase on her drive home to LA. "You've been working nonstop. You have to be tired, too. I bet you're ready to kick back and relax."

"I guess you don't agree I can take care of business here without your watchful eye," Jordan muttered under her breath. The last thing she wanted was to argue with Sarah before she left Colorado. It would be weeks before she'd see her older sister again.

Although Sarah was keen to get back to Prospect quickly.

The fact that her older sister had raced through falling in love and was turning the corner toward until-death-do-us-part with Wes Armstrong had made the lodge decision even more interesting. Meanwhile, Jordan and Wes, who was the local lawyer overseeing the lodge property in Sadie's absence, could handle anything that came up with the real estate agent. If they managed to get an offer, Jordan could confer with her sisters over the phone to make any decisions. Easy.

"I know you don't want to leave Prospect," Jordan said. "Or you don't want to be gone any longer than necessary."

Sarah sighed. "If Sadie were here…" She and Jordan laughed.

"The way she would hoot and yell, 'I told you so,'" Jordan added. "How many times did she tell you to fall for a cowboy when we were kids? It didn't make any sense. We lived in LA. What good would a cowboy do us even if we found one? And then she always told me…" Well, no one needed to know what Sadie had told her about the risks of charming, chivalrous cowboys during the Summer of Exile. Teenage Jordan might have forgotten her vow to avoid Prospect for the rest of her life and jumped headfirst into love otherwise.

Sadie's warnings had protected a certain cowboy as much as they had Jordan.

"I don't know that there is anyone else in this world who could turn what's happened into a victory like this. She got us back to the mountains she loved, when I said I never would return, and then you go and fall head-over-sneakers for a cowboy."

When her sister didn't argue that last fact, Jordan knew Sarah was a goner. Smitten. Never to see single again.

"Does a Colorado Cookie Queen museum make sense? In Prospect?" Sarah chewed her bottom lip. "Am I doing this to satisfy my need to move here because of that cowboy?"

She'd successfully worked out a deal with Michael, who was stepping up to lead the Cookie Queen Corporation. In exchange for curating pieces of Sadie's memorabilia for the corporate headquarters, the rest would find a permanent home or small tourist spot somewhere in Prospect. Michael had agreed to pay a generous salary and rent on a Colorado Cookie Queen museum. There wasn't much of a downside for Sarah here.

Jordan shrugged. "So what if you are?" Sarah followed her as she motioned toward the sparkling lake they could glimpse from the parking lot.

Jordan didn't see a problem either way. Life and shepherding her three great-nieces had taken Sadie away from her rustic home in Prospect to fancy places in LA and New York; her death was bringing the Hearsts back home.

"It's going to be expensive if I'm doing this museum on a whim," Sarah murmured. "If the place doesn't draw visitors, how long will Michael bankroll it? I'll be back at square one, needing a job and a place to live."

Common sense was necessary here. Sarah depended on Jordan to tell her the truth at all times.

Jordan edged closer to where the water lapped at the banks. The days and nights were cooling, but the water was cold all year long. She could still remember the shock of running full speed ahead and leaping into the lake when she was a kid.

"Michael's sentimental bone is missing. If he calculates some value in preserving and curating a collection of Sadie's memorabilia for her fans and the customers who buy Cookie Queen–branded products, there has to be a solid, long-lasting angle for the business. You know the rest of the family wants to keep Sadie's memory alive, too. What better way to do that?"

Sarah opened her mouth to argue.

The weird grumbling noises her sister made told Jordan she'd won this round.

All three of them were sore losers.

"Go to LA. Start working through the collection Sadie's lawyer had collected from her LA house and New York apartment. Take the step that's in front of you." Jordan inhaled slowly as she heard those words in Sadie's voice. It was good advice. She'd never forgotten it, and every now and then, since the day Sadie had forced her to listen and understand instead of staging a protest in the spare bedroom with the beautiful purple quilt and Cookie Queen poster, it popped back up when she needed it.

Jordan had been lost that summer.

Sadie had cut through the noise in her head with that piece of advice: *take the step that's in front of you.*

Now Sarah needed to hear it, too.

Jordan could see the perfect answer cantering down through the Rocking A pasture that lined the lake, a shiny black horse trailing behind his. After the sale of the land to the Rocking A, Wes Armstrong's first order of business was to make sure that the gate between the Rocking A and the lodge was in good working order.

Since Sarah's cowboy who lived next door obviously planned to use it frequently.

"Oh, great, here comes your boyfriend," Jordan murmured, channeling her inner teen angst to annoy Sarah.

"With Starla," Sarah said.

Her tone was the same as if she'd said, "With a dozen roses, a winning lottery ticket and a hot pizza," which would be the most roman-

tic way a man could ride into Jordan's life...
no riding required. She didn't do horse things.

Jordan watched her sister dig around in her
pocket to fish out her keys, feet fidgeting as
if she was preparing to race across the yel-
lowing grass and hurl herself romantically
into Wes's arms.

Sarah shoved her keys at Jordan as Wes
stopped, a nice six feet away or so. That was
fine. Horses were acceptable at that distance.

"Arrow told me that Starla wanted to take
a trip up to Larkspur Pass. Would you like
to join us?" Wes asked Sarah, who was already nodding and on her way. Wes slid out
of Arrow's saddle and waited to give Sarah
a boost up onto the beautiful black horse the
Rocking A stabled for the Hearsts as a part
of their purchase terms for the pasture.

Sarah didn't need much help into the saddle. She rode as beautifully as she did most
things.

It was hard being her younger sister sometimes.

"Hey, Wes," Jordan said as she watched
him check to make sure her sister was secure.

"Sorry, Jordan, I forgot my manners." Wes
stepped closer to wrap his arm around her

shoulder. They'd progressed to hugs as greetings, which was fine, because it was clear that they were going to be family someday. "Your sister didn't give me enough time to properly greet you right away. If I don't catch up with her, she and Starla will ride off into the sunset without me."

Jordan nodded. She understood. Tackling more than one Hearst sister at a time was tricky. Good thing Brooke had become thoroughly citified and clung to the New York burbs. "I get it. Sarah's a terrible influence."

His chuckle was nice.

"Why don't you head back to Prospect now?" Sarah said as she took the baseball cap Wes pulled out of his back pocket for her and tugged it on to cover her eyes. "You've worked so hard, Jordie."

Hearing her sister say that boosted Jordan's failing energy, not that she'd tell Sarah that. They both knew how much work there was left to do inside the lodge. "A warm shower would be nice."

Jordan didn't need to hear Wes and Sarah's telepathic conversation to know that he was asking whether Sarah had changed her mind about having a plumber check on the hot water at the lodge. They'd discovered it wasn't working when they were gathering Sadie's memorabilia, but the three sisters had agreed not to put a dime into the lodge, since they were likely going to have to sell it to someone who'd only tear it down.

"A working shower would mean we'd save the money we're spending on lodging at Bell House while we're settling everything here." Jordan didn't whistle, but she pasted the most innocent expression she could manage on her face.

"Your sister is making a valid point there," Wes said to Sarah.

Jordan's opinion of her someday-brother-in-law improved in an instant. Taking her side was an excellent personality trait, she thought.

"Fine," Sarah groaned. "I'll tell Brooke we authorized the repair, but you don't need to be at the lodge by yourself, Jordan. Wait until I come back to Prospect to move out of the B-and-B. We still have to get to the bottom of…what's happening in the kitchen." Sarah waggled her eyebrows in an obvious hint to the "ghost."

"You told him about it five seconds after it

happened." Jordan shook her head. "I think you made the whole thing up about the noise and whatnot. We haven't heard any rattles or crashes or things that go bump in the night since, and we've been working out here every day."

Sarah tried her mean glare. "Listen to your older sister and stay in the B-and-B."

Since they'd be arguing over what was definitely not a ghost until the mountains crumbled, Jordan held up her hands in surrender.

"Fine, you win." For now. She wasn't sure how long it would take to make Sadie's cozy apartment at the Majestic safe and comfortable, but there was still plenty she could do after Sarah left.

And she'd move in as soon as the hot water was on. What could Sarah do about it from LA?

Jordan waved as Sarah and Wes rode off. They passed through the pasture to the foothills that rose up into the mountains, forming the backdrop for the Rocking A and the Majestic Prospect Lodge.

Choosing to do whatever she wanted to do when she wanted to do it had become Jordan's guiding philosophy ever since the Summer of Exile, when she promised herself no one would ever force decisions on her once she was grown.

Jordan could be stubborn, too.

She had a lifetime of being the middle Hearst sister.

She sighed when she stepped back inside Sadie's old quarters where she and Sarah had been working. There was still a lot of stuff to clear out, things that could be donated and worn-out items that should be trashed, but it was going to make a nice apartment someday soon.

The more effort she put in now, the sooner she could move in.

Sarah made plans; Jordan made decisions.

Jordan Hearst couldn't change now, could she?

CHAPTER TWO

CLAY ARMSTRONG SLID out of his truck Friday night in front of the ranch house he was lucky enough to call home. He wanted a shower, a sandwich, a bed with cleanish sheets and at least ten hours of uninterrupted sleep. He'd been working sunup to sundown in Colorado Springs for the past five days to tie up a number of his projects and salvage the budget on the subdivision he was building, so that he could come home to the Rocking A and make some progress on it.

Both were important.

Every extra dollar and the bulk of his company's resources were tied up in Fountain Estates, the subdivision in question. He and his business partner, Chaney Lee, were overextended and sweating the schedule. He needed to be there, watching closely, as three houses were nearing the final walk-through stage; once the punch lists were cleared up, he could meet the buyers at signing, hand over the keys, collect checks and breathe easier. For months, his days had consisted of spreadsheets and never-ending phone calls from concerned buyers and to suppliers hunting for reasonable prices and qualified tradespeople.

They had sacrificed so much to get where they were, and it was finally paying off. Instead of outbidding a field of competitors for their next job, they'd been approached out of the blue to take on a luxury retirement village and golf course in Pagosa Springs. Opportunities like that didn't come along often, but climbing the next step depended on finishing Fountain Estates on time. This trip home would jeopardize both.

The remodeling and updates needed at the Rocking A ranch house had a deadline, too, so he'd left stacks of notes for Chaney to follow up on. When they'd parted ways that afternoon, she'd already drawn up three to-do lists for Monday morning and seemed energized by the battle. That was why they'd always worked so well in business. Clay could see the big picture; Chaney nailed every detail.

They were successful together.

If Chaney decided he had his priorities out of order, would the partnership fall apart? All the work and worry had him worn out.

This "vacation" to come home to improve the ranch wasn't going to provide rest or relaxation, especially now that almost all Armstrong sons were under one roof with their father again. And he and his brothers were too old to settle their differences with clumsy roughhousing. They might break something.

Instead of the window he and Matt had shattered by throwing boots at each other in the messy bedroom they'd shared when he was eighteen, it would be bones.

This renovation would open up space for the next generation of Armstrongs, foster kids who needed the place as much as Clay and his brothers had when they'd landed here. It would also give his brothers room to breathe and fast-forward the interior from its worn 1980s slump to the present day.

If they all survived the experience.

"Hello?" Clay called out as he walked inside, immediately swamped with memories. Nothing had changed since the freezing day he'd met Prue and Walt Armstrong for the first time. His first foster mother, who'd been his safe place for almost ten years before that day, had been admitted to hospice with stage four pancreatic cancer, and losing that lifeline had sent him into free fall. Clay had grown up in the foster system, one of the lucky ones with a stable home, but this new place was nothing like what he'd known. The Armstrongs had seemed nice enough—the other kid, Wes, was less terrible than he'd feared—but country life was foreign. Home had been an apartment complex filled with people and kids and noise. Clay had learned early on the dangerous places and people there.

The Rocking A Ranch located outside Prospect, the tiny town they'd driven through that day, had been a sheet of white snow drifts, and his caseworker had been in a hurry to get back to Boulder.

The living room was still brown. Brown furniture, brown paneling and a large television in a large brown wooden console. Wallpaper with pink flowers tied in blue ribbon covered the kitchen wall that he could see from the doorway. His parents had poured every extra penny back into the ranch business that kept the family fed, paying for more livestock and better equipment and the feed and vet bills and unending fence repairs. The house was warm and comfortable, but it had been out of fashion twenty years ago and it had never risen to the top of the priority list.

Until now.

Tonight was summer-turning-to-fall October, so there was a chill in the air at night but not a snowflake to be seen.

Happily, the place was also empty of Armstrongs right at that second.

A shot of relief made it easier to head for the bedrooms. He'd expected to act as referee for Travis and Grant, his brothers who were doing most of the work to the house so far. He'd lost count of the number of phone calls he'd taken while they were putting in the foundation for the new addition. Technical questions, sure, but more often, they needed a final decision and quick. Both were prickly, with too much empty time on their hands, and all it took was the wrong word to get an argument started. Hence, the need for a ref.

Clay checked out the bedrooms to assess his choices. All four of the rooms had been claimed. On his occasional overnight stays, he slept on the couch in the living room, but he'd come for a month this time. Bunk beds remained in one of the rooms, so he dropped his bag on the bottom bunk, shoved the dirty clothes that had to be Grant's onto the floor, stripped the comforter and sheets, and headed for the washing machine.

"Bunk beds," he muttered and tried not to remember how comfortable his king-size bed in his neat, boring apartment in Colorado Springs would be at that moment. When everything was washing, he moved toward the kitchen. At least Wes ran a tight ship in here. Their mother would lose her cool when she visited from her place in town if her former kitchen was as messy as the bedrooms. It was a good thing she dropped in now and then. At first, he and his brothers had been certain their parents' separation would never last, that they'd reunite at any moment; instead, they remained close although not together.

Maybe that was a good thing tonight. There was no room for another person in this place.

Clay opened the fridge, took a quick look inside and closed it. He steadied the ceramic goose cookie jar that rattled on the top of the refrigerator. Then he took it down in a fit of optimism and put it back carefully when he discovered there were no cookies to be had.

"Peanut butter sandwich it is." He grabbed the loaf of bread and the jar and moved to the kitchen table. A folder was open there, paperwork arranged around it in neat piles. The form in the center was labeled "Application for Foster Family Home License." The *Foster Parent Handbook* was underneath it with yellow flags poking out along the side, presumably to mark important spots. Pamphlets for CPR training, first-aid classes and resources for parents of children with special needs were tucked inside the pocket. Travis had been doing his homework at the kitchen table.

His brother's dream had been to take in boys who needed foster homes at the Rocking A, like Walt and Prue had done for Clay and Travis and the rest of his brothers. All five of them had a family thanks to this foster care system.

That dream was important enough for the whole clan to make the sacrifices it took to have the ranch house ready for reinspection when the November 1 deadline rolled around.

That was why he was here, crammed in with the rest of them and leaving his business and his ability to pay his bills in someone else's hands. Travis, Grant and Wes were living there through the renovations as well as lending a hand. Only his brother Matt had escaped the close quarters by way of leasing an office space for his veterinary clinic in town. He was camping out in his office there.

Lucky, lucky Matt.

Money was as tight as space was, but it was all worth it.

Peanut butter sandwiches were not going to cut it for long.

When his phone rang, he pulled it out of his pocket. "Hey, where you at?" he said instead of a normal greeting. He and Wes could cut through the niceties like that. "And can you bring me food when you come back?"

His brother laughed. "I'm in town and yes. Where are you, little brother?"

Clay rolled his eyes. Wes was technically older by five weeks and two days. Standing in their bare feet, it would take some careful study to decide which one of them was taller, but Wes had been there the longest, so he was "big brother." None of them had been able to convince him otherwise.

"Just got home. I see you forgot to make my bed for me," Clay drawled. "Grant never has learned to hit the clothes hamper. Not sure the bunk beds are rated to hold the weight of two grown men."

Wes sighed. "He has learned to throw punches at me for nagging too much, so you are on your own there. Not sure where everybody's going to go once we start the interior demolition."

Since they were doing this renovation on a shoestring budget, Clay had a feeling they were eventually looking at sleeping bags on the living room floor instead of comfortable hotel rooms for the duration.

"No money for a cleaning service here or a place with room service, huh?" Clay asked as he opened the cabinet doors to see if he'd missed something better than peanut butter.

"We're tougher than that. Not sleeping on cushy mattresses won't kill us," Wes said, a touch of uncertainty in his voice. "I'm glad you're there, though. I'll bring you whatever you like from the Ace High, if you'll do me a big favor."

Clay closed his eyes. He should have let the phone go to voice mail, curled up like a cat in Grant's laundry and postponed all of this until daylight.

But no, he'd gone a different way. That came back to get him more often than not.

He wasn't going to like this favor. He could hear that in Wes's voice.

"What do you need?" he asked reluctantly.

"It's Jordan Hearst," Wes said slowly, as if he expected a loud retort. Clay and Jordan were the only ones who knew of their actual history, but his brothers had picked up on the tension.

Probably because all she did was glare at him when they were together.

Some of the glares he deserved, but Jordan had some explaining to do herself.

Clay bit his tongue and waited.

"She's working at the lodge and not answering her phone. Sarah is sure she's fine, that the phone is in the car or somewhere that Jordan can't hear it ringing, but it has been hours since we left her there and..."

"You want me to go over to tell Jordan to answer her sister's calls." He'd somehow put Jordan Hearst's return to Prospect out of his mind for a while. That was surprising. Ever since she'd appeared right here in the kitchen with her sister for a business meeting regarding the sale of Sadie Hearst's land, he'd spent a lot of time thinking about her—how little she'd changed in fifteen years, how she'd disappeared without saying goodbye and reappeared without saying hello, as well as how much they'd missed in between.

He'd been Jordan's "boss" for one summer while they both worked at the Majestic Prospect Lodge's marina; he'd also been a pain in her neck often. That much Clay remembered.

She never knew he had been more in love than hate in their love-hate relationship that summer, and he planned to keep it that way.

Clay tilted his head back to study the ceiling. It desperately needed paint.

Refusing to go would get him to bed sooner, but it would also make him feel like a fresh cow patty. His brother and his no doubt future wife were moderately concerned about Jordan. What were the chances he'd end the call without being infected by that same concern?

"Sure. I expect you to bring dessert and two cold beverages of my choice, as well."

"Can do. Call me when you track her down and I'll tell you what's being offered from the Ace's kitchen tonight. Thanks, Clay." Wes hung up before Clay could agree to the plan.

There were no menus at the Ace. His choice would be This or That. Simple.

Wes also knew there was almost zero chance that Clay would deny any of his family's requests.

Clay was again in the truck and headed down the lane to the lodge before he let himself consider what he was going to say to Jordan Hearst. They'd had a tense conversation in the Rocking A's barn after that business meeting at the breakfast table, where they'd shoved their brief will-they-or-won't-they flirtation as kids under the rug and then nailed the rug down tight to cover it up. But they weren't on easy speaking terms yet.

Also, Jordan had never been quickly swayed by logic or reason or even stubborn will, so if she didn't want to answer her sister's calls, what was he supposed to do about it?

He was glad to see light spilling out of the few uncovered windows along the front of the lodge. Jordan had taken it upon herself to handle that before she and her sisters had even made the decision to list the lodge for sale. But breaking the window in the Majestic's lobby had halted her plan to uncover every window. Repairing the broken window was on his to-do list, now that he was in town for a stretch. Part of the terms of the sale of the parcel of pastureland to the Rocking A had been his assistance as an unpaid "consultant" on repairs to the lodge. He intended to uphold the obligation, whether it was awkward with Jordan or not. That was an Armstrong trait he'd always try to live up to.

When he didn't see a car, Clay parked and tested the front door. It wasn't locked. The lobby was the same as the last time he'd seen it: dusty, open, wood beams, scuffed floors and almost empty. A large rectangle draped in an old sheet rested against the back wall behind what had been the check-in desk. Cobwebs dangled here and there from the exposed beams, and Clay tried not to imagine where their builders might be. Cleaning up the lobby would be a big job.

Clay immediately discovered the problem with the calls. There was a cell phone on the long check-in counter. By process of elimination, it had to be Jordan's. When he picked it up, he could see six missed calls and numerous texts.

The restaurant side of the lodge was dark, so he turned down the hallway toward the rooms. A sweet scent floated there in the doorway, as if someone had been in the kitchen cooking. There was a brush of air, as if someone was passing by, but it stopped after he paused to listen. Had they opened up the kitchen again already? "Jordan?" he called in case she was actually in the kitchen on the other side of the restaurant. No one answered.

Clay moved faster down the lighted hallway and was relieved to hear someone singing very badly as he turned the corner. It was easy to follow the music, and as he stepped inside a nice apartment built onto the back of the lodge, he saw Jordan dancing around an island in the small kitchen there. Boxes lined the wall, and it was clear she'd made impressive progress. All the cabinet doors were open, as if she'd cleared them. She had a sponge in one hand that was also her microphone. He could see a bucket of dirty water in the sink before she turned back to empty it. She hefted the bucket and turned it over to drain it and then braced both hands on the sink to stretch.

"One more bucket, then I'm calling it a night," she said. She brushed the messy dark hair that was tilting precariously on top of her head upright as a show of determination.

Normally, Jordan's voice was strong. Bossy. She didn't back down in conversation, but tonight, she was wavering.

When she started humming again and moved a pot under the sink faucet to fill it, he realized she was wearing headphones. There was an old CD player attached to her waistband. How long had it been since he'd seen one of those? It might have been the same one from years ago, since she'd worn it everywhere the summer she worked at the Majestic.

The thing had to be an antique by now.

That explained why she was humming a George Strait song, too. Jordan had been a California girl and fan of Top 40 hits when she'd arrived, but Sadie Hearst had insisted the Majestic was all country, all the time.

How would he get her attention without scaring her?

When she started an improvised two-step around the small kitchen, he decided to prop one shoulder on the wall to watch and wait for her to spot him. The entertainment was top-notch.

When she completed a full circle, she stopped in her tracks. A scream made it halfway from her lips before she clasped her hands to her chest. "Oh, you scared me." She collapsed back against the counter.

Clay held up her cell. "I'm supposed to tell you to answer your phone. Your sister has been calling." He moved closer to her and noticed that the floor was wet, too, as if she'd washed it at some point and a few spots were still drying. "Why are you here all by yourself, California?" She should have some help.

Jordan frowned at the old nickname before she took the phone to scroll through the messages, her lips twisted in a grimace. "Sarah was here. We've packed up a lot of Sadie's memorabilia, but I wanted to clean. Wes brought Starla over and convinced Sarah to knock off early to go for a ride." She wrinkled her nose. "I was supposed to do the same thing. I didn't follow orders."

Wow. He was not shocked. Not at all.

Sadie had named him an assistant manager the summer he and Jordan had worked at the marina, which meant he was responsible for training Sadie's great-niece and locking and unlocking the doors every day. Since it was his third summer at the marina, Clay had expected it to be easy. Almost boring.

Then Jordan had splashed onto the scene.

Clay crossed his arms over his chest. "You know they hate it when we don't follow orders. The big brothers and sisters of the world."

She nodded. "Yes, but we have a sacred duty to thwart them whenever we can. It keeps them humble."

He hadn't expected this from her. Fighting with her was frustrating, but moments like this reminded him of why he'd never been able to walk away from her.

"Maybe forget the final bucket tonight. Have dinner. Reassure your sister." Clay studied her red hands and the fatigue on her face. "You look tired."

"Thank you." Jordan rolled her eyes. "If only I'd known I was going to have a gentleman caller, I would have dressed for the occasion."

"Didn't look like you needed a caller. You were two-stepping nicely on your own." Clay motioned to the CD player. "Don't tell me you're still wearing that wherever you go." He'd tried to get her to take it off while she was running the cash register and meeting customers at the dock with no luck.

"No," Jordan said and patted her hip. "I found it while we were packing. Took the batteries out of one of the flashlights we brought when the electricity was turned off, and it worked like new. A whole bunch of George Strait to keep me company."

"George is good for that." Clay's stomach decided to rumble a contribution to the conversation at that point, so he said, "I'll wait for you to lock up and follow you back to the road."

"I was going to heat up more water and do one more pass over the floor tonight." Jordan bit her lip. This was a much weaker argument than he'd expected. Eventually, her shoulders slumped. "Okay. I've got to get Sarah's SUV back to Bell House, anyway, so she can leave early in the morning."

"You weren't staying out here tonight?" Clay asked, the urge to poke and prod tickling there in the back of his brain. It was dark. Deserted. Should a woman alone be there... alone?

"Not until the hot water is working. Probably. Maybe." Jordan moved quickly through the apartment, shutting off lights as she went. He followed her out through the lobby. "I'll lock the front doors and walk around back to get the SUV. You can go ahead. If you don't eat soon, the bear that's in your pocket might get us both."

"I'll drive you. It's dark out there." Clay moved toward his truck. When he stepped out of the light, he was convinced she wasn't safe on her own. Nor was anyone. It was already too dark. Eventually, the stars would seem close enough to touch, but she'd be better off in town.

"No problem. I can go in and leave by the apartment door instead." Jordan paused by the door.

"I'll drive you. It's dark out here, too." Clay waited patiently. He wasn't going to lose this argument.

Her annoyed sigh was all too familiar, the years between now and when they'd last stood at the Majestic as teens collapsing. He shook his head and carefully kept his expression neutral when they slid into his truck. If he let one little curl of his lips betray his victory here, she'd barrel back out of the truck like her hair was on fire. They were silent as he drove around the lodge. Jordan clicked the SUV fob to turn the headlights on and illuminate the darkness.

"This truce we called…" Jordan motioned between them. "How long will it last?"

Clay shrugged. "Not sure. It's only holding tonight because we're both worn out. One good night's sleep, and you'll return to ignoring me."

"While you pick and pick and pick at me like you always have." Jordan paused with her hand on the door handle. "Why do you do that, Clay?"

He couldn't help it. That was the only answer he'd ever found, but it wasn't good enough and he knew it.

"You ever going to apologize to me? Do you know how to apologize?" he asked.

Because he was never too tired to face off against this woman.

"You keep saying that!" Jordan expelled a gust of air. "For what? For just going home years and years and years ago?"

And breaking his heart.

Not that she knew his heart had ever been involved.

"I thought we'd become friends." Then he'd

kissed her and she'd turned tail and run away. "But I guess you're right. It has been a long time. I forgive you."

Jordan grumbled but he couldn't make out the words.

That might be a blessing.

"The truce needs to hold a bit longer, Clay, so I am sorry I hurt your feelings." Jordan spit out the words, so he had serious doubts about how from the heart they were.

It was the best apology he'd ever get. "Thank you."

She rolled her eyes and pushed open the truck door. "You don't have to follow me," Jordan said as she hopped out. "But you will, so I'll stop wasting my breath." She closed the door and got into the SUV, saving them both from any more conversation. Clay waited for her to take the lead down the long lane back to the highway that went into Prospect. Jordan honked when she passed the sign for the Rocking A, and Clay turned back toward home.

The urge to continue all the way to town for dinner at the Ace High caught him off guard.

"More time with people" had been nowhere on his list of things to do for the evening.

If he rolled into town behind Jordan, he couldn't predict her reaction, but he could imagine his brother's raised eyebrow about why Clay had changed their plan. Wes was so far gone over Sarah Hearst. In Clay's experience, people like that, newly in love, were determined to share the joy with everyone around them. The last thing he needed was his brother matchmaking for him and Jordan.

Everyone around the two of them was trying to figure out what had happened between them. Matchmaking would not help.

Instead of following Jordan, Clay walked inside the house, went to the washer, moved his sheets and comforter to the dryer, and called his brother. "Jordan should be pulling up at Bell House in less than fifteen. What's on the menu tonight?"

"Would you rather have chicken fried steak or chicken and dumplings?" Wes asked.

"One of each, a slice of pie and two iced teas to go," Clay answered.

His brother groaned. "Got it. Everything okay out at the lodge?"

"Yeah, Jordan was working herself into the

ground. Her phone was too far away to hear the ringing." Clay sighed. "Wake me up when you get here."

"I'll do it. Thanks, Clay," Wes said before he hung up.

Clay hoped his brother hurried home with the food.

He probably wouldn't rest easy until he knew Jordan had made it safely back to Bell House.

And if he thought about that for too long, what that meant, he might not sleep at all.

CHAPTER THREE

JORDAN WAS FROWNING at her broken fingernail and trying to convince the rest of her aching body to roll out of bed the next morning. She heard the loud jangle of tiny bells from the wreath on the door to her sister's room at Bell House. Instead of boring numbers and high-tech key card locks, Prospect's only bed-and-breakfast had gone with metal keys on old-fashioned rings and wreaths that represented the unique decor found inside each room.

Sarah had thought she was so clever when she'd booked Jordan into Wedding Bells, the honeymoon suite. It was spacious and comfortable, with an antique four-poster bed draped in white fabric. Unfortunately, there was also a bathtub large enough for two dead center by the wall across from the bed. Jordan hadn't used it, but the fact that it stood there meant the vision of other people splashing around in it kept popping up like soap bubbles.

At least the wreath on her door, a fluffy arrangement of white tulle and tiny pearls, was quiet.

As payback, Jordan had moved Sarah from Liberty, a heritage room dedicated to the silent Liberty Bell, to Silver when she'd made her second visit to Prospect. Her excuse to Sarah? It was the second-finest room at Bell House, after Wedding Bells, obviously.

Sarah wasn't fooled by that.

The room was Christmas themed, complete with a dazzling, multicolored lit faux tree, and the wreath outside was covered in small, jingling bells.

Unfortunately, Jordan's excellent revenge had backfired. How many times did her sister have to go to the bathroom at night? Too many.

Every single entrance and exit were announced by the annoying, musical wreath.

A quick knock was her second warning that Sarah was about to catch her lying in bed after sunrise.

Something many happy people did, but in Prospect, it seemed to cause concern.

"Good morning," Sarah said before she pounced on the bed beside Jordan. "I'm ready to hit the road, but I wanted to make sure you're okay. You weren't yourself last night."

Jordan had forced herself to shuffle down to the Ace High, Prospect's only full-service restaurant, after she'd driven Sarah's SUV back to Prospect. Bell House and the Ace High were in the heart of Prospect's historic neighborhood that had been preserved since the days of Colorado's silver rush. On Friday night, the old saloon-turned-restaurant had been crowded, louder than usual, and her dinner companions had been preoccupied with each other.

But skipping dinner would have worried Sarah and meant Jordan would wake up starving at midnight. Chaperoning two adults who were trying to make every single second before they had to say goodbye count would normally be enough to dampen her appetite, but the chicken and dumplings Faye had deposited in front of her had smelled like heaven on a plate.

"I was worn out. I should have quit when you suggested it." Did she honestly mean that? No, but Sarah would gobble up the veiled "you were right" and it would power her all the way back to LA.

"Take it easy today, then. Rose has already served up breakfast and done away with the dishes, but you can grab lunch and then take a nap." Sarah pointed. "Or you could find a chair or hammock and take a book out to the lake to read."

Jordan wrinkled her nose. "That was Brooke's thing, not mine." She'd always been about action when she and her sisters came to visit Sadie. Out on the boat with their dad. Digging in the flower beds with Sadie. Climbing trees while her mother yelled at her to get down. Jordan rubbed the dull ache in her chest that those childhood memories always brought up. It was a lot easier to focus on the Summer of Exile and annoying Clay than the family vacations to Key Lake and the Majestic that had ended when her mother died.

The first time Sarah had left her alone in Prospect for a week, Jordan decided to start opening the lodge without either of her sisters knowing. It was never smart to leave Jordan with too much free time on her hands. "I could go for a nice nap without the constant jingling coming from next door and the woman with the world's smallest bladder."

Sarah's broad grin made Jordan giggle. "I prefer the Liberty room. Remember that."

Jordan huffed as she scooted out of bed. "Let me change clothes and I'll walk down with you." After she'd brushed her teeth and her hair, Jordan put on her last pair of clean jeans and an almost-clean sweatshirt to carry her sister's suitcase down the stairs.

Sarah expected to be in LA for a month this time, and Jordan was already missing her sister.

Not that she'd admit it.

It was a long time to stay in a small town with no friends and no entertainment.

And no real income for the moment, either.

The smart thing would be to go back to LA herself, get serious about the job search and let the real estate agent do her thing in Prospect. Wes could handle any lodge business for them. Sarah might even stop worrying about her for a hot minute.

Sadie's death, spending time with her sister, all the memories the lodge brought back of her mother and Sadie...

If she left Prospect, this might be the last

time she experienced the power of the Majestic and Key Lake.

"Promise me you you'll take it easy," Sarah said as she gripped Jordan's shoulders. "Any buyers Erin convinces to tour the Majestic will have to see the potential through the dust and cobwebs."

"I can't promise that. You know how I am with a project," Jordan said. "It keeps me out of trouble."

"You know what else might do that? Finding a job." Sarah closed her eyes. "Or not. I don't know. My great-aunt created a job for me in her company. I'm not a career expert, and besides, we're going to end up with a lot of money when we sell the place. Why rush home?"

"It's nice that you worry about me." Jordan hugged her tightly. "But I promise I'll stick to tidying up, that's it. Just to keep me busy. Really, I won't do too much." Jordan held a hand solemnly over her heart, content with the way she'd created a giant loophole in her words that she could slip through if she needed to.

Her older sister was wise to her ways. "That's not what I asked." Sarah shook her head. "Never mind. Come back to LA with me."

It would be easy to agree. Her sister could definitely use the help, and the effort Jordan was putting into the lodge might turn to nothing, but she couldn't say yes. She needed more time at Key Lake.

"I'm not ready to leave yet." Jordan spoke the truth as she gripped her sister's hands.

"Fine, but remember Brooke is trusting us to make the best choice for all of us. There's a lot of money at stake. None of us can afford to throw it away on repairs to a place we aren't keeping," Sarah said.

Jordan narrowed her eyes at Sarah. "I don't need a manager, Sarah, or a babysitter while you're out of town."

"No, but Sadie's lodge does. Wes has been watching over it for years and he knows who to call to get things done. Let's decide what's essential." Sarah walked around to the driver's side of her car. "And don't move out there by yourself. It's not safe. Wes has orders to snitch on you immediately if you try it."

Jordan bit her tongue because, babysitter or not, she planned to do exactly as she pleased the second Sarah drove away. Time to change the subject. "Where is your true love this morning? Isn't he going to kiss you goodbye?"

Sarah grinned. "He did. Last night. After you went upstairs. Did it excellently, too." She waggled her finger as Jordan groaned. "You know what the lodge needs? A good swing, a porch swing. You know that kind of thing?" Her gaze turned distant and Jordan knew she was remembering the excellent goodbye kiss that must have occurred on Bell House's porch swing. That was where their hello kiss had taken place, too.

Jordan squeezed her sister tightly. "I'll miss you."

"You're going to ignore everything I've told you and go stir up trouble. Don't pretend otherwise, Jordie." Sarah opened the car door. "At least promise me you'll be nice to Wes. He's an innocent bystander in our epic battle of wills that's spanned decades."

"I have no idea what you're talking about. Text me when you stop for the night." Jordan waited for Sarah to agree and then let her older sister close the door.

Jordan watched Sarah's car drive out of Prospect. Then Jordan spun on her heel to survey the town.

Prospect's version of the big-box store, the Homestead Market, had a fair amount of bustling traffic going in and out. It sat on the edge of Prospect's old town district, so the face of the combination grocery store and one-stop-shop was originally a livery stable. Exploring there was high on her list of priorities. Prospect's growth could be traced like the age of a tree, in the rings that radiated out from the buildings built in the late 1800s.

In the center of town, carefully preserved facades housed modern businesses like the market. The Ace High had once been the fanciest saloon in town; it was probably open, but the lunch crowd hadn't hit yet. Down the block, the Prospect Picture Show, a beautiful historic movie theater, was only open on the weekends and special occasions. Today the marquee stated that *Destry Rides Again* would have a matinee showing at three and evening showings at seven thirty on Friday, Saturday and Sunday.

There was more busy traffic up and down the boardwalk on both sides of the street— weekend tourists pausing to take pictures of the onetime jail or peeking in the windows, as they walked toward the Mercantile at one end of town or the Homestead Market at the other.

Where to start?

Jordan could see only a few cars now parked in front of the Mercantile, so she crossed the street and stepped inside the foyer. The space had been divided into two businesses after the Armstrongs had divorced. Sarah passed along any gossip she picked up and had related these details when she'd dragged Jordan into Prue Armstrong's half of the building, a craft shop called Handmade, a couple of times to talk about embroidery and pillow finishing.

Finding out that the Armstrongs had been married for so long wasn't a surprise. Discussing how they were still so friendly after the divorce had kept her and Sarah occupied more than one night. Instead of bitter enemies, Prue and Walt squabbled and flirted like on-again, off-again teenagers.

Sarah loved Prue's store, but Jordan was more interested in the hardware that filled the other half of the historic Mercantile.

Walt Armstrong's hardware store might carry the same inventory as the big-box places, but it would take a treasure hunt with a detailed map or an experienced guide to find whatever she needed. Getting hot water was her biggest hurdle at that moment, but she wasn't sure where to start. She hoped Walt would know.

Walt himself was her favorite kind of guide. He didn't do anything without telling a story. There were no bells over the door on this side of the Mercantile. There was also no crowd. The cars out front must belong to Handmade shoppers.

"Mornin'," Walt called from his comfortable seat at the cash register. "How's life out at the Majestic Prospect Lodge?"

Jordan sighed. "Messy? Dusty? Hard work? All of the above."

"But it sure is pretty out there, ain't it?" He nodded when she did. "Ain't another place like Key Lake, neighbor."

"That is impossible to argue with, Walt." Jordan bent down to rest one elbow on the counter. This seemed to be a universal pose for shooting the breeze in the hardware store. Walt immediately followed her direction and propped his elbows across from her.

"What can I help you with today?" he asked.

"Do you know anything about hot water heaters?" Jordan asked. "The one in Sadie's apartment isn't working. If it's a repair instead of a replace situation, I'd love to have hot water."

He tapped his jaw. "Well, now, could be a fuse. Or a thermostat. Is it gas? Electric?"

Jordan wished she had the answer.

"The age of that place," Walt murmured as he straightened, "could be gas like ours. First thing I'd do? Check the pilot light."

Jordan nodded as if she had any inkling what that meant.

Walt's rusty chuckle confirmed he was not fooled.

"I'll find a video online." Jordan waved a hand as if it was no problem. A determined woman could find all the instructions she needed if she was ready to put in the effort. Gas made her nervous, but she *probably* wouldn't cause an explosion that wiped the Majestic off the map.

Walt tipped his head to the side. "Jordan Hearst, you remind me of my dear ex-wife. Prue would rather stand on her head than ask anyone for help." He tapped the counter. "Since she's impossible to forget—that is a compliment, but also, sometimes a complaint—we won't tell her I said that. Wait here."

As he hurried away, Jordan squashed the urge to ask nosy questions about how the two of them had ended up divorced when it was clear he still had feelings for his ex. She studied a wind chime hanging from the rough wood beams overhead. Silver cowboy hats and boots were strung together. Before she could stir the long strings to hear the chimes, Walt hustled back to the counter.

"If it ain't the pilot light, most likely that's a fuse and a heating element, one, the other or both. Easy fixes, all of 'em." His expression was both confident and reassuring.

As if everyone in the world was capable of repairing a water heater without blowing the Majestic off the face of the earth. Probably.

Jordan chewed her bottom lip as she asked herself if she was repair-appliances ready. The water heater was already not performing the way it was intended to. How much worse could she break it?

"Okay. And what about lawn chairs?" Jordan asked as she studied the store aisles.

Walt nodded and slid off his seat with a low grunt before walking around the end of the counter. "Kinda out of season for lawn furniture, but I keep some of them bag chairs on hand year-round. They sell pretty good when the lake's busy." He motioned for Jordan to follow him, and she was delighted to observe the ramshackle aisle that included plumbing supplies, charcoal and a few grilling necessities, and large bags of birdseed. Along the back wall, there were the chairs that folded up to fit in bags that could be slung over a shoulder. Walt had five to choose from. They were all army green, so style and fashion were not factors. "How about one of these?"

Jordan nodded. "Good. After I get the water heater working, I'm going to try to relax." She knew her lips twisted as if she'd said "eat brussels sprouts" when he laughed.

"Not good at sitting? I know someone like that." He patted his chest. "Only way to get me to do it is to tell me I can't, you understand? Even then, it took a little heart attack, a stern talking-to by my sons and an 'I told you so' trembling on Prue's lips." He sighed. "I'd tell you to never get old, Jordan, because your heart will plumb act like a fool, but retirement comes for us all if we're lucky."

"How is that working out for you?" Jordan asked as Walt rang up the purchases. She didn't wince as she slid her credit card across the counter.

Walt finished the sale and passed her the receipt. "Well, now, that is a good question."

He settled into his chair and propped his boots up on the counter before waving a seed catalog around. "When Prue walks in? Taking it easy is always going well. She's the one who said it couldn't be done. I make it look like a dream." He motioned at the laptop next to the cash register. "But when she ain't watching over my shoulder? I'm busy enough."

Since Jordan was familiar with his strategy of stubbornness and subterfuge when required, she admired it. "Doing what?"

Walt pointed at the laptop. "Would you believe day trading? There ain't never enough money for ranching, and right now, the boys need what extra we've got to go after the things they want. Our house? Needs top-to-bottom renovation, but the money says we better stick to the bottom. The boys don't want to sell this place, which would help, so…I dabble. I gotta help somehow. Picking these stocks don't feel much different to me than gambling at a horse race, you know? You study your options, check out how the horse has been runnin' lately and you place a bet you can afford to lose. Big winners know how to find the right long shot. Trading's like that but with less beautiful scenery." He frowned.

"Now, Jordan Hearst, you and I are coconspirators here. I'll advise on the repairs you aren't supposed to be doing at the Majestic and you protect my secrets, you understand?"

The twinkle in his eyes was adorable. Wes and Clay might be adopted, but it was easy to see they'd learned how to charm from Walt. The resemblance was clear. Jordan would guess all five of the Armstrong boys had been taught very well.

"Yes, sir," Jordan said as she snapped to attention, happy to be on the inside of Walt's plan. "You can count on me. I will spread tales far and wide of how relaxed you were when I came in."

He nodded. "Good. You're what I needed. An accomplice. You seem like a woman who understands it's necessary to prove people wrong sometimes. My wife said I couldn't change, that I couldn't slow down." He held his hands out as if he were proving Prue wrong.

"Can you pretend to have changed for… forever?" Jordan asked. This was something she mulled over at night when dreams about what the Majestic could be again wouldn't leave her alone. If she could pretend to be the kind of person who started something and finished it, would she be able to reopen the Majestic herself?

Did she even want to do that? What would life be like in Prospect over the long haul? One restaurant. One movie theater that showed old Westerns and only on the weekends.

And how long would it take to convince her sisters she'd changed?

"Oh, I'm not pretending. I have changed. I may not be doing it the way Prue expected, but I have made advancements in my life." Walt tilted his head to the side. "More important, I made some in my thinking that she said were impossible. I just gotta show her."

"How long will that take?" Jordan wondered if the two months or so she had to try to find someone to reopen the Majestic were long enough.

Walt's slow smile eased some of her fears. "As long as we don't quit, Jordan, we've got all the time we need."

His words settled in her chest with a warm glow, the sort of encouragement she needed in that exact moment.

From a stranger who seemed to see through to her heart.

"Hope the chair and the view do the trick for you. It's good to slow down every once in a while, I will admit that. Time is short. You gotta enjoy it along the way," Walt said. "Took me too long to figure that out."

Jordan knew he was right, but it required practice. "That is good advice. I'll stop by the Ace and pick up a picnic to go with my chair and the view. That will help."

"Can't hurt, that's for sure." Walt offered her the bag of water heater pieces and parts.

"I don't need any special tools for this job?" Jordan asked uncertainly.

He shook his head, his expression once again saying anybody could do it.

So she nodded and left the hardware store.

At the Ace High, she ordered the club sandwich, a slice of pie and a tea to go.

Faye, who was the owner, the best server on staff and sometimes the cook, brought her the order and said, "I hope it's okay if I send this other sandwich with you. You don't mind, do you?"

Jordan accepted the large paper bag Faye held out and the two plastic cups with lids. "No." Did Faye hear the uncertainty in her voice? Obviously not, because the woman nodded happily. "Good. That's good." First, plumbing parts she didn't know she needed. Now, an extra meal that wouldn't be wasted.

Living in a small town took a lot of adjustment.

"I guess Sarah left this morning," Faye said as she pulled money from her apron and dropped it in the large tip jar next to the cash register. "I'm surprised you stayed behind. Figured LA would be calling both of you by now." She propped her hands on the counter. "Not a lot of action around here."

Jordan shrugged. "It's a nice change."

Faye pursed her lips before nodding. "Well, I will have to take your word on that. I do know it's fun to see new faces, so don't be a stranger, Jordan. I got all kinds of secrets I can share about those Armstrong boys if you happen to need any leverage."

Jordan's mouth dropped open. She hadn't expected luck this good. "Really?" It was easy to imagine tossing out some juicy tidbit the next time Clay called her California to knock him back in his boots.

"Grew up right next door." She wrinkled her nose. "Dated more than one of them, but everyone makes mistakes when they're young." Faye winked to show she was joking, surprising a laugh from Jordan.

"When I come back in for dinner, we will need to talk about this. Do you ever get a break?" Jordan asked on her way to the door.

Faye's grin faded. "No breaks, but for you, I'll sit down for a glass of tea every now and then." The phone rang and Faye waved back to Jordan before turning away.

After Jordan loaded all of her purchases in her car, she made the trek out to the lodge, grateful again that Wes Armstrong had had the lane to the lodge graded. The potholes had been intense, but now it was a beautiful drive through green pastures and tall trees. When the clearing opened to show the lodge, she could see a large package against the front door, something wrapped in brown paper, and a familiar truck parked in the shade nearest the best view of the water.

And the lightbulb came on over her head.

She hadn't needed any tools or any special knowledge because she hadn't been the one who was going to complete the water heater repair.

Because there were boots hanging off the tailgate of the back of the truck.

Not cowboy boots.

Steel-toed work boots like a man might wear on construction sites.

Clay Armstrong was waiting for her. Walt must have known that. Had he included Faye at the Ace in his plans? Jordan wasn't carrying an extra sandwich for herself. She'd picked up Clay Armstrong's lunch for him.

The efficiency was impressive.

She parked next to him and got out to see that he was comfortably asleep in the bed of the truck.

The weight of her stare must have been enough to disturb him because his eyes slowly opened. "Well, now, I am happy to see you." The lazy stretch he gave caught her attention, long arms and legs shifting as he rolled to sit up. "Good morning."

"Afternoon, but close enough." Jordan pointed over her shoulder with her thumb and frowned to cover her wonder at his friendly greeting. "Did someone around here order lunch?"

He tugged down the bill of the ball cap he preferred to a cowboy hat. "I did not, but I could use one."

Jordan laughed. "Okay, it must have been Walt looking out for us both, then."

Clay ran a hand over his face. "That sounds right. He ordered me into town to pick up the replacement glass for your window." He pointed at the large rectangle.

At the reminder of how her plans to be "helpful" sometimes backfired, Jordan winced. "Oh, yeah. That. I'm sorry but I definitely need your help repairing the window. Then you can show me again how to remove the plywood without breaking the window underneath."

Clay covered his heart with one hand. "You admit you need help? Are you okay, Jordan?"

She rolled her eyes and marched back to her car to get their lunches.

"I'm out of my depth with the repairs, Clay." She forced herself to be pleasant. "Does that make you feel better?"

Clay pursed his lips. "Not really. I mean, I didn't think I'd ever hear it, but I like confident Jordan a lot." He shifted on the tailgate. "But it is nice not to have to fight my way through the project. This day is improving. Nice nap. Good lunch delivered by a beautiful woman. And no arguments." He pinched the skin on the back of his hand. "No, you better do it. Pinch me so I know I'm awake."

Jordan clambered up on the tailgate and bumped him with her shoulder instead.

She had to do something.

If she stayed there and let the words *beautiful woman* repeat endlessly in her head, he would know he'd knocked her for a loop. Clay Armstrong had been good at that, once upon a time.

"How are the renovations going at your place?" she asked. Maybe he'd be gone soon.

"I'm dreaming of calling in a few guys who work for me to speed things up," Clay said as he yanked off his baseball cap and tossed it down in the truck bed. "Bunk beds, Jordan. Do you have a guess as to how much strain two grown men put on the weight restrictions of wooden bunk beds? I'm amazed I lived through the night."

Jordan could tell every word was heartfelt. Clay was expressing his emotions and it was wrong to laugh.

Right? She bit her lip, but the image of grizzly bears tossing and turning in tiny bunk beds kept popping up in her mind.

Why were they wearing old-fashioned sleep caps and nightgowns in her imagination?

"Are you laughing?" Clay asked suspiciously.

"No," Jordan said firmly. "I am not laughing."

"But you want to," he added.

"Food will help. It always does," Jordan said meekly.

Clay held her stare for a long moment before he chuckled. "Can we make it through a sandwich without debating something?"

"Let's give it a shot. We both need a good meal and some time with Key Lake right now." Jordan sorted out the contents of the bag. "And if you show me how to fix the water heater, I'll give you the piece of pie I ordered for myself."

He studied the container. "It's really good pie." Some of the humor had sparked in his dark eyes when he faced her again. "I accept your terms." He offered her his hand to shake, and Jordan did her best to ignore the pleasure that came from his skin pressed to hers.

"This is much nicer than fighting. Have we grown?" he asked.

"Matured, obviously." Jordan crossed one leg over the other and picked up her sandwich, pleased with how well her day was turning out. By the end of it, she might have hot water. Getting along with Clay was a new thing, too. She might even learn to enjoy it.

CHAPTER FOUR

THE THIRD TIME Clay reached behind him to straighten the flashlight—his dedicated assistant was supposed to be aiming the beam under the restaurant's oven so that he could see to restart the pilot light—he swallowed the order to pay attention and forced himself to count to ten. He'd learned that trick working alongside Jordan at the Majestic's marina. Going into the job that summer had been about earning spending money for college. Little did he know when Sadie Hearst offered him a pay bump in exchange for more responsibility that her beautiful great-niece was about to march through Prospect. He'd been knocked sideways, but he'd learned a lot about accomplishing tasks even when he was fascinated by his coworker.

As a coworker, Jordan had been sarcastic, funny and adorably out of her depth. Coming to her rescue had kept him busier than the actual boats on the lake, but her sharp wit had hooked him and reeled him in.

That fascination hadn't changed at all, but Jordan had. This time, she realized the problem before he could address it.

"I'm doing it again. Sorry." Jordan nodded once, tightened her grip on the flashlight and assumed her best intense expression. "I get distracted, but I won't let it happen again."

"Look at you. My number one apprentice." The light helped. He could see the tube for the pilot light now, but he was also aware of Jordan's elbow resting near his hip. "Didn't even have to repeat myself this time."

"You might have been my first boss, but you weren't the best one, Clay," Jordan drawled and inched closer with the light. "I'm a much better employee now, paid or unpaid, and don't you even say I couldn't have gotten any worse."

Since that was something he might have said at one time, Clay chuckled. "Wouldn't think of it."

"Right." The word was so long and drawn out; Jordan's disbelief dripped from the last letter.

"I never doubted you'd be good at anything

you decided you wanted to do. It was just selling bait was never your dream job." Clay recognized that she would tackle anything that she was passionate about. This whole episode had started with hot water, something most people would be enthusiastic to have; it had ended up with crawling around on the floor, but Jordan hadn't ghosted him yet.

"Once we finish this, we can go play in the lake." Clay had dared her to jump off the dock at quitting time every day that summer.

And she'd answered every dare.

As a teenager, Clay might not have understood life in small-town Prospect that winter day he met the Armstrongs for the first time, but it hadn't taken long for him to settle in and learn the rhythms. Life on the ranch in Larkspur Pass was comfortable, the seasons inspiring. He always had chores. Some days were for school. Others were for riding anywhere and everywhere he wanted to explore. Some days there were celebrations in town, and the family made trips to bigger cities for supplies and other events now and then.

But overall, nothing much disturbed the smooth surface of his life then. He'd known what to expect from every day.

Until Jordan arrived with a splash.

It was no wonder he'd fallen in love.

Clay rubbed his nose to chase away the sneeze that had been threatening ever since he'd scooted across the floor to peer under the stove. They'd started with the water heater for Sadie's apartment; after it lit successfully, they moved methodically through the rest of the lodge. They'd checked all the gas valves and pilot lights: the furnace that heated the Majestic, all the water heaters for the lodge rooms and the commercial kitchen. If he could make it through this last appliance in the restaurant without snapping at Jordan, they'd have worked together beautifully. Not a single argument, real or manufactured.

That showed true progress.

Two minutes. He could do anything for two minutes, even ignore the distracting pressure of Jordan's arm against his side. Clay grabbed his last long match, a happy discovery from Sadie's personal kitchen, lit it and stretched forward to light the pilot. When the flashlight jittered crazily, he knew Jordan was half a second from celebrating. "Give it a minute before you stir up a breeze, California."

She rolled her eyes at the old nickname, but

her lips curled and she wrapped both hands around the flashlight to steady it. At least she didn't try to change his mind about the nickname. More than once, she'd informed him she was a Coloradan at heart, having been born here, and had the birth certificate to prove it. He could still remember the way her eyes had flashed when he'd told her he'd heard Denver might as well be California.

Then she'd left that summer to go "home" to California without telling him goodbye and she'd never come back.

When he was certain the flame was good, Clay returned the oven drawer and closed it. He reset the oven temperature and watched the flame spread before sighing with satisfaction. Everything worked exactly how it was supposed to.

"This place is in great shape for being closed up for so long. We might have had some trouble getting these things started, but all the appliances are in working order," Clay said as he eased away from Jordan to stand. He offered her a hand and waited to see what she'd do. When she put her hand in his, he happily pulled her up to stand next to him. That was another satisfying thing about the day.

Clay was a builder. He loved house specs, custom detailing and every decision that he got to make that turned out one-of-a-kind houses. Homes that would weather all the ups and downs of life.

But the further he moved away from hands-on construction into the land of spreadsheets and sales meetings, the more he enjoyed small jobs like this one.

Restoring order always felt right.

Having a beautiful partner might have sweetened the project, too. When he realized how closely he was watching Jordan smooth loose strands of dark hair back into her ponytail, he started to worry he might have a problem. The world was full of beautiful women. He'd learned that between eighteen and now, but another thing that had gotten so much clearer: when a man was mesmerized by a woman who'd been crawling around on floors with a large smudge on her chin, he'd slipped into something other than appreciation. Loving teenage Jordan had been one thing, almost as inevitable as a sunrise.

But he'd learned a lot about himself and what he wanted from life since then. Building something for himself mattered, and Jordan would be nothing but a distraction. Falling for this version of Jordan would be a mistake.

Even if it was impossible to take his eyes off her.

Jordan moved to the sink, turned on the hot tap and ran her fingers under the water to test the temperature. He watched her chew her lip nervously and knew without a doubt what she was thinking. "Let it run for a minute. Don't give up yet."

Her eyes met his. "There you go, reading my mind again. I wasn't giving up."

How many times had he said that to her as a kid? At some point, someone had convinced her quitting was the only option when things didn't work, but Clay had never gotten that message. Whatever was broken could be made right with enough time and attention, even the hot water and the cranky marina cash register.

The words were achingly familiar.

Her cheer when the water turned hot made him laugh. "I guess it really is the little things, isn't it?"

She enthusiastically scrubbed her hands, even though there was no soap, and he decided to follow her lead. Getting rid of the dust bunnies might address the need to sneeze.

"Now," Clay said as he shook his hands to dry them, "what were you searching for while we were crawling around on the floor?"

Jordan motioned to the large, empty kitchen. When the Majestic had been running, this kitchen had served lodge guests and Prospect customers daily. If he recalled correctly, fried fish had been the menu staple, but Sadie Hearst's desserts had been the real draw. The quality of her pies, cakes and cookies had built her reputation and the restaurant's regular crowd, and the view of Key Lake from the large windows across the dining room meant every visit was a special occasion. Clay's father had treated his mother to anniversary dinners at the Majestic.

Today the kitchen was completely bare. Nothing on the shelves or counters. The spacious pantry had also been emptied. Any chef who needed an equipped kitchen would find plenty of space to fill, and now the appliances were working.

"Does it seem strange to you that we haven't seen any sign of critters?" Jordan raised her eyebrows as if she were illustrating what she meant by "sign."

Amused, Clay scanned the countertops and

the baseboard cabinetry. No holes. No damage. No "sign" of anything invisible yet alive in the kitchen. After so many years standing empty, it was impressive.

"Sadie wouldn't have had it any other way, would she?" he asked. She'd been larger-than-life, always making an impression. As a kid, he'd learned never to give Sadie a smart answer or a bit of trouble because she would return either without hesitation.

"But if you don't see a mouse or a rat—" Clay took her flashlight and held it under his chin as if he were about to tell a spooky story around a campfire "—then it has to be a ghost." He flicked the light switch on the wall off and on to make the overhead lights flicker.

Jordan crossed her arms over her chest, her lips twitching. "Fine. It can't be a ghost. On that we agree. Option C?" She inhaled slowly. "And why do I smell vanilla at the oddest times? It's so weird. When Sarah and I first got here, it was nice to find these little pockets of Sadie here and there around the Majestic. There were framed news stories hanging in the restaurant, one of her publicity shots, and her apartment had all these pieces that reminded me of her. This kitchen doesn't have any of her left, but that smell… It's like Sadie is still working away in here."

There was a beat of silence between them where he had to imagine how that might feel. The closest he'd come to losing someone he loved as much as the Hearst sisters had loved Sadie was his first foster mother. He'd been young, but the overwhelming sensation of drifting with nothing to anchor him in place had stuck with Clay. Some of that showed on Jordan's face now. He wanted to wrap his arms around her and pull her close.

She'd made him feel the same way when she was sixteen and angry and lost because she'd been sent away from home. The only way he'd known to help then was to distract her from her sadness. It would definitely still work in this case.

Clay pursed his lips. "Is smelling vanilla occasionally that odd? We're standing in the kitchen."

"It has been empty for years and years and years, Clay." Jordan's dark eyes flashed and the usual déjà vu kicked in. They might not have had this conversation before, but he'd been caught up in those eyes more than once at eighteen.

He offered her the flashlight. "Pretty good reason to continue your stay at Bell House if you ask me. Nobody wants to be squatting in a ghost's territory all alone. Of course, if the ghost is going to scare you by preparing some of Sadie's cowboy cookies, it might be worth the risk."

"You could have told me ghost stories were too much for you, Clay." Jordan tilted her head to study him critically.

"I love my family. I miss them when I'm not home. I'm trying to bond with them, you know?" He sighed. "But I'd bunk with an angry poltergeist right now as long as the snoring was quieter than Grant's." His hangdog expression tickled her as he'd intended.

"No fair when I'm determined to give you a hard time." Jordan covered her mouth until she could speak without giggling. "I have plenty of space here. You're welcome to some of it, but the question of who or what is going on in the kitchen remains unsolved. You don't know *everything*, cowboy. Ghosts might be real."

"What would you do if I took you up on

your offer?" he asked. It was a sign of how uncomfortable the bunk beds were that staying in a haunted hotel was enticing.

Jordan patted her shoulder. "Congratulate myself for finding an excellent loophole in Sarah's last instructions to me. If you were with me, I would no longer be alone." The triumphant fist pump she gave to punctuate her statement was adorable.

Clay lost track of how long they stood there, grinning at each other, until she blinked. The world came rushing back between them.

"Have you been down to the marina since you've been back?" he asked. "Want to take a walk there to see what kind of shape it's in?"

She hesitated so long that Clay was almost sure the answer was no. "When I made it back to LA that summer, I promised myself that I was never walking near the worm cooler again."

Clay drawled, "Did you ever walk by it when you were working at the marina? As I recall, I handled all the stocking of the live bait." He'd done it happily to be near her.

"I didn't think it was fair that you got to spend all the time out on the dock, gassing up boats, and I had to stay inside. It was a more equal distribution of labor," Jordan said airily as she moved past him and led the way out of the restaurant to the lobby. "I needed the vitamin D from the sunshine, you know."

Clay hurried to beat her to the front doors to open them for her as they stepped out into the dying afternoon sunlight.

"And how many times did you pump gas?" Clay tapped his chin as he bumped her shoulder. Matching her stride had always been natural. Jordan marched, as if she never had a doubt. There was no pause. When she changed her mind, she also changed direction immediately. She might move fast, but the length of his stride made it easy to keep pace with her.

"Not many. Good thing I was related to the boss, huh? I might have gotten fired." Jordan's laugh floated along the breeze. Had he heard her laugh so easily since she'd come back to Prospect? It was hard to picture her doing anything other than firmly avoiding his direct gaze or chewing her lip nervously. "You were pretty patient with me. I was certain my life ended when my father dropped me off here that summer. I had all these dreams of lazy days at the beach, not making change, pumping gas and dishing out live bait, but I got lucky you were trying to save up money for college." She darted a quick peek at him. "Anybody else would have made me work a lot harder."

"They might have tried, but you were equal to all my efforts." Clay shoved his hands in his pockets. "And I imagine any guy who got to work with you that summer would have been half in love and willing to do almost anything to make you happy."

As soon as he said "love," he regretted it. He'd already made it clear how her disappearing act from Prospect had devastated him.

Her laughter faded slowly.

"Love? That's impossible to imagine, Clay." Jordan shook her head wildly. "You certainly never had to struggle against your *overwhelming feelings for me*." She clasped her hands and pressed them to her chest, where her heart was. "I am not the kind of woman who inspires crushes. I was spoiled, annoying at sixteen." She waved a hand. "Forget that. I still am. I'm not telling you anything new. Brooke? She has this all-American girl kind of aura that makes everyone stumble over their own feet when they're around her. If we were flowers, she'd be a perfect rose." Jordan grimaced. "I'm more like a carnation, pretty but also common, you know? No thorns, but no one's going to pick me to declare undying love, either. I figure I got lucky with my boss that summer because you're old school. Chivalrous. Kind."

Clay wasn't sure whether to disagree with her about how unlikely it was for a man to fall for someone as smart and challenging as she was or to let her keep going. He liked the direction she was headed.

More than one woman had called him old-fashioned. That had to be the less polite version of antiquated. But no one had called him kind before. That landed differently, hitting him in the chest and lighting up with a little glow.

"When I talked to your dad in the store this morning, I could see the resemblance between you two. You and Wes both have that steadiness and charm. Believe me, it's rare." Jordan started down the path toward the lake and the marina.

"If I didn't know better, I'd think you like me, California," Clay murmured as he fell into step behind her. When there was no response from her, he didn't know if that was because she hadn't heard him or she hadn't wanted to comment.

Letting the moment go was the smart thing to do here.

They were on the edge of unfamiliar territory. A place neither of them had been to before, where love and hate or like and dislike melded into something different when honesty was added to the mix. Jordan would steer them back to familiar ground if he followed her.

Clay wasn't certain that was the direction he wanted to go.

CHAPTER FIVE

JORDAN WAS STILL analyzing their "love" conversation as she watched Clay open the door to the restroom. The short walk down to the marina had been beautiful and silent. It was impossible to read Clay's face while he stopped and assessed, but his last words had confirmed that she was as good at hiding her emotions as he was. He was only *beginning* to understand she liked him?

Clay Armstrong, the boy who had changed her summer and her mind about so many things, had no notion how deep that "like" went. Jordan wasn't sure whether to congratulate herself on protecting that sensitive girl's heart or to apologize to him for not making it clearer how much his friendship had meant to her that summer. Being embarrassed by her feelings then and now was a confusing place.

He paused in the doorway, one hand wrapped on the frame, and quietly performed his careful catalog of details, including the condition of the ceiling, walls and floors, just as he had in every room they'd entered that afternoon. First, he scanned for evidence of leaks or other damage. Then his head tipped down as he surveyed the floor, always from right to left. This time, he stepped inside to flick the light switch on and then off. He flushed the toilet and ran the water. She recalled Clay had always had a system for doing things, a particular order that made the most sense to him. So as he'd been showing her the ropes at the marina, she'd delighted in "forgetting" the correct order and following her own drum.

Mainly to cause low-level chaos that ruffled his feathers.

His response to that had always been to move closer to Jordan to demonstrate whatever it was she needed "help" with.

Getting his attention was a victory then. Somehow, in the years away from him, she'd assumed her true form of a cussedly independent person who didn't need assistance ever. It was nice to find somewhere in the middle with Clay.

"How did you decide to become an architect?" Jordan asked, ready for a distraction.

"You were planning to be something practical the last time we were here together." Was his major accounting then? A subject like that.

He stepped out of the restroom. "I had this history class that required a research project." He leaned against the door frame, one knee bent. There, in his jeans and flannel, there was no mistaking that Clay had grown into a strong, handsome man. "I never have done things the easy way." His ironic smile was cute. "I picked Sullivan's Post, the ghost town in the hills above the Majestic."

"Oh, I remember the ghost town that Sadie would never let us go see because it was in such bad shape," Jordan explained with a pout. "You were supposed to take me."

"But you left before I had the chance to." He waited for her to acknowledge her disappearing act before continuing his story. "I researched the buildings. Sadie was a great resource because her father had written down what he knew of the people and businesses. My simple paper about this silver-mining town transitioned into building materials, tools and construction processes of the late 1800s. I included careful sketches of how the Ace High might have been built at that time."

He shook his head. "I got an A but I will never forget the professor's comments. 'Become an architect. No one else cares this much about construction.'"

Jordan nodded. "So you did. That was solid advice."

Clay agreed, "Yeah. Only I don't draw up a lot of plans anymore. These subdivisions my company is building at the moment seemed like the natural evolution. They used all my skills, right? Planning, drafting, construction, people. But I had no concept of how much I hated financial spreadsheets. My partner hates them, too. When I can't charm her into attending sales meetings with the agency listing the lots for sale, I go, but then I always wonder how I ended up there."

"Sounds like me in my gray cubicle staring at a screen all day long," Jordan said.

Clay's eyes met hers. "I would hate that, too. Quitting was the smart choice. You deserve something better."

The way his affirmation landed like a warm hug startled Jordan.

She wasn't used to anyone supporting her choices so easily, but he had a history of reacting differently to Jordan than the other people in her life. There had been no worried sighs or well-meaning lectures from him. Instead, his usual response had been to affirm or encourage.

Handsome golden boy Clay Armstrong had never been short of female admirers on the lake.

He had treated them exactly as he had Jordan, offering a teasing grin, clever words and patient assistance.

For Jordan, who had been bruised from her father's lectures about her bad decisions and the out-of-control direction her life had taken after her mother's death, Clay's presence and words had been a blessing.

Sometimes irritating, but never disappointing.

And then she'd left without saying goodbye, stayed away for years and returned to Prospect without telling him. Thank goodness they'd worked through all that. He'd already done more to make it possible to live at the Majestic than she would have ever dreamed of asking him.

"How did you decide to start your own business?" Jordan asked.

Clay shrugged. "Not sure it was ever really a choice." He propped his hands on his hips. "My whole life has been about starting with nothing and building something. It's easy to get discouraged as a kid when you look around and see what you don't have, you know?"

Jordan nodded but she wasn't sure she did, not the way Clay and his foster brothers understood that.

"Walt and Prue told us from the very beginning that if we worked hard they would support us with everything they could. I believed them. I studied. I made good grades. Those were things I could control, right?" Clay said. "That hard work led to more hard work but more success, too. So, when it was time to figure out a career, I didn't want to be limited by what other people said I could do. Flipping houses was simple enough. Buy the worst, work day and night to fix it up, sell and pour every bit of profit you make into the next one. We're doing the same thing today, just with more houses and larger investments. Each step moves me upward, but the higher we go, the smaller the safety net feels."

Jordan considered all the trouble she'd had stepping out and saying she wanted to give the Majestic a try herself. "Seems pretty brave to me."

"Walt and Prue wouldn't let me fail," he said firmly.

Jordan was just as certain Clay Armstrong would never let himself fail.

"Everything satisfactory in there?" Jordan pointed toward the restroom. As soon as they'd come back to the marina, she'd immediately sat on the laminated counter that held the cash register and folded her legs tailor-style.

It was as if she'd never left the place. It had been her favorite perch between customers.

"I guess I can't get you to move this time by telling you your aunt Sadie better not catch you sitting down on the job, can I?" Clay ran his hand down the painted door trim. "It's amazing how well this place has held together. Do you have a guess when the marina was added on?"

Jordan shrugged. "No idea, sorry. Aren't you the construction expert?"

Clay pursed his lips as he seemed to be considering that before he nodded in agreement. "I don't remember a time when there was no marina. The style of the building makes me think of the fifties, but it could be a lot earlier."

"I concur." Jordan enjoyed his snort. "Why do you ask?"

"All the materials are solid." He knocked on the wall. "I appreciate the skill it took to make all this, that's all. Standing here, I feel as if this marina, the Majestic, are special to this place, could only have been built here and by the people who did it. A one-of-kind result with real history." His eyes met hers. "Sure would be a shame to tear down buildings that have stood the test of time to replace them with a generic mansion that could have been put together yesterday in any city on the map."

On that, they agreed. It was that same emotion or unnamed feeling that Jordan and her sisters were wrestling with. If they sold the Majestic, that unique time-place combination that had made Sadie Hearst a legend would be gone forever. The places she'd walked, where she'd worked and laughed, enjoyed moments with family and friends would disappear.

The longer Jordan stayed here, the more memories that resurfaced, the better she understood that losing it would mean losing an important piece of what had made her and her sisters who they were, too. How many people were lucky enough to have that connection to the past?

When Jordan's mother died, everything changed. Her father had needed new surroundings, so they'd moved to California, drawing Sadie along, too, eventually. The ties to the Majestic had frayed, but spending time here now, regardless, strengthened them.

She knew Sarah understood that.

If they could get Brooke here, would their decision about what to do with the lodge change?

"It could be worse, you know? I mean whatever takes this spot could definitely be worse than a boring box with zero personality. You'd have hated the monstrosity of glass and metal that the casino developer was proposing." Jordan grimaced. "I did. All wrong. If the mansion was vanilla ice cream, boring but edible, the casino was a strange combination of, like—" Jordan tried to dream up the worst blend of flavors "—mint and bacon."

Clay's disgusted expression delighted her. She'd nailed the metaphor. Simile? Whatever. He understood her.

"That's what I love about my job." He held up a finger. "Not the paperwork, but the ability to explore a new site and dream up the design that fits." He studied the open space of the marina. "Even now, this place is perfect. Completely outdated, but it would be simple enough to change the fixtures, paint and refinish the floor, and that way you could hold on to the history without losing function or style."

Jordan would have never used the word *style*, but she got what he meant. Even the marina could be a one-of-a-kind experience in the right hands.

She stared at the room lined with cleaned shelves and counters and thanked the stars above that the dreaded live bait cooler had been emptied. If the spotless condition of the kitchen and carefully cleared convenience store here at the marina were evidence of anything, it was that the temporary manager had taken their job seriously. The small storage room next to the kitchen held carefully labeled boxes, all neatly stacked. A new owner could come in tomorrow, scrub hard, restock and open the doors for business.

Like with the restaurant kitchen, all this place needed was the right person to step up.

"In my mind, this was so much bigger." Then she patted the heavy, ancient cash register that had given her actual fits as a teenager. "Can you believe no one has broken in to steal this beauty?"

"I'm not sure it can be removed from its spot. The whole place was probably built around it." Clay's lips curled. "Might be worth something. It's definitely an antique. You should take it with you as a souvenir. I remember how much you loved putting a new roll of tape in."

"Right. Sadie laughed so hard her mascara ran the day she came in and heard me cussing and lamenting this stupid cash register. Said it was expanding my vocabulary every minute." Jordan slipped off the counter, immediately regretting the spray of dust that went up.

Clay sneezed twice, loudly, before Jordan followed with her own.

He pointed to the dock. "Seems like some cleaning is still required. Let's get some fresh air."

Jordan followed him out and locked the doors. As she expected him to, Clay meandered down to sit at the edge of the dock. She was drawn to follow him. She had been at sixteen, too.

Every day, he'd dared her to jump into Key Lake. Jordan had spent a lot of time in her head that summer, thinking, worrying, vowing, but Clay had given her one choice of her own at the end of every shift: jump or don't jump.

That summer, up until she'd stood toe-to-toe with Clay, she had been certain that she was too mature, or worried about her hair or her clothes or her aunt Sadie's opinion or what she was missing out on in LA or whether her family would ever forgive her for her bad decisions or if she'd find the place she truly fit in to respond to his silly little game.

And then she'd jumped.

Just to hear him whoop and clap and then the satisfying splash when he did the same.

"We aren't going into the water today?" Jordan asked as she eased down next to him.

"My estimation of the water temperature gave me frostbite in my boots." Clay stretched back to rest on his elbows. "But if you're around in June, we'll talk about it again."

Jordan memorized the fading golden light

spreading across the mountains that framed Key Lake in the quiet moment. The trees ringing the lake and spreading up over the mountains were reds and golds and evergreens. "This has to be the prettiest month to live in Prospect."

"It's tempting to say that in every season. Spring has all the new blossoms and the joy of green grass, summer means this water is absolutely perfect, clear and cold, and winter has days with the brightest blue skies and pristine snow." He turned to face her. "But I can't argue that fall is gorgeous all the way around."

"Wow, Clay Armstrong is a poet." She wrinkled her nose to soften the teasing.

"I prefer artist." They sat in companionable silence as the sun set, the only sounds the wind in the trees, crisp falling leaves rustling and small splashes on the water where fish were hunting for dinner.

Had she ever experienced this kind of peace anywhere else?

"While we're getting along so well, I need to know something." Jordan waited for him to turn his head and raise an eyebrow. "Why don't you ever wear a cowboy hat? Isn't that one of the rules of being a cowboy?" She tapped the bill of his ballcap and knocked off a small dust bunny he'd picked up somewhere along their tour.

"I do." He shrugged. "But the cap and the work boots make sense on the job. I don't worry about losing them. The cowboy hat comes out on special occasions."

"Like when?" Jordan asked.

"Business meetings where I'm determined to impress. Holidays with my family." He grinned. "Important dates with beautiful women."

The reminder of how he'd called her a beautiful woman when she'd been offering him lunch shot through Jordan and she straightened.

"If you see the hat, you know I'm doing something I can't afford to mess up," Clay said.

Jordan inhaled slowly, caught off guard by his answer and how much she suddenly wanted to see him in that hat. "I guess you had plans for today? Other than catching a nap in the bed of your truck." She squeezed his arm. "I didn't mean to keep you all afternoon, but I could never have done any of this without you. I appreciate it. Thank you. When Walt handed me parts to repair the hot water heater myself, I was worried."

He chuckled. "The thing about my father is that he will never pass up an opportunity to tease you. To tease anyone. The next time he tries something like that, call his bluff. Think of the most dangerous tool you can, something with teeth and power, and ask him to add it to whatever it is he's recommending. He'll get fatherly and serious quickly."

Jordan laughed. "I like your dad. I love the store. Hidden pockets of things here and there. You never know what you'll find."

"True. It's his hobby. Always has been, but now he gets to spend time there, telling stories to whoever comes in. It makes him happy to be that close to my mother, like they needed these separate lives to be able to get along. Actually, it's more than that. To be whole, I think. He talks about selling the business, but that would break everyone's heart." Clay shook his head. "As much as I love the place, I do wish I knew how to find things in there without plenty of spare time and a miner's helmet."

His eyes met hers, spinning the invisible string that drew them closer.

"I don't want to go home." Clay sighed. "It's chaos. Growing up there, we were crowded but we didn't know any better. I've gotten comfortable with my own space since. The snoring, Jordan."

His tone was despair, a man facing a terrible prospect.

She, Sarah and Brooke had spent more than one night in the pillow fort their father had built in their living room, but that had been decades ago. Could the trio live happily together now for any amount of time?

Probably not. It was easy enough to picture how Brooke would take over a bathroom at fifteen. She couldn't have improved much.

"I have lots of rooms. Lots of space. A lot of it covered in dust, possibly worse, but you're welcome to use any of it." Jordan bumped his shoulder. "I have hot water now."

"And it would keep you from being out here all by yourself." He tipped his chin down to give her his serious face. "I don't like that idea, California."

Jordan mirrored his expression. "You do realize I am all by myself all the time, don't you, cowboy? LA or Prospect, I've only got me. Surely crime is lower here in the heartland than the big scary city."

She thought she'd won the argument until he raised his eyebrows. "How many bears do you meet in the mean streets of the City of Angels?"

Jordan pursed her lips. "You'd be surprised that the answer to that is not zero as you might expect."

He chuckled. "Fine. I guess I can't argue with that."

Pleased, Jordan straightened. "I will take your warnings to heart."

"And then do whatever you had planned to do all along," Clay said.

Jordan got up slowly. "It's nice to reconnect with old friends. We don't have to go through all that 'me, being me' again for you to get how I operate. I like it." She watched him rising, the present and the past overlapping since it was easy to picture lanky Clay, with his sunburned nose and board shorts, in the man who stood across from her in flannel and work boots.

Both versions of Clay were too handsome to be real.

"Are we friends?" he asked. "Were we friends before?"

His uncertainty caused a sharp stab of pain. "I thought we were. Was I wrong?"

Clay tilted his head back to study the darkening sky.

Jordan followed his lead. The sky was cloudless. When dark fully fell here at the Majestic, the stars would be clear, almost close enough to touch. He'd been the one to convince her to stop long enough to look up and admire them that summer.

Surely that meant they'd been friends.

"What I know is…" Clay said slowly as if choosing his words carefully. "I owe you an apology, too."

Jordan turned back to face him so quickly she almost lost her balance. She gripped his arm to steady herself. "You do? For what?"

One corner of his mouth curled. "Don't tell me you've forgotten what sent you running back to LA. The kiss? Right here on this dock? I kissed you without your permission, scared you off and you left Prospect." He shook his head. "I would have apologized then if I'd had the chance."

Stumbling to catch up in her head, Jordan

crossed her arms over her chest. "I didn't hear an apology when I came back to town, weeks ago, although you were certainly happy to ask for one from me for taking off on you and Prospect unexpectedly."

Clay cleared his throat. "I'm sorry. I shouldn't have done it. You were right about reacting the way that you did. My father would have pushed me into the water himself if he'd seen me that afternoon. I wish you had."

She hadn't ever considered shoving him away. Instead, she had run up the trail to the Majestic like her hair was on fire, begged Sadie to take her home and tried to block the embarrassment from her mind.

All because she'd been absolutely certain that she'd kissed her handsome boss without his permission. Jordan had known deep down in her cringing soul that she'd shown this man that she liked him, when he was simply being Clay—patient, kind, cute, charming Clay, who could do much better than misfit Jordan Hearst.

Sadie had taken pity on her, loaded her up and driven to LA to start hunting for her own home there.

It was a good thing she'd insisted Clay explain what he wanted an apology for or she would have confessed to the wrong thing. Leaving without saying goodbye had hurt his feelings. Confessing that she'd had a crush on him and finding this out would have caused intolerable embarrassment.

Jordan cleared her throat in the effort to contain the laughter ticking under the surface. There would be plenty of time to secretly laugh at teenage Jordan later. "Well…" Was she going to tell him the whole truth here? If she did, she was sure she'd be forced to issue another apology. "It was a good kiss. No hard feelings." She tangled her fingers together to wait patiently.

Clay tipped his head to the side as he absorbed that answer. "No hard feelings."

Jordan was relieved. "None." She patted his shoulder as if he were the helpful kid who'd loaded her groceries in her car for her. "It's been a long time. We've done a lot of growing up since then. It was certainly not a disappointing first kiss for me, down here beside the lake."

"First kiss," he repeated.

"It wasn't your first kiss, though, was it?" Jordan pointed at him. He shook his head.

Of course not. Why did that take some of the wind out of her sails?

And when had the suggestion of Clay becoming overwhelmed with attraction and the urge to kiss her blown those sails in the first place?

"We talked about how you didn't belong in LA or in your house or anywhere, remember? I understood what you meant because life as a foster kid had convinced me that I'd never fit in the spaces I should, until I got here." Clay untangled his knotted fingers. "Key Lake washed all that away for both of us. I was so close to you."

Jordan rubbed the aching spot between her eyebrows. She didn't want to remember that conversation. That nagging misfit label was still her biggest worry. At work. With her family. So far, Prospect had treated her better, but telling him the things she'd kept bottled up before and since then had been a mistake.

The kiss had made that as clear as the stars above them.

Her wild emotions had stilled when his lips touched hers.

That had scared her like nothing else could.

What would happen if they kissed now? The anxiety that welled up at the thought nearly stole her breath, but the restlessness that accompanied every important decision Jordan ever made was there, too. She knew what she wanted, even though kissing Clay made no sense, and not grabbing it would continue to itch under her skin. Running away became a solid option.

"Be my friend again, Clay. Please." Jordan didn't want to go down memory lane any farther. Those wild emotions? Keeping them carefully contained had been the work of a lifetime. He'd been the catalyst before, but if the dam broke again, here, with Clay, Jordan wasn't sure where the flood would take her.

That summer, she'd had Sadie to keep her from being swept away, but Sadie was gone.

"Fine, but I need a promise." They stood and headed along the path that led up to the lodge. Dark shadows from the trees were spreading across it, and Jordan was glad to have his company. Despite her big words about the possibility of running into bears in LA, she was not a wilderness girl. Having his hand wrapped around hers turned this into an adventure instead of an opportunity to imagine all the hungry wildlife that might be lying in wait.

"You won't leave without saying goodbye this time, will you?" Clay said as he pointed out a log that might trip her up. "Before, there was a chance you'd visit or Sadie might drop tidbits of information about how you were, what you were doing. This time, you won't be coming back. Ever."

That was the heavy pain that work kept at a distance. Selling the lodge made sense, but losing it would be like saying goodbye to Sadie again. Grief threatened to overwhelm her, but Jordan opened the door to Sadie's apartment and sighed with relief as they returned to familiar territory. She'd avoided the storm this time.

"Okay, I'll make that promise." Jordan crossed her arms. "But I need you to answer something honestly for me. I trust you not to sugarcoat the answer."

He raised his eyebrow before agreeing. They both knew he would always tell the truth.

Jordan trusted him to do it without hurting her.

"If you were in my spot," Jordan said as

she held out her arms to indicate the apartment, lodge and surroundings, "would you try to convince your brothers to reopen the lodge?" Before he could answer, she held up both hands in the "stop" position. "You have to imagine you're me, undependable Jordan Hearst, who runs away when handsome boys kiss her or when jobs get too boring, who has two sisters who could definitely use the money from the sale and there are no funds for renovation or even the basics until customers can actually stay in the lodge or eat in the restaurant. In that situation, is it ridiculous to dream about how you would start up the Majestic again?"

She could tell he was waiting for her to finish, so she tacked on, "And you have no experience running fishing lodges, restaurants or businesses in general." Hearing it all laid out like that, Jordan was sure she'd tell herself it was an over-the-top silly suggestion.

Clay's lopsided grin eased some of the tension knotting her stomach. "Anyone lucky enough to have this place land in their lap? To me, it's wild to ever consider selling it. It's a treasure you don't let go of."

The way their eyes locked reignited the

uneasy tremble in her abdomen that accompanied the anxiety of those emotions that slipped out of her control. His answer was perfect. Only stepping into his arms to press her lips against his felt like the next correct move. The way she wanted to jump into his arms reminded her of the freedom of taking his dares.

"It will take hard work, but you seem to have gotten better at that." He grunted when she poked him in the stomach in pretend outrage. "So long as there are no live worms in the fridge."

"I can work. I will work. It's the money this place will take to get it going…" She huffed. "Forget that. It's the money my sisters will lose if we don't sell that worries me." She rolled her eyes. "That and the fact that my sisters have watched me pull the same disappearing act far too many times. They won't trust me to do this, even if I can overcome the other problems. I don't see how I can do this without them."

His slow smile increased the jitters. "Maybe you've found the one thing that can finally convince you to hang around and fight. All that stuff's true, but none of it changes who you are, Jordan."

"What does that mean?" she asked with a sigh. That was the big question, wasn't it? It was the one she'd been struggling to answer her whole life.

"Sadie was able to build a career and a fortune from this small start, and anyone who ever met both of you would say you were made from the same mold. What can you accomplish if you decide to dig in right here?"

Before she could answer, and Jordan had no clue what she'd say, Clay's phone rang. "Hello, big brother." He rolled his eyes and smiled at Jordan's laugh. Soon she realized Wes was only doing Sarah's bidding and scowled. "Yes, we're locking up for the day. Hot water is working. All the pilots are lit. Window is repaired and Jordan and I had a workshop on removing the rest of the plywood covering the windows. We've been busy."

She listened in to his list and realized how much help he'd already given her.

And on a place she wasn't even sure she'd own tomorrow.

Clay Armstrong was a good friend at eighteen.

He was a good man now.

And apparently she hadn't embarrassed herself into oblivion at sixteen by kissing a boy who'd only been nice to her. Jordan had made a lot of progress for one day.

"Yes, I'll follow Jordan out, but you'll have to convince her not to pack up and move out here tomorrow. She informed me that she spends a lot of time alone in the big, bad city and bears mean nothing to her. Please tell her sister that. If Sarah is still worried, I'll grab a sleeping bag and come stay in one of the lodge rooms, but you will both definitely owe me for that." Jordan grinned at his tone. Some things were universal. The younger siblings tormenting the responsible, bossy older siblings had to be one of them, and selling what he in fact wanted most as a great sacrifice was one of her favorite tricks, too. "I want the fried chicken and all the fixins. What's for dessert?" He listened intently. "Two helpings of the peach cobbler, please."

Then he put his phone away. "The Armstrong Dinner Delivery Service is annoying, but they do good work in the end."

Jordan sighed. "Guess I'll have to take myself to the Ace High. I want peach cobbler, too." As she went to grab her phone and turn off the lights in the small kitchen, she realized she'd be able to buy groceries and make her own dinner tomorrow night if she moved into Sadie's apartment.

If she did it without telling anyone, she wouldn't have to worry about anyone worrying about her, either.

The idea settled her a bit, made her feel more like herself. The Jordan Hearst who did exactly what she wanted to do.

Except kiss Clay Armstrong.

When the lights were out and she'd locked up, Clay trailed her to where their cars were parked.

"Thank you for everything you did today. If you want the space, I'll clear out a room or rooms for any or all of you while you're renovating." Jordan knew it might be a mistake to have the Armstrongs underfoot if she wanted to attempt further updates on the sly, but offering them an out from their own crowded house was the right thing to do. "Only if you can clear out the ghost." There was no sense in being sacrificial here. She didn't want to investigate if outside creatures had made their way inside. He would do an excellent job with that.

"Thanks. I might take you up on it, whether you're being haunted by a cookie-baking ghost or not." Clay motioned her to her car. He wasn't leaving until she did.

Jordan grinned as she climbed into her sedan and then drove back along the road into town, with his headlights in her rearview mirror. Talking to Clay had settled some of her worry about stepping forward to ask her sisters to trust her to reopen the lodge. He hadn't hesitated or hooted with laughter.

If she could convince him not to bring up the kiss or her previous escape from the jumble of emotions it brought, he would be a steady advisor. Turning onto the town's main street, she enjoyed how reassuring it was to have Clay Armstrong nearby.

CHAPTER SIX

FIVE DAYS AFTER he'd enjoyed his afternoon crawling around in the Majestic's dust with Jordan, Clay was perched on a ladder asking himself how he'd ended up putting a hip roof on the Rocking A farmhouse addition with only his brothers' help. Growing up on the ranch meant they'd had plenty of time to build basic fix-it skills. Upkeep on the house, the barns, the fences—they'd all had an opportunity to learn.

The problem was that it had been a long time since the boys had had to work together. Clay'd been overconfident in his management abilities and in how well his brothers could be managed. Framing the walls for the addition of his father's new apartment had gone so smoothly that he hadn't realized it was because they'd done their tasks independently.

Following orders was not in his brother Grant's genetic makeup.

Getting along with Grant was not in Travis's genetic makeup, apparently.

And Wes and Matt disappeared whenever Clay wasn't watching them. They said it was to take care of "important business."

Now that the sun was setting, Clay was contemplating vanishing himself. All the way back to Colorado Springs.

He'd take a loan out, finance some other poor crew to come and finish this job, happily make payments for the rest of his life and still come out ahead of trying to put up the trusses with the Fighting Armstrongs as his muscle.

Tonight he was going to sit down and calculate how far this farmhouse reno project had fallen behind. Their deadline was only a little over two weeks away, and it had been tight but doable in the beginning. Now he was starting to worry. His hunch was that he should not be staring at open sky where the new bedroom ceiling for these foster kids should be.

Clay had gotten so much done himself today because Travis had spent his time in a class to complete his CPR training, which would meet one of the foster care requirements. And he had sent Grant to Frisco to pick up paint and whatever he could add to the list. Seeing he was shorthanded, Wes had taken pity on him and they had worked together efficiently, crossing things off the list, until Dr. Singh had arrived from town for an appointment to go see the house available for rent that Wes was coordinating on behalf of one of their neighbors. Could Clay build the whole roof himself? Maybe, and it would be a lot more fun, but he'd never make the deadline.

Clay peered over his shoulder as Wes's truck rolled back into the yard. He and Dr. Singh strolled around the house to stand next to the addition. They both propped their hands on their hips and stared up at him.

"Sun's setting. You're going to have to come down from there, eventually," Wes said.

"Doc, do you concur with his diagnosis?" Clay climbed slowly down the ladder before offering a hand to Prospect's only general practitioner.

Dr. Singh pumped his hand down once in a firm handshake before trotting up Clay's ladder to take a look around. "I do, yes, I do. This is coming along!" He craned his neck to see everything he could in the setting sun before hopping back down. "You do good work."

Before he could say thank you, Wes said, "Dr. Singh's about to head to Haiti for a medical mission. He's going to rent Sharita's house so his replacement will have somewhere to stay."

"Not a replacement," Dr. Singh said as he held up one hand. "Or, at least add on 'temporary' there. Prospect is home and my wife had made me promise we're coming back at the end of six months. She's concerned the grandkids won't remember us."

"The town will miss you both," Wes said.

"Dr. Keena Murphy's taking a break from her Denver emer oom to spend some time in Prospect. I will write a prescription that everyone here makes her welcome." He beamed at them as if he had no doubts. "I know the Armstrongs will be the first to step up. Glad she will have you all for neighbors."

Wes clapped him on the back. "Can you stay for dinner, Doc? No idea what it'll be, but I'll round up plenty." The doctor waved his hands and started backing up toward his car. "No, I better get home. We are making so many arrangements for travel and getting the clinic ready for Dr. Murphy. The to-do list never stops, but thank you for helping me cross this one off the list, Wes." He waved at them both and trotted toward his car.

Wes and Clay followed slowly behind and watched him drive down the lane toward the highway from their spot near the paddock in front of the house.

"He's always running. I guess that's how he gets so much done in this town. Hope the new doctor can keep up." Wes sighed. "Being the only lawyer in town keeps a man busy, too, but I was glad to get down off the ladder." Wes held up his hand to show Clay a bruise. "I'm wounded."

Clay resisted the urge to poke the bruise out of orneriness. "How'd you do that?"

"Dropped a hammer." Wes shook his hand as if it still hurt.

"Were you holding the hammer in your other hand?" Clay asked slowly, trying to picture Wes functioning on the job with one of his usual crews. It wasn't happening.

"We made a good team today," Wes said, instead of answering his question.

"Got all the plates on. When the trusses arrive tomorrow, we'll be ready to put them on." And the hardest part would be done. Without the pressure of meeting the deadline, the hopes of his entire family weighing on his shoulders, the project's budget crunch and the hammer-dropping crew, he would have enjoyed the work.

His usual team would have had this done in half the time, and Clay would have had no new gray hairs to show for it, either.

"Where is everyone?" Clay asked.

Wes climbed up to sit on the top bar of the fence and rested his elbow on the post. "Matt's having equipment delivered early to the office tomorrow, so he's in town."

"What does that have to do with working tonight?" Clay asked.

"Not a thing." Wes shook his head. "But you also couldn't have talked him out of leaving. He yelled his excuses as he reversed out of the yard."

Clay could picture it easily. "You'd think a veterinarian would have a better work ethic."

Wes frowned at him. "In Matt's case, don't know why you would. He makes sure to tell everyone he's the baby of the family so he can get away with anything."

Since he'd mostly said it to make conversation, Clay didn't argue. The "kid" was less than two years younger than the rest of them, but Matt had arrived last and graduated behind his brothers. In his mind, that made him the youngest and worthy of spoiling. The kid worked as hard as the rest of them, traveling all over the county to take care of animals large and small, so even though they teased him, he still got away with escaping a few chores now and then.

Clay inhaled slowly and enjoyed the cool air. This was the perfect time to be on a job site—not too hot or cold. Dry, sunny days would soon run out and leave snow on the ground.

They had to get this addition closed up before then.

"I'm guessing you were calculating how far behind we are," Wes said as he squinted into the setting sun.

"It'll be a close finish." Clay waited to see if the answer he'd been giving anxious Travis would satisfy Wes. They stood there in silence for a long minute.

"If we could find the funds, you got a crew who can come in and finish up the roof?" Wes asked. "I'm afraid there will be real arguments and a whole lot of disappointment if we don't get some real help and soon. Not sure if it will be you coming after us or if Travis will finally let off some of the steam that's been building, but either way, it will be a smart investment to keep the peace."

Relief settled in Clay. Of course Wes was watching and doing his best to find solutions. They'd all come to depend on that.

"All day, I wondered the same thing. Winter will be here before we're ready if we don't pick up the pace." Clay weighed the pros and cons. "We need to keep spending down. That has been the goal all along, right? Postpone other add-ons so that we can get the essential part of the house ready for the foster kids. That's got to be priority number one. Then we make the whole place more livable for you sad sacks that are dead set on living together again."

Wes grunted. "Realistically, how many days are we talking about to get the roof on and shingled?"

Clay closed his eyes. "Two likely? Possibly three? If we have all the materials and professionals who don't drop their hammers on their own fingers, it'll go fast. But out here, if I've forgotten something that Dad doesn't normally carry at the store, we'll be running the roads."

"You didn't forget anything." There was not a drop of doubt in Wes's delivery. "You check and check and check again. I've watched you. Grant may have fallen for this errand run you sent him on today, but it won't work again. No way you'd miss the details twice."

"You been keeping an eye on things from the cushy comfort of your office?" Clay asked.

"You bet. Someone has to, and keep the bills paid," Wes answered loftily. "Although, now that Travis insists on handling feeding the livestock and dealing with the ranch repairs, I do have more free time to keep a closer eye on all of you."

Clay knew they'd have few opportunities like this one to talk freely, so he asked the question that had been bothering him the most. "What are we gonna do if we don't get approved to foster these kids? Travis has put everything, including himself, into this…" Clay trailed off because it was hard to describe how his brother seemed stretched so tightly that one wrong move might shatter him.

Wes sighed. "We'd figure it out. We always do."

"Any idea what's eating him?"

"The first home study with the caseworker rattled him. He's never been good at waiting." Wes pulled his hat off and scrubbed a hand through his hair. "And having Grant prowling around doesn't help."

Clay tilted his chin up, as if asking a question. But Wes understood it correctly to mean "what's his deal?"

"Too much spare time on his hands is my guess. Don't know what happened that sent him home from the rodeo circuit but he has jumped on any job he finds," Wes added.

They weren't going to solve whatever was bothering Travis or Grant tonight.

"I'll make a call to the crews I usually hire to see if anyone's got time to come here." Clay pressed his hand over his eyes, relieved to have help on the way even if he couldn't quite figure out what they'd have to lose on the project to pay for it. "Have you talked to Jordan about housing them for a couple of nights or do you want me to?"

He and any crew he could find would stay at the lodge until this house was finished. It might be dangerous to be that close, because no one could mention her without him feeling that spark of attraction, and this time he had no one to blame but himself.

He'd resisted driving over to the Majestic to check on Jordan because this construction project had consumed his days. And not sleeping while Grant grumble-snored next to him in the living room, rather than their newly painted bedroom, had preoccupied his nights.

"She's been working hard," Wes told him. "I went over there yesterday because Sarah was concerned, and she had mattresses propped up behind the lodge. She was beating them with a tennis racket." Wes held up his hands to make a small circle. "One of the antique wooden ones? No telling where she found it."

Clay pictured Jordan whaling on the mattresses. "It was probably good for her. Therapeutic."

Wes sighed. "She did appear happier than I've ever seen her."

"Did she tell you why she was working out her issues that way?" Clay couldn't connect the dots, but he would bet money that Jordan had taken the tiny snowflake of reopening the lodge herself that she'd floated between them and was rolling it into a giant snowball at this point.

"My guess is she wanted to see if the mattresses could be salvaged. For the lodge. To use them." Wes was studying his face so hard as he spoke, that Clay started picking at a splinter he'd gotten stuck in his palm that afternoon. "What's your best guess?"

Clay nodded slowly. "Wouldn't surprise me, but I can neither confirm nor deny."

Wes huffed out a breath. "Why?"

"Because anything I say to you will go directly to her sister, and Jordan deserves to talk to Sarah when she's ready." Remembering their teenage kiss had stirred up so many other memories.

Standing on the dock at the marina, he could recall young Jordan explaining to him what it was like to be in the middle, with an older sister who was so capable and a younger one who was beloved. She'd wanted to be able to fit in and make her own decisions about her life instead of being uprooted. At sixteen, Jordan had been confused and hurting and lost.

Clay understood those parts of Jordan even better now. As a kid, he hadn't been able to name the fear that pushed him. Since then, he'd worked so hard to build his business, to prove his second chance at the Rocking A had made a difference in his life. Now that he'd reached the make-it-or-break-it point, he was scared of what would happen if he failed. The worried kid who'd met Prue and Walt Armstrong that snowy first day was still with him.

There were parts of that Jordan still inside her, too, he knew. They'd come out when she'd asked for his honest opinion about whether she could reopen the Majestic herself.

Her uncertainty had shown in the wrinkle between her eyebrows, the way she nervously tangled her fingers and chewed her lip, but there had also been hope in her eyes.

Her dark eyes had always been so expressive. When they'd been there in Sadie's apartment, he could see Jordan had faced him with a mixture of fear for his answer, trust in his honesty and hope that he would have faith in her.

There was no way he was going to betray that confidence. Whatever happened to the Majestic, he was firmly Team Jordan. He liked Sarah well enough, which was a good thing since he knew without a single doubt she was going to be family someday, too.

He loved Wes, had come to trust him the same as if they'd been born into the same family instead of adopted, but on this one issue, Jordan would have his loyalty above everyone else.

"Fine." Wes cleared his throat. "Say I had this theory that Jordan was cogitating on re-opening the Majestic, but I had made this promise to her sister as the official manager of the property that I would not release any funds for major repairs until the end of the contract with the real estate agent. No use putting money into the buildings that will only end up being torn down."

Clay rolled his head on his shoulders and waited patiently. There was more coming.

"But if we were to work out some kind of barter system with Jordan, I wouldn't be tech-nically breaking my promise." Wes's reason-able tone was amusing. This was a man who was tiptoeing through a minefield, hoping a loophole would save him.

"We negotiate with Jordan to get rooms at the Majestic for the roofers and in exchange—" Clay stared off across the paddock to the break between the mountains in the distance "—we pay the roofers for an extra day or two to do some repairs on the Majestic's roof?"

Wes nodded slowly. "It's not quite an even exchange, is it?"

It wasn't. The Armstrongs would be paying more than empty rooms with busted mattresses would deserve, but he wanted to make this work, too.

"She already offered to let us stay there, too. While we're renovating." Clay glanced over at his brother. It still wasn't enough, but it might help.

Wes scratched his temple. "Will Jordan go along with us?"

Clay laughed. "Oh, Jordan is not only going to take this plan but improve it, don't worry. She's been trading promises with built-in loopholes for as long as I've known her. For her, it's a talent."

Wes propped his elbow on the fence and rested his chin on his hand. "Do tell. I'm all ears."

There was no escaping it. At some point the story was going to get out. And the longer this "secret" went on, the worse the investigation would get and the bigger the disappointment everyone would experience when they found out the simple truth. "Jordan worked at the marina the summer Sadie made me assistant manager. I was her boss." He sniffed as Wes nodded because neither one of them expected he could end the story there. "I kissed her. She left Prospect the next day with Sadie at the wheel. That was when Sadie bought a house in LA and made the final move."

Wes whistled long and loud. "Well, I am shocked."

Clay groaned. "I've regretted it for years, but my kissing Jordan wasn't this decision I made, you know? I was locked in the moment with her and it was completely right... until my head cleared and I realized Jordan was gone."

Wes nodded. "I've been there." He turned back to the paddock. "A thing I've learned about the Hearsts is that they don't hesitate much. They jump in with both feet. Impressive, really. Was it like that?" Wes clapped his hand on Clay's shoulder as if to comfort him. "You should feel bad, but you gotta move on."

"I've apologized. She accepted. We're friends again. No more kissing." Clay was pleased at how firmly the words came out.

"Uh-huh." Wes didn't argue, but the sarcastic tone made his feelings clear. "The way you two spark is definitely not like a couple itching to kiss each other." And if it was Opposite Day, his words might have been true.

If he spent too long dwelling on Jordan kissing him back, the whole situation was going to get chancy.

"We've negotiated a truce. No kissing," Clay repeated.

"Fine," Wes said. "Do you want to talk to her about this plan or should I?"

"I will," Clay said and realized he should have hesitated. He was only confirming Wes's suspicions. "I'll call Carlos tonight to see if he can get a small crew together. The shingles and other supplies are coming tomorrow along with the roof trusses. If the roofers follow the next day, we won't have wasted too much daylight waiting." Clay knew he should be more worried about how the money was going to happen, but the promise of having his crew on hand to rely on was like a reassuring handshake.

"Please talk to Jordan tomorrow. I'll hold off on telling Sarah until we have an agreement in place." Wes pursed his lips as if he were carefully weighing the alternatives.

So Clay shot back with his own "Uh-huh"

to show that his "big brother" wasn't fooling him.

"We'll all breathe better with some help." Wes sighed. "I'm not excited about the next step. Got any concept on how to tackle the kitchen redesign?"

That was going to be the second renovation priority, making the house comfortable for that many people to eat and congregate going forward.

"Two or three." He needed to talk to Chaney for part of the plan.

"Can we convince Mama to get involved?" Wes asked.

Since that was the second part of his motive for this part of the project, Clay grinned. Of the five of them, he and Wes were often on the same page.

"Depends on whether it's a love or hate day, I guess." Wes settled his hat more firmly on his head. "What if changing this place, putting in more room, was the magic that could save them?"

Clay nodded. "Surely it can't be that easy, but I have every intention of getting Mama's opinion on the kitchen. Dad wouldn't want it any other way."

Wes nodded and wandered back toward the house.

Clay pulled his cell phone out of his pocket and headed for the corner of the barn that had the best cell reception. The sooner he got Carlos and his team lined up, the sooner he and Jordan could put their heads together and come up with a plan that left the Majestic with a new roof, Clay with a full-size bed to sleep on for the duration of their renovations and...

Well, whatever he and Jordan did next, it was bound to be interesting.

CHAPTER SEVEN

ON FRIDAY, JORDAN knelt next to the last mattress she'd dragged through the lodge and out into the grass behind it to beat any dust and lingering infestation inside. Exposure to fresh air and warm sunshine, a solid thrashing with a handy tennis racket and a thorough pass with the ancient vacuum cleaner she'd discovered in the utility closet behind the lobby desk had been her diagnosis for treatment of the twelve mattresses she'd been willing to salvage. Jordan was half a second from patting herself on the back for dedication and ingenuity when the vacuum coughed, sputtered and died.

"I wasn't ready to say goodbye," she said mournfully as she shook the hose. When it refused to be revived, she tossed it down and decided to take her chances by stretching out on top of the mattress. "I've had a good run, I guess." Not a single one of the appliances left at the Majestic had given her a spot of trouble, other than needing Clay's help with the pilot lights. It made sense that after all this time, something would wear out.

Jordan was feeling the strain of doing all the work herself.

"At least I have room for a new vacuum cleaner on my credit card," she muttered as she gazed up at the blue sky. She was almost certain that was true, anyway. Could she find one in Prospect or was replacing it going to turn into a road trip?

From the corner of her eye, she could see sheets she'd washed and hung to dry on the clothesline, drifting in the easy breeze. If she were running a lodge such as the Majestic, she'd be pretty proud of herself for everything she'd accomplished with elbow grease, powerful cleaning supplies and a few old but reliable time-saving devices like the two large washing machines in the utility closet.

It was like the Majestic was aiding and abetting her stealth-like renovations.

Until the vacuum had given up on her.

It was tempting to lie there and rest, Jordan told herself. She hadn't done much resting since she'd moved out of Bell House earlier in the week, mainly because the jobs surrounded her on all sides right now. If she wasn't plotting ways to resuscitate the mattresses, sweeping and mopping up dust and cobwebs, or waiting outside the restaurant's kitchen, on the alert for any signs of outside life being inside, she felt like she should be. Lunches were lakeside, though, no matter the temperature.

Someday, the work would be done, and she'd have so much time to enjoy the views from the windows she'd uncovered.

Jordan pulled out her phone and stared hard at Erin Chang's number. The real estate agent had toured the Majestic at a low point. Her opinion of their ability to find buyers who would want to reopen the business instead of tearing down everything to build a vacation home had been low. Really glass-half-empty-of-optimism low.

Was the agent's opinion affecting her ability to sell the place? If Erin could see it now, cleaner, the windows opened to the light and the golden colors of fall, would that change the outcome?

Jordan dropped her phone on the mattress. She wasn't certain she wanted to change Erin's opinion. Without the right buyer, the odds of her sisters listening to a pitch for allowing Jordan to start the lodge herself increased.

"You're doing it again. Thinking in circles, which only stresses you out." Jordan knew she was embracing her bad habit of talking to herself. That had driven the guy in the cubicle next to hers to complain to the boss more than once. No one agreed her explanation that it helped her think to hear her own voice justified distracting her coworkers.

"I'll die if I have to go back to a cubicle," Jordan muttered as she rolled over to stand up. The twinges in her muscles were lessening, or she was growing accustomed to changing positions without regretting it immediately. Still, she pressed her hands to the small of her back for a stretch and stared out at the lake, before picking up her phone and heading inside to change clothes. Apparently she was going into Prospect today.

Her phone rang while she was digging through the small stack of her clothes she'd put away in Sadie's dresser. She'd bagged up all the old items she'd found in good condition and donated them to a women's shelter in Denver.

"Hello, sister," Jordan answered before yanking her sweatshirt and T-shirt off. She'd learned to be prepared for any temperature there in the mountains as the seasons changed. "How is New York?"

Brooke sighed. "I don't want to talk about New York, Jordie. It's just…"

Jordan sat on the edge of the first mattress she'd treated before rolling her sleeping bag out on top. It was more comfortable than she'd expected.

"Talk to me. What's going on?" Jordan tried to gentle her voice. Brooke hated it when Jordan was bossy. Jordan never meant to be bossy; just her voice never got the memo.

"Paul is…" Brooke hesitated. Jordan waited tensely. She and Sarah had wondered if there was trouble between Brooke and her husband, but this was the first time her little sister had opened the door to the discussion. The fact that she'd called Jordan instead of Sarah made her wonder if Brooke needed immediate help. Sarah was about planning, but Jordan was all for action.

Brooke said, "We're…"

Jordan closed her eyes. "How bad is it? Are you arguing or going to counseling…?"

"He moved out while I was with you and

Sarah, hearing Sadie's will. I was gone for one day, and when I got back, he was clearing out the last of his books from his home office. We have lawyers, an agreement with signatures. It's…done. Today I got his signed copy." Brooke inhaled shakily. "And this seems the worst part, telling you about it."

Jordan's eyebrows shot up. "Telling me? That was the worst part?" How? She loved her sister. More than anything, she wanted to magically teleport to the nice Brooklyn apartment Brooke had sent them pictures of on moving-in day and squeeze her little sister close. "You can tell me anything, Brooke."

"I don't know. I guess I expected you to tell me exactly how I messed up by trusting him in the first place." Brooke cleared her throat. "Thank you for not doing that."

Jordan bit her lip and faced the mirror over the dresser. Did that sound like something she would do? Hearing her sister say those words hurt her heart, but she was mature enough to know that now was not the time to let that take over. "I will deal with him if you need me to. You know that. I shouldn't have to say it every time someone needs sorting out. That's a standing offer for family."

Brooke's watery laugh made Jordan feel a bit better. "I was hoping you could tell Sarah for me." The silence on the phone might as well have been an actual physical cringe. Jordan could picture her beautiful sister braced for impact. Instantly, she remembered Brooke once waking her out of a deep sleep to say she'd wrecked Sarah's car.

Had Sarah loaned Brooke the car? Not exactly, which made telling her about it even trickier, but they'd done it together the next day...after they'd cleaned the entire house and weeded the small flower bed out front to soften Sarah up to receive the bad news.

She and Brooke might disagree about almost everything, but Jordan would always back her sister up.

"I can tell Sarah, but she's going to want to talk to you, you know." Jordan tilted her neck to one side and then the other to ease the tight muscles there. She didn't want to be the one to break this news, but she could see how it would simplify Brooke's life. "You better get your guest room ready. Sarah will be on the way."

"Okay, that's part of the reason I need your help with this. It's not a good time for a visit.

Everything is up in the air right now. Paul is being lower than a snake about the apartment and the money, so I need some time and space." Jordan enjoyed the touch of Sadie in her little sister's comment.

Brooke sniffed and her voice was stronger when she added, "I'll call for help when I'm ready to move, because I've never done that by myself and I'm not sure I know where to start."

Jordan rubbed her forehead. "We'll be there whenever you need us, but give me a few days' warning."

Brooke laughed. "So you can start driving cross-country?"

Jordan hated flying. She'd done it twice and was certain she was going to die both times. Her sisters never quit their teasing. "Sarah can administer the meds and take me on and off the planes as needed."

"Thanks, Jordie. You hate the idea of even stepping foot in an airport. But I know you'd do it for me."

"I would. I might complain the whole time, but it would be done with love." Jordan relaxed as Brooke giggled. She meant every single word. It was important to Jordan that

Brooke understood that disagreeing didn't mean there was less love.

"Are you going to be okay?" Jordan asked. "Forget that. Of course you're going to be fine. It will take time."

"Yeah," Brooke said, "I'm going minute by minute right now, but I'll be okay. How is the lodge? Any interest yet? That buyer matters more than ever now."

Jordan pinched the denim fabric over her knee. "Not yet, but I've done a lot of cleaning up. It's starting to show more promise, so we'll be ready when they call."

"I'm surprised Sarah hasn't convinced you to go back to LA to find a new job yet," Brooke said. "It's not like her to let us…linger like that. No worried phone calls at all lately."

"If I had to guess, she's working dawn to dusk to get everything of Sadie's cataloged as quickly as she can so she can get back here to her cowboy."

Brooke's sputtering cough illustrated her reaction perfectly. "Living in Prospect? How, Jordie? There's nothing there."

Jordan sighed. "You ought to come for a visit. The place might grow on you."

Brooke's gasp was loud and dramatic. "Don't

tell me you're falling for a cowboy, too, Jordan! I won't believe it!"

Clay's face floated through Jordan's mind before she gave her head a small shake. "Not a cowboy." Not yet, anyway. "But this place is special, Brooke. Like whatever is broken, it can be fixed." Jordan bit her lip. She hadn't meant to admit anything as heartfelt as that, but she understood that the truth had slipped free.

The silence between them was filled with so many questions and Jordan didn't have any answers, but Brooke didn't pursue them. "Thank you for letting Sarah know, Jordan. When she calls, I'll connect you so we can hash out whatever we need to, okay?"

Jordan frowned as she considered Brooke's words. She wasn't sure what needed to be discussed.

Unless she meant scheduling a trip to New York to help her move.

Or she was reading between the lines and guessed that the Majestic wasn't for sale, after all.

The fact that Brooke didn't immediately reply with how much she needed the funds from the purchase, or how the town wasn't all that special, convinced Jordan that this might be enough for one day.

"I have to drive into town to find a vacuum cleaner. Wish me luck." Jordan smiled as her sister hooted.

"Jordan Hearst is doing housework! The way Mom would have celebrated that. She couldn't get you to stay inside long enough to fold a pair of socks!" Brooke's grin was easy to hear in her voice.

"It is pretty funny to see how things work out. Love you, Brooke." Jordan shook her head, reminded again of how much she loved her baby sister.

"I love you, too. Thank you for listening." Brooke's voice was so soft. The strain was clear in her voice, but there was nothing else to do in the moment, so they hung up. Jordan stared at her phone for a long while. Was she prepared to talk to Sarah?

Instead of dialing, she pulled out a clean sweater and tugged it on over her head. She'd go to town, buy the vacuum and a nice, filling meal at the Ace before tackling the call to her older sister.

The drive into Prospect from the Majestic had not grown boring yet. When Jordan had first arrived in town, summer had been on its way out, but the trees and grass were still green. Today, the autumn colors were so brilliant that the drive required sunglasses.

"And when winter comes…" Jordan couldn't finish that thought. She'd realized lately that thinking that far ahead had been habit. Funny, though, she wasn't worried at all about what would happen when she returned to LA, just how life in Prospect would change with the seasons.

"It might be time to address this weird fixation with the Majestic and have it out with my partners," Jordan muttered as she made the short turn into the Homestead Market parking lot. The crowd was smaller than she expected, but that was a good thing. The first time she'd visited to get groceries had been during the after-work rush, so she'd picked up a few things but quickly left. The giant collection of mums of all colors outside the doors was tempting her already, so Jordan put three of them in a shopping cart and said a quick prayer for her credit card limit.

It was easy to see the history of the rough wood facade of the building. When Prospect had been built to replace Sullivan's Post, the old mining community not too far away, the livery stable and blacksmith were here. As soon as she stepped inside the sliding doors, however, Jordan found modern lighting and busy shoppers.

Jordan accepted a sample-sized bite of spicy sausage from a woman wearing overalls and an apron near the dairy section before turning right to head for home goods. The men's clothing section was front and center and heavy on the practical: denim pants, denim shirts and denim jackets. A spark of Kelly green caught her eye; the bargain price caught her attention, so Jordan tried on one of the warm jackets on the aisle and dropped it in her shopping cart. She was scanning the magazines on the end of the checkout lanes when she heard her name.

"Jordan! Jordan Hearst," Prue Armstrong called as she hopped up and down, one arm in the air to get Jordan's attention. Rose Bell, the proprietor of Bell House, was frowning up at Prue from the depths of her favorite Broncos hat.

"Hi, Rose, Prue," Jordan said as she hurried over.

"Well, now I was excited to see you stroll

in. We need a stylish young person's assistance here." Prue motioned at the circular rack of women's sweaters she and Rose had been inspecting. "Rose hasn't purchased anything without a football team logo since shoulder pads were all the rage. Save us from making a boring, old-fashioned decision."

Jordan glanced at the duo.

Prue's beautiful smile convinced Jordan that she knew she was as far from stuffy and old as she could be. Clay's mother was the kind of cool person Jordan aspired to be but would never accomplish. She had an artistic flow, even bundled up in a wool coat for the cooler temperatures. Her hat was a kind of floppy design, knitted in a fantastic purple yarn, and there was a silver button for accent. Somehow, she was practical and posh at the same time, and Jordan just knew Prue had crafted the sophisticated yet simple hat.

It was no wonder Walt was still in love with Prue. Her style was one of a kind. Even if Jordan copied each piece, she felt she wouldn't be able to carry it off and would still somehow look like she'd been doing laundry and vacuuming all day long.

"I'll be happy to give my opinion. What's the occasion, Rose?"

"My best friend is deserting me." Rose had never been talkative unless someone offered an opinion of her team, but Jordan was hoping for more information.

"I said two games. I'll go with you to *two* games. I don't even like football." Prue huffed out a breath. "Name another person who can turn winning season tickets to Broncos home games into betrayal."

"Name another friend who'd ruin the best thing to ever happen to me like this." Rose was muttering when she walked away.

"We're only going to build the profile, Rose. Imagine taking someone with you who understands the game. But you don't have to go out on a date if you don't want to." Prue held up the sweater to study it.

Jordan froze. Profile?

"Dating apps at our age." Rose snorted.

"This is perfect." Prue held up a sweater the same blue as Rose's hat.

Jordan considered warning Prue that dipping a toe into the dating app world would likely bring frustration and stories that might be funny…someday. "That is a lovely color. I like it."

Satisfied with Jordan's answer and undisturbed by Rose's frown, Prue put the sweater in her basket. Rose wandered off. "How's life out at the Majestic? I haven't seen you in town much, at least not since you stopped in at the hardware store."

Jordan wondered if the Mercantile had security cameras up. She hadn't visited Handmade, Prue's domain, that day.

"It's going well." Jordan nodded forcefully. "Clay was out to help with some chores, and since then, I've made a great deal of progress tidying up the place." She tipped her head to the side. "There's still a long way to go, of course, and I can't even touch the big projects, but I've been busy." Jordan motioned vaguely toward the parking lot for some reason that wasn't entirely clear to her except that Clay's mother made her so nervous. "This morning, the ancient vacuum gave up on me, so I'm hoping to find a replacement. I'll wander the aisles and then take myself on a date over to the Ace High for dinner."

Jordan knew she was talking too much, but it was like trying to stop a runaway horse. She had to hold on until her brain and her mouth ran out of steam to come to a stop safely.

Prue patted her hand. Could she tell how nervous Jordan was? How embarrassing. "That is a great idea. I get so tired of my own cooking sometimes that being able to sit at a table and eat off dishes I don't have to wash later is a real treat." She crossed her arms at her waist. "And I sure am glad Clay was able to assist you. He is so wonderful at his job, but I miss him when he's away in Colorado Springs. It would be nice if he had something bringing him back here to Prospect more often." Prue smiled pleasantly.

Jordan tried to mirror her expression but she wasn't sure what they were discussing.

"Something, or someone, I should say." Prue raised her eyebrows. "Prospect is an amazing place to raise a family." She waved a hand. "Clay has probably already told you all about that, though."

Nodding as if she understood when she absolutely did not was going to get Jordan in trouble someday, but at the moment, she had no other options. The conversation had taken a left turn and she was lost.

"How are the renovations going at the ranch?" Jordan asked awkwardly.

"Oh, I have no idea." Prue sniffed. "That is obviously none of my affair. Hasn't been for a while." Then she waggled her finger. "But if they ruin the kitchen, those boys will never hear the end of it from me."

Jordan bit her lip, dying to ask why, if the place was none of her business anymore, she was issuing this sort of warning.

"I'm sure they won't. You're absolutely right. Clay is the man you want in charge of the task." Jordan hadn't forgotten how much relief she'd felt that afternoon that they'd worked together. All in all, she might have been able to do everything all alone, but the anxiety would have been overwhelming. Having Clay on hand had wiped all of that away.

"You're right, of course. I forget… How is it you know Clay, Jordan? I mean, from before you walked into my…" Prue cleared her throat. "Before you and Sarah came back to Prospect. How did you and Clay first meet?"

Jordan was impressed. She'd gotten hints, raised eyebrows and broad suggestions from others who wanted her to explain their history. But Prue came right out and asked and it was politely done. That was talent.

"When I was sixteen, my father brought me to Sadie for the summer. I got in a bit of trouble in LA and…" Jordan realized she was giving too much information and cleared her throat. "I worked at the marina and Clay was one of the managers. He had to keep me focused on my job. I didn't make it easy for him." Jordan wrinkled her nose because it was the absolute truth. "I was going through a rough patch. I wasn't interested in making peace with anyone at that age."

Prue nodded wisely. "Oh, honey, we all went through that. Might have appeared different from the outside, depending on how those hormones acted out, but I swear, when I had four boys all turn sixteen within months, I began to second-guess every single one of my life decisions. I considered running for the border. Canada. Mexico. It didn't matter. I needed a place they couldn't track me." She nodded and chuckled as Jordan's jaw dropped. "Motherhood is not for the faint of heart, and if you don't have solid conditioning, they will conquer you. They have more energy than you, so you've got to have a steel spine."

Jordan's laughter bubbled out because Prue was so matter-of-fact in her delivery. In Prue's mind, it was all true, not a bit of exaggeration. Did all mothers feel that way?

Jordan couldn't ask her own, but she wondered what her father would say. Her smile died as she understood his Hail Mary of sending her to Sadie for the summer. To save Jordan from her bad decisions. Was that his version of running for the border? He'd had only one shot left: Sadie and Prospect.

What would have happened if she hadn't had that summer?

"I can tell I got you thinking about something serious. I hope it's not sad." Prue wrapped her arm around Jordan's shoulders and squeezed. It was the comfort Jordan needed in that moment.

"I was remembering how lucky I was to have Sadie. The Majestic saved me and..." Jordan nodded. "Apparently Sadie and Prospect kept my father from changing his name in Mexico to escape me."

Prue chuckled more. "That's how families go. We make it through those rough patches. I wouldn't trade those boys for anything in this world."

Jordan nodded. "Yes, you should be proud. Wes and Clay have been good neighbors for us."

Prue bent her head closer as if she had a secret to share. "When will the wedding be?"

"Oh, I don't know." Jordan stumbled over the words as the hot fire of embarrassment spread over her cheeks. "Clay and I… We're friends now. And then. We were friends then. One kiss wouldn't change that. And I'm sure he's got…" She pressed a hand to her chest and tried to slow her heartrate.

Prue's jaw dropped, which was Jordan's first clue that she'd gone off the rails.

"I was referring to Wes and Sarah." Prue tried to hide her amusement. "Rose and I were considering drawing up one of those pool things, you know, where you pick a month and date and put down a dollar and whoever gets closest collects all the money?" Prue waved her hand. "Rose lectured me about gambling and how she refuses to be drawn into that, but I am telling you that she's the one who gave me the notion. You mean to tell me if the Broncos made it to the play-offs that she wouldn't bet her dollar on them? Ha!" Prue rolled her eyes as if the suggestion were completely ludicrous.

Everyone in Prospect knew Rose was the world's most devoted Bronco fan, so it did seem that she'd gamble on them winning.

Most importantly, she wanted Prue to stay on this track instead of turning back to the track Jordan had been on when she'd so spectacularly fallen off by mentioning the kiss.

"So, you and Clay are friends." Prue pursed her lips. "I haven't heard of that before. Kissing friends. Hmm… I'll have to take your word for it." She patted Jordan's hand as she moved on. "For now. Never forget that friendship has to be the firmest foundation for real love that there is."

Rose had returned with a scarf in one hand. "I like that." She pointed at the sweater in Prue's basket and dropped the scarf on top. "I'm ready to go get my picture made." Her tone was more like "jump out of an airplane without a parachute" but she moved toward the checkouts. Prue shook her head in amusement. "She and I have been friends for a long time, Jordan. I know some things take a minute to settle in for Rose. She doesn't make decisions as quickly as I do, but that doesn't change the fact that we understand each other." She patted Jordan's hand one more time. "When you find a friend like that, you hold on to them." Then she waved goodbye and followed after Rose.

Jordan's feet were frozen to the floor as she weighed her options. Should she chase down Prue Armstrong and explain very badly that she had the wrong picture? Or should she say a quick prayer that her faux pas passed over quickly and get on with her shopping?

Since she wasn't sure she could get her tongue to form any words, much less the right ones, Jordan turned on her heel and began searching for small home appliances.

It might be a friendly thing to do to call Clay and give him fair warning that his mother would be pursuing more information. Although, the last thing she wanted was to talk to him any more about the kiss. The urge to tell the whole truth, that she'd been convinced she kissed him, not the other way around, would get her in trouble.

She'd have to be ready to deal with an annoyed Clay the next time she ran into him.

Jordan was torn between anticipating the occasion and pulling up a map on her phone to find out how far away the safety of the Canadian border might be.

CHAPTER EIGHT

CLAY WAS RELIEVED when he arrived at the Mercantile after a long day. Other than the truss delivery, the house renovations weren't much further along, but he was glad to have a new, solid plan in place. Carlos and his crew were planning to drive down on Monday. They would bring lumber, shingles and everything they needed to complete the ranch house roof. While they closed up the addition, he'd take the Fighting Armstrongs and set them loose on the kitchen demolition. As that was taken care of, it was finally time to talk with his mother and get her buy-in on the updated kitchen.

"Hey, partner, how's it going in Prospect?" Chaney said as she answered his call. When he and Chaney started out together, doing quick flips in the Denver suburbs, neither one of them had much money or much satisfaction working for other people. Their partnership had been the key to their mutual success.

She was a no-nonsense leader who never struggled to get what she wanted from the crews and tradespeople they worked with. It helped that her husband, Kai, was a huge support—built as big as a defensive tackle and with a mug you wouldn't mess with. Clay didn't know where his business would be without Chaney.

"It's going. I'm pulling Carlos up here to help out with the roof. How is business on your end?" Clay asked.

"Yeah, Carlos mentioned we needed to push back the repairs on the house we're flipping for the veteran over in Woodland Park. But that's no problem. It shouldn't take more than half a day, and his family doesn't expect him home from the rehab facility until mid-November." Chaney tip-tapped on her computer. "Slots in perfectly with the following week's schedule, but don't do this again. You should have my lecture about project timelines memorized by now."

Clay was relieved he hadn't messed up her plans for the subdivision, but he hated the tension in her voice.

"Not quite as handy as you remembered, your brothers?" Chaney asked.

"If we had an apprentice with their kind of bad attitude, we'd be hiring a replacement ASAP." Clay rubbed his forehead at the prospect of returning to the struggle to find enough skilled employees to start a new development. Even though they were based in Colorado Springs, they still scrambled to fill out crews some days.

"Well," Chaney said, "we're back on schedule for now, but I had to hire that electrician we used two years ago in Pueblo, so the budget is so tight it's squeaking again."

Clay winced. The electrician had done a fine job, but his rates were the highest around and he kept whatever hours he pleased, so short delivery times didn't affect him in the least. At one point, he went on vacation and held them up for over a week.

More than anything else, Clay wanted time off. A real vacation. Possibly on a beach. No hammers allowed.

"Okay, let's talk about this kitchen," Chaney said, all business. "I sent samples of the cabinets we have in stock, but I wanted to remind you about the order that we had to replace a couple of months ago. The cabinetmaker sent the wrong color? It was for the lady who insisted every permanent surface in the house be white. All white. Nothing but white. Remember? Somehow we got navy bottom cabinets delivered?"

Clay tried to picture them, but in his head, all he could remember was the panicked phone call he'd gotten from the interior designer who had made her daily visit to check on progress, found the cabinets and immediately got in touch.

"It would be good to get them out of here. They're taking up a ton of space, which we need. You could paint them at that ranch of yours. Even the arguing brothers can paint and save some cash." Chaney waited for his response.

Clay immediately estimated the room that would add to his budget and relaxed a bit.

"Yes, if there's space available on Carlos's trailer, get someone out there to load them. Otherwise, I'll have someone here come pick them up." This would be an excellent errand for Grant.

"Good. You can pull fixtures up on the manufacturer's website. I'll get them ordered and sent before you're ready to install. Flooring... You wanted to go with tile. I put some choices in the box. Send me measurements and I'll get that ordered, too." Clay pulled out the three tiles she'd chosen. They were all sedate shades of white and gray. Any of them would be fine. "What else do you need from me?"

Clay checked the window of the Mercantile. His mother was watching him and waiting for his response to her wave. He returned it from his truck and said, "I'll email all the specs tonight to get the orders going."

Chaney said, "I sure hope I don't sound as exhausted as you do, Clay."

Clay closed his eyes. Was he going to tell Chaney he was daydreaming of walking away from all of it?

"One other thing we need to discuss," Chaney said before he could answer. "The developers with the Pagosa Springs deal were hanging around the site yesterday in expensive suits." Her skepticism about the cost of their outfits was funny, but he knew what she meant. Real developers knew job sites were for wash-and-wear fabrics only. "They're *anxious* to get a contract in place."

"You don't seem as interested as the last time we talked about it. What about the five-year plan?" Chaney had always been big on planning and goal-setting and timelines. She kept them on course. "It's the kind of project we've been dreaming of. True luxury homes. No constraints on the plans or the materials. Enough lots to keep us building for years. The kind of project that makes a name and reputation." That had always been her goal, that reputation for excellence.

"It is. I can't argue with that. Something about it feels all wrong. Kai says I remind him of his mother, with all the intuition stuff, but he's probably doing that to get a response out of me. He's also sending texts to ask me what color my hair is." Chaney huffed. "Because for days I haven't been home before he went to bed. My husband is a saint most of the time, but he never lets me push him into the background for too long, thank goodness."

Concerned that his absence was causing more trouble than just extra work for Chaney, Clay said, "If you don't like the deal, we won't do it." He winced as he realized he might be jumping at the chance to drop out without having to disappoint his partner, so he added,

"Ask around. See what else you can find out about these guys before we sign anything." Clay would take the same time to get his head together.

"Good advice, partner. I'll be in touch."

She said goodbye and hung up, already making the to-do list of everything that Carlos would need to collect before Monday, no doubt.

More than anything, Clay wanted to talk to Jordan. If anyone understood about being at a crossroads with big career decisions to make, it was her. They had such different backgrounds, but they'd always gotten each other so well. Turning his back on guaranteed work and money wouldn't make sense to a lot of people, but he knew Jordan would support the changes that he was thinking of making in his life.

But Clay noticed his mother cross her arms over her chest at her window perch and he reached for the box of samples. Jordan would have to wait because his mother definitely would not wait much longer.

When Clay made it inside the front door of the Mercantile, he shook his head as he always did at how his parents had divided it up as a requirement of their divorce. His mother had insisted she wanted her own place, and she didn't want to be crowded by his father. It was a unique situation, but it was working for them. They were each standing in the doorway of their respective establishments, waiting for him.

"Good afternoon, Mother and Father. Is this the usual welcome visitors can expect?" he drawled.

His father gestured to him. "Stop in to see me before you go." Then he tipped his imaginary cowboy hat. "Ladies always go first."

"Such a gentleman," Clay's mother said, her lips curled in a half smile.

When he watched them like this, it was even more confusing how they'd ever ended up apart.

Clay followed his mother inside Handmade, her craft store, and weaved through the displays. Fabric and thread and scissors and so many things, all of them in a riot of colors and styles.

"I wondered if you were going to peek in after all," his mother said.

"I was on a call with Chaney, trying to smooth out some problems," he answered.

"My boy. I was thinking of closing up for the day. I'm glad I didn't." His mother wrapped her arms around him and squeezed tightly. That had been the first thing he loved about Prue Armstrong. She didn't do polite hugs with a mere impression of warmth and the faint scent of her perfume left behind. Prue held him close, her cheek pressed to his shoulder, and gave him time to settle in, to feel that connection.

That was the kind of mother she'd been his whole life, too.

"I can't believe you'd chance missing a customer. To one of the top ten quilt shops in Colorado?" Clay carefully picked up the pile of fabrics stacked on the work table in the center of the room and moved them to the side before sitting down. Not a single one of Prue's sons was ever careless with her projects. They'd grown up with them covering the kitchen table, which was also the scene for every breakfast and dinner, so transferring things carefully had become a habit early on.

It could not have been easy herding them to adulthood.

She now spent five days a week at the shop,

more in the busy summer months. Neither of his parents were good with idle time.

"Well, now that Bell House is empty again, no Hearsts and no reservations until the quilt retreat I have set up for December, Rose offered to watch the place." His mother surveyed the store. "Not sure I'll ever accept her offer, but it's nice to dream about taking a short trip somewhere warm."

Clay propped his elbow on the table. "You could hire real help."

She pursed her lips. "Right, with all the money I'm making hand over fist around here." She waved her arms to show her empty store. "No matter. Leaves me plenty of time to work on my projects. Now that we have the quilt finished for the Western Days raffle in the spring, I can do anything I want." She tangled her fingers together.

Why didn't she seem happier about that?

Clay cleared his throat. "That is a natural transition to what brings me here today." He dragged the box closer and relaxed as she scooted forward immediately to see what was inside.

"Kitchen finishes." He rattled the box. "Do you have time to work with me on what we need for the ranch house kitchen?" She'd said she had loads of time, right? How could she say no?

His mother pursed her lips and then shook her head. Firmly. "No."

That answered his question about *how* she would say no, but not necessarily why.

Clay made the "keep talking" motion with his hand. "More information, please."

"It's not my kitchen." She shrugged her shoulders as if it was perfectly clear. "I don't live there anymore."

Clay started emptying the box slowly. He'd never expected her to refuse, and her reasoning was even harder to understand.

"The five of us currently crammed inside that house don't think of it as anyone else's kitchen, so…" He left the sentence open-ended. Her answer still didn't compute.

"Even your father, who called it his mother's kitchen for the first ten years of our marriage?" she asked as she tilted her head to the side.

At that point, Clay knew he'd landed in deeper water than he'd ever intended. He and his brothers had never understood the divorce from the outside. He didn't want a closer look from the inside, either.

"We didn't ask him." Clay wondered if that had been a miscalculation. "His direction was to make it shine since it was the heartbeat of the home."

She scoffed. "He never said anything like that."

Clay scratched his chin. "You think I made something like that up?" He wasn't sure who had said it while they were in the early planning stages, but it had been the goal since the beginning.

Her laughter erased some of the tension in the air. "It honestly doesn't sound like either of you. Have you been coached?"

Clay immediately shook his head. He knew the right answer to that one.

"I asked Chaney to pull together some options for the kitchen. You know we're working on a budget here. Can you give me your opinion?" Clay knew it would all come together. Chaney's taste was excellent and she understood customers like no one else he'd ever worked with, especially what fit their individual personalities.

So he flipped through the stack of paint samples and arranged the navy one next to the stark white sample Chaney had opted for, the gray-and-white tiles and the stone they'd picked for the countertop. Then he found the website that showed the sink fixtures and scrolled through several choices until he landed on one he thought would work.

Clay crossed his arms over his chest. Waiting her out might be the only option.

The second she touched the navy sample door, he knew he had her hooked.

"Is this for the bottom cabinets and white for the top, so it's not dark and overwhelming?" Her eyes darted to his face, so he nodded.

"We have those navy cabinets in storage, so I can use them here at no charge. That will save on the budget." He considered offering her a nicer stone for the countertops, but then he remembered the state of the floor, and hoped she would ask for less expensive finishes instead.

Which never, ever in the history of his business, had happened before. Everyone wanted to upgrade, never downgrade.

She picked up the tile with the boldest gray pattern. When it was laid, the tiles would create gray diagonals on a white background. Smart.

"I like this as the backsplash." His mother then frowned down at the stone for the countertop. It was pretty plain. Would that be her objection?

Clay stacked the backsplash tile on the paint colors and waited.

"Could you do poured concrete instead?" his mother asked. "Don't know how expensive that is." She smacked the table. "No, butcher block. That's better. This stone is too glossy for that house and that family and the years it'll have to stand before another Armstrong decides to spend money on anything other than cattle, barns and fences." She shrugged as if it was unimportant, but Clay was convinced this was another clue to the trouble between his parents.

"We can do that." He squinted his eyes as he tried to picture the kitchen with the more rustic counters. As far as he could tell, it worked. "What about the floors?" He tapped the two tiles remaining.

"Refinish the wood." She shook her head. "No tile. It has been there for generations. You don't cover something like that up, do you?" She sighed. "I never wanted to rip it all out, just make it ours, you know?" She propped her elbow on the table like he had done and then dropped her chin in her hand. "Get a pretty rug for under the table, navy and white or gray. It'll be beautiful."

The sadness in her tone was something Clay was unprepared for. "Will you enjoy cooking in that kitchen, Mama?" She still came out to the ranch to make meals for family occasions. "When Travis works through all the red tape, we're going to have a new generation that needs to know the joy of your biscuits."

Her slow smile reassured him. She flapped her arms like a chicken. "My cute apartment kitchen is too small. It's nice to have room to stretch now and then. You know you won't be able to keep me out of this new kitchen."

He nodded. "The good news is that you've helped me out here, with the decisions and the budget." He showed her the tablet. "Sink?" She pointed. "What about cabinet hardware?" He switched over to another site and passed the tablet to her. She frowned critically and then scrolled down before tapping the screen. "This one."

Clay took the tablet, braced for an expensive choice and noticed that she'd chosen one at a reasonable price he could make work. It was like she was limiting her decisions to the constraints.

One tour around her shop and a person would understand that Prue liked beautiful things and she didn't worry a lot about the cost.

"It's going to be perfect, Clay." She beamed at him. "I am so proud of you. Thank you for spending this time on the house. I know it's a sacrifice, taking days away from your business, but I know how important this is to Trav and to your father. He's a broken record about the Rocking A's history, his mother's furniture, the way his dad handled the livestock. I love to see you boys working together on something that fits you all."

Pleased at how easily he'd persuaded her to offer her opinions, Clay packed everything back up and mentally patted himself on the back for not listing all the ways in which her other sons were problems in the ranch's construction process.

"Any idea what Dad wants to talk to me about?" he asked casually.

She fidgeted with a stack of fabrics. "Nope, but I have something else we need to discuss in depth." She reached across the table and clasped his hand in hers. It was the kind of pose he associated with the delivery of fatal news, so he snapped to attention.

"What is it?" When she paused for dramatic effect, Clay got even more nervous. "Tell me."

"Guess who I ran into over at the market at lunch?" She waggled her eyebrows and he instantly knew that the answer she wanted was Jordan. Something, intuition or sixth sense, warned him not to give in easily. "No idea. Who?"

She wrinkled her nose as if he were being too adorable for words. "Jordan. Hearst. Your neighbor, Jordan."

Clay tugged his hand free. Was it sweaty all of a sudden? Just in case, he wiped it on his jeans. "Okay. Wes said she has been busy over at the Majestic. Glad she left the place for some company."

His mother pursed her lips. "She did. Mentioned she was going to the Ace for a nice dinner." She dipped her chin. "I bet she's still over there, seated at a big empty table all by herself."

Clay tried the counting-to-ten thing again. It worked with Jordan. "I have something I need to run by her. If we're done here, I could stop in to see if she has time tonight."

His mother nodded and his relief was overwhelming.

It was also too soon because she held up one finger. "When I was speaking to her, she mentioned your friendship?" It wasn't a question, so why had she made it sound like one? "Your history?"

Clay nodded impatiently.

"How nice it was you two were on good terms," she said as she propped her chin on her hand again. "And I don't know how I misled her, but Jordan seemed to think I knew something about a kiss." Her beaming expression would have been funny if it had involved anyone else but him.

Clay sighed. "When we were kids, Mama. Not last week or anything."

A faint wrinkle appeared between her brows as she weighed that information. "She's single. You're single. You're both here." She patted his hand. "You should try it again. I'm sure you've gotten much better at the whole kissing thing since then. Don't let one miss knock you out of the game."

At this age, Clay could tell she was employing reverse psychology, but seeing it in action only lessened the power a fraction. "It was a good kiss then, but we were young." Before his mother could jump in to remind him that that was no longer a problem, he took a step back. "I know. You tell me quite frequently that I have reached the perfect age to settle down. Jordan is—" it was impossible to find one word to describe her "—temporary. So am I, for that matter. My business is in Colorado Springs. Falling in love in Prospect doesn't make much sense for us. Right now, we're friendly." The way they had always circled each other, one day friends and the next day foes, Clay wasn't sure how long it could last, but he didn't want to tip the scales himself.

Prue frowned. "You know love doesn't care where you are, right? I was happy in Denver, living a nice single girl's life until I fell in love with a cowboy who brought me to Prospect. There's a way to make it work if you and Jordan both want it to."

Clay bent closer to her. "I'm not sure you're making the point you want to make here. You and Dad? You didn't make it. You're divorced. Sometimes love doesn't conquer all, right?"

Her face was filled with love and regret. "Honey, if you think we don't still love each other, you are sorely mistaken. Love did its thing. We messed it up. If you're as smart as I hope you are, as I know you are, you won't make the same error."

Frustrated, Clay asked, "I don't get it. If you still love each other, why split up?"

Prue closed her eyes before saying, "Whether or not it's Jordan, when you find the woman you want to spend a life with, make room for her, Clay. That's the answer. I don't know how to tell you how to do it, though. Make room for her. Work is important. The ranch is important. So is your family and hers. But if you fall for someone, she needs to come before all that other stuff. You should expect the same from her. Make your decisions together. Even if you think you know her better than you know yourself, you've got to be in the thing together."

Clay wanted the right response to wipe the sadness away but he couldn't find it.

When Prue was certain he'd gotten her message, his mother relaxed. "Don't let your father keep you too long. Jordan won't wait forever."

"Okay, Mama. Thank you for your help."

"Love you, baby," she said as she wrapped him up in her arms again. "Keep your eyes open. That's all I'm asking. You're here together now. I love that, but it would be okay if you found the perfect woman and followed her to LA…or wherever. When you have the one who makes life better, don't let an address split you up."

Clay grunted. "Wes made your life so much easier by falling for the girl next door, so we all ought to do the same?"

She tapped her chin as she pretended to think before nodding wildly. "Yes, I agree. But it helps that I like Sarah and Jordan. Sadie Hearst, as much as I've cussed her name for leaving us high and dry when a celebrity could have put this town on the map, was a decent person with a good heart. Great even. That kind of person raising those girls tells me all I need to know. I would like two daughters-in-law this time next year."

"Should I warn my three other brothers that there's one sister left?" he asked as he paused at the door that led to the foyer between the businesses.

"She's married." His mother studied the ceiling. "Let's wait and see how that works out, but I'm not saying no, not yet."

He was still shaking his head when he stepped inside the hardware store.

"Decades later, your mother still has that effect on me, too." His father had his boots propped up on the counter, but he plucked a piece of paper and waved it in the air. "Got somethin' for you."

Clay shifted the box under his arm, very aware of the time ticking away. "It's a check." The amount surprised him. "What's this for?"

"I leave that to your discretion, but I want to invest a little personal money in the renovation game here." He shook his finger. "My only criteria for how you use it is that it needs to go into the kitchen."

Clay tapped the check on the counter. "The kitchen. Why?"

He knew why. His father was still hat over boots in love with a woman who loved her kitchen.

"Heart of the home and all that," his father announced. "One of them pot fillers could be an unexpected luxury, and I would be pleased to see one in my kitchen." He folded his hands together in his lap.

"A pot filler." Clay immediately reconfig-
ured the kitchen plumbing in his head to run
water over to the wall behind the stove. "You
make a lot of pasta, do you, Dad?" He couldn't
contain his amusement.

"I do like a good noodle." His father cleared
his throat. "If there's anything left…"

Clay stared down at the check again. "There
will be. What else?"

The way his father hesitated immediately
caught Clay's interest. What could be more
surprising than his father, who had never
made a pot of spaghetti in his life, asking
for a nice-to-have-but-not-really-necessary
thing like a pot filler in a house that had run
on nothing but practicality since it had been
built decades ago?

"Soaker tub?" His father wrinkled his nose.

"We aren't touching the main bathroom,
Dad." Clay folded the check and slipped it
into his pocket.

"Not the family bath." He cleared his throat
again. "The one you're putting in my quarters. The addition. The spot for me."

Clay blinked. The picture of his father in
a soaker tub didn't compute. In Clay's mind,

there were foamy bubbles and a tiny yellow ducky.

He didn't want to ask any more questions because he was afraid of where they might lead, so he nodded.

"Okay, I'll see what I can do."

His father immediately relaxed in his seat. Making the requests must have been as painful to him as they had been to Clay hearing them. "Good, and make a note that if anyone asks where you got the inspiration, I had something to do with it."

"Anyone?" Clay studied his face. "Or Mom?"

His dad sighed. "You know the answer to that. She made sure to sigh wistfully for years every time we watched a home improvement show with one of those pot fillers. She thinks I wasn't paying attention." He met Clay's stare. "I want her to know that I was. I paid attention and I remembered all this time. Might have taken a ridiculous amount of years to get around to giving her what she wanted, but it wasn't because I didn't care."

Clay wished his mother wasn't involved in this breakup because she was the only person he knew who could put such a sorry couple back together.

"Do I want to know where the money comes from?" Clay asked on his way out the door. "Is it legal?"

His father scoffed. "Of course it is, but keep this our little secret just in case."

Clay paused. He definitely needed to ask more questions about the source of this funding, but Jordan was waiting over at the Ace High.

Instead of staying and grilling the suspect, Clay dropped the box in his truck and trotted down to the Ace High, conscious of the time he'd spent with his parents and afraid he'd missed Jordan completely. He tried not to be too obvious as he surveyed the dining room.

"Hunting for someone in particular, Clay?" Faye asked as she hustled by. He waited for her to return to say, "Has Jordan already left?"

Faye stopped in her tracks. The sly grin that spread across her face was fair warning. "Another Hearst-Armstrong pairing in the works?" She patted his shoulder. "I like it. Last time she was in for dinner, I made sure to tell her about that one homecoming dance we went to and how good a dancer you are."

Clay inhaled slowly because that was not

the kind of answer he'd expected, but arguing with Faye would accomplish almost nothing, so he waited.

"Haven't seen her. Try down at the Garage. Lucky was planning a big blowout this month since the weather will be changing soon. Had to move it up a weekend because of Halloween in the Park next Saturday." She poked his arm. "And if I see your girl, I'll be sure to send her the same way."

Before he could say "thank you" or "don't poke me" or anything that might convince her not to tell his mother about how he'd been searching the crowd for Jordan, Faye had hurried away. She moved like a dragonfly, sometimes in straight lines, other times zigzagging, but always fast.

Clay headed back out to the wood boardwalk and passed the Mercantile and the Homestead Market. The Garage, more formally known as Garcia Auto Repair, marked the southern end of the downtown section of Prospect. The buildings and homes in this section of town were newer, most of them built during the 1950s or 1960s. The Garage had been maintained by the Garcias for generations. Lucky and her husband, Dante, worked on cars five days a week. On special weekends, Lucky organized food trucks and spread the word through social media. Everyone in town enjoyed those nights, and the crowd milling around this evening next to the Garage was larger than he'd expected.

The relief that settled over him when he spotted Jordan seated at one of the picnic tables was sweet. She was laughing at something Dr. Singh had said to her as he hurried toward the food truck with the longest line.

That satisfaction was also a sign that he was farther underwater, in over his head, than he liked. His mother would be so pleased.

He had to discuss business with Jordan, but it would be smart to wait until he had his thoughts in order.

Clay had a long history of doing the smart thing. In fact, there were only a few minor blips in that history.

This woman had been the reason he lost his head before. Taking a minute to get himself together made perfect sense. There was no rush to speak to her right now… As long as he got her permission before he showed up with a crew and a stack of sleeping bags, everything would be fine.

Then Jordan spotted him in the crowd and shrugged at him. It wasn't the warmest greeting, but for her, it was an invitation.

As he moved through the milling crowd, unable to walk away from temptation, Clay knew that when he lost his head again over Jordan Hearst, he'd have no one to blame but himself.

CHAPTER NINE

Jordan had never expected to find nightlife like this in Prospect. To be fair, she hadn't expected any nightlife in the tiny town that gave the appearance of being closed even when everything was open, but food trucks and a party atmosphere were her kind of entertainment.

When she'd left the Homestead Market with her new vacuum, at least one hundred dollars' worth of critical cleaning items and miscellaneous impulse buys, and four of the gorgeous dark red mums she hadn't been able to leave without, she had intended to settle into her usual booth at the Ace. That would give her time to script her phone call to Sarah while she scrolled on her phone. She'd had her fingers crossed for more chicken and dumplings, but then someone had passed by her on the sidewalk carrying an amazing concoction.

Jordan hesitated too long to ask for a name

or directions, but she followed her nose and her heart in the direction the person had been coming from. Fortunately, she'd found the group of food trucks stationed on a broad paved lot a block off the main street. White lights were strung over picnic tables that dotted the half circle in front of the trucks, and the atmosphere was definitely welcoming and comfortable. Nothing was too loud. Kids darted in and out of small groups here and there.

And most important, she discovered the Calories Canceled food truck selling something called Nancy's Dessert Nachos.

Were they authentic Mexican or Tex-Mex? Had she had dinner or anything resembling a healthy meal all day? No. Once Jordan got a second look, a long, lingering gaze at the heaping pile of cinnamon-dusted puffy tortillas covered in chocolate sauce, strawberries and whipped cream, none of that mattered.

So she was unemployed, covered in dust and bored of having conversations with herself.

Nothing bothered Jordan anymore after she took the first bite.

Not even finding Clay Armstrong frowning at her from the edge of the happy crowd.

Her single, minor complaint was that she hadn't purchased a drink.

When a woman had this much goodness to enjoy, sometimes she needed to cleanse her palate, to get the blast of flavor for the first time again.

"California, I hope you had a good meal before you started on dessert," Clay drawled as he stopped in front of her. Flannel shirt. Dark jeans. Work boots. Clay fit in with the crowd perfectly.

Why did he catch her attention when he should fade into the background?

Jordan plopped one of the cinnamon chips in her mouth and chewed slowly. The nickname didn't even bother her at that point.

"Should I give you two some privacy?" Clay raised his eyebrows as he waved a hand in front of Jordan's face.

"If you're going to pick a fight, keep it moving, cowboy. I'm busy." Jordan chose one of the dark red strawberries and popped it in her mouth. "Tomorrow is soon enough to argue."

He ran a hand over his nape. "You're correct about that."

Before she could hit him with a clever zinger about always being right or some other thing that might eventually come to mind, he walked away. Jordan was sadder about that than she expected, but she chuckled at a woman who was doing her best to keep two toddlers from taking food off people's plates. Jordan hadn't been able to determine whether these toddlers knew their targets, but the way their mother apologized, she knew it didn't matter. Mom had said no, so they were pushing their limits.

When the twins zeroed in on Jordan, their mom grabbed a hand in each of hers and tugged them to a stop.

"I don't mind sharing," Jordan said. It was almost true. The pair were adorable. Nothing less than that would have convinced her to give up part of her glorious meal.

The beautiful woman shook her head firmly. "Teaching them not to talk to strangers is a lost cause at this point, but I refuse to give up on not accepting candy or food of any sort. The whole town is in love with my children and I appreciate that, but we're all going to have to learn to say no." She shook her head. "As soon as I figure out how, I will be teaching classes. I'll put you on the list." She held her hand out. "I'm Lucky. This is my family's garage. And you're Jordan Hearst."

Jordan stared at her chocolaty fingers and waved her hand instead.

"No problem. We can do the handshake-thing later." Lucky laughed. "I am happy to meet you."

"Oh, me, too. I wish I'd looked more prepared to meet new people before I drove into town this afternoon, but this has been a truly lucky…" Jordan wrinkled her nose. The pun had definitely not been intended, but her new acquaintance waved it off. She must be accustomed to that by now. Jordan brushed her messy ponytail over her shoulder, self-conscious that she wasn't making a better first impression. "A happy discovery. I needed dinner. I didn't know I was going to find heaven on top of a puffy tortilla."

When Clay stepped up beside Lucky, Jordan spotted his stack of tacos in a paper dish and two bottles of water. "Lucky, I almost missed food truck night at the Garage. I gotta get connected back into Prospect's network while I'm in town."

Jordan was interested to see Clay making conversation with someone who wasn't…her. He was completely at ease in this setting.

Because he belonged here, even if he didn't call Prospect home right now.

"Food truck night is early this month. Next Saturday night is the big high school fundraiser in the park," Lucky said after she stopped one of the girls from crashing on the asphalt. "The kids set up a costume contest. Different age groups with trophies and bragging rights for the winners. Your picture will go up on the Prospect social media pages, which is our version of the local newspaper nowadays." Lucky smiled at Jordan. "And there will be a chili cook-off, bake sale, all of that, so come hungry. Every purchase supports programs at the school."

Jordan watched the two little girls run circles around Clay. Their boots smacked the pavement as the kids chanted a silly song about elephants. Lucky huffed out a sigh. "I swear, the *abuelas* used to warn me that whatever mischief I committed would be returned to me twofold by my children. I was not prepared for this level of shenanigans." When one of the twins tugged free to run toward a tall man who was talking to one of the food truck owners, Lucky pointed. "I should go. Her father has less ability to say no than I do. It was nice to meet you, Jordan."

"Women of all ages can't get enough of Clay Armstrong."

Jordan grinned when Clay held out a bottle of water to her. She reluctantly set the paper container of nachos down to accept it. After she twisted off the cap and took a welcome sip of water, she said, "Thank you. How did you know that was the only thing I needed to make the night perfect?"

"I pay attention." He sat down next to her and picked up a taco. "In my experience, that's a big step for impressing women. Am I right, California?"

Jordan tilted her head back. He paid attention enough to see that she had nothing to drink. Had any other man, friend or foe or combination of the two, ever detected anything of the sort? None came to mind.

"Brilliant. I cannot argue with clear success, either." Jordan waved a hand. "I give you permission to call me California for the rest of the night and I will not snarl or snap one time."

He whistled and offered her the container of tacos. "That is a big concession. I am honored." He seemed to be watching and waiting patiently for something. "I won't take the nachos from you. But I am offering you real food. Your prize is safe."

Jordan accepted the offering and took a bite of the most delicious taco *al pastor* she'd ever put in her mouth. "Nancy did not make this taco, did she?" Each morsel was so delicious that Jordan was mentally reviewing how much cash she had in her pocket. If she purchased a few to go, she could take them back to the Majestic and enjoy them in private, no awkward conversation required.

"No, Lucky's sister makes these. She doesn't have a food truck yet, but when she does, she'll be extremely popular." Clay ate his first taco before taking a drink. "I'm glad I found you. I have a proposal."

Jordan coughed and sipped her water.

"A business offer. A proposition? Is it the word *proposal* that's choking you?" he asked, amusement lighting his face.

She shook her head. "No, too spicy." That was a lie. The taco was perfect, but there was no reasonable way to explain why one man saying a completely innocent word caused her throat to tighten.

"Talk to me." Jordan glanced longingly at

his tacos but she knew she was being greedy. No one liked greedy people.

Clay took a taco and slid her the other one.

For a split second, she considered trying to achieve the high road by thanking him graciously and sliding it back, because she'd certainly had enough to eat. He propped an elbow on the table and waited some more.

Instead, Jordan took a bite and mumbled, "Thank you," before offering him her precious leftover nachos.

The corner of his mouth curled. "If I touch that, are you going to speak to me ever again?"

Jordan shrugged. "Guess we'll have to wait and see."

Clay pushed it back.

Of course he did. Clay Armstrong was comfortable on the high road. He was a frequent traveler.

"After several frustrating days framing the ranch house addition, Wes and I have decided to bring in one of my crews to finish the roofing. We were hoping we could work out a deal with you to let them take some of the rooms at the Majestic. I hear you've been beating mattresses into submission. They're bringing sleeping bags."

Jordan nodded. "Sure. No problem." She slipped one of the cinnamon chips in her mouth and licked the sugar off her thumb.

"You don't want to know how many guys?" Clay asked. "Or for how long?"

Jordan frowned. "No, there's plenty of room. If we have a buyer who wants to come through, things need to be fairly neat, but we should have advance warning." She sighed. "No calls yet."

He nodded. "What about your fee? What are you planning to charge?"

"You have got to be kidding me." Jordan snorted. "Charge you, the man who has helped me have hot water for days, or your brother, the man who has done so much for the Majestic already, the cost to let someone stay in a dusty, run-down fishing lodge? Zero. I'm charging you zero dollars." She held up a finger. "But I am revoking my agreement to let you call me California. I'm back to snarling now."

Clay chuckled. "I can't tell if it's the sugar talking or are we friends again?"

Jordan bit her lip and she weighed the answer. "Could be both at this point."

He nodded. "Well, if you aren't charging,

then I have a suggestion. We barter. I'm going to have Carlos examine the Majestic's roof. He can give us an estimate to repair, and if it's in decent shape, he might even be able to take care of the leaks, patch the roof."

Jordan's mouth dropped open. "You're kidding! No way. That is not an equal trade at all."

More than anything, she wanted to accept his offer. The biggest hurdle to anyone reopening the Majestic would be the amount of money it would take to get it repaired and ready for business. The roof was one of the costliest requirements. Most of the renovations could be done piecemeal, a block of rooms at a time, but it didn't make sense to do any of those until the roof was solid and they were sure no more damage would be done over the winter.

But how many times could Clay Armstrong save the day?

He had another long sip of water. "Hold on. We haven't settled all the terms yet. If you don't get the roof repaired before the snow falls, the melting and refreezing will definitely create more problems inside. That is certain. If we keep the cost low, Wes can help us sell this to your sister as a preventative re-pair instead of an investment that will never earn out when the place sells."

Jordan studied his face. If she could see the flaws in this argument, surely he could. No matter how good the deal was, the roof would be an investment.

But Jordan wanted this to happen.

She was suspicious. "Is this a strange form of charity? Or a new sort of romantic gift Wes dreamed up?" Jordan wrinkled her nose. "Sarah won't see it that way. When she gives orders, she expects us all to follow them."

Clay rubbed his forehead. He usually did that when he was trying to be patient.

"Do we have a deal?" Clay asked. "The two of us can find add-ons at a later date to even the exchange. Maybe you can… I don't know. How are your electrical skills? Can you rewire a kitchen?"

Jordan pursed her lips. "For you, I'll give it a shot."

His low chuckle landed in her chest with a glow. Clay was serious. He was smart and dependable and good at everything he tried. Being able to make him laugh made her feel smart and strong and dependable, too.

That was a precious feeling for the Hearst who managed to leave every mess she ever made.

"Okay, not electricity. I can paint. I can scrub. I can…" She tapped her lips. "I'd offer to cook but I might be better at wiring outlets."

He waved a hand. "Okay. We have options. If it's okay with you, I'll bring Carlos and his crew over Monday."

"Do Carlos or his employees have any issues with unexplained noises in the middle of the night?" Jordan asked.

"Have you heard any?" Clay's patient expression was so familiar. She'd never forgotten it.

"No, but I know that's why you haven't taken me up on my offer for one of the rooms. You're afraid." She poked her bottom lip out in a fake pout.

"So we have a deal." He offered his hand to shake.

Jordan held up her no-longer-chocolaty fingers and said, "These were my utensils. Are you sure you want to shake this hand?"

He blinked, but before she could threaten to hug him, he'd wrapped his arms around her and pulled her close. "How about a hug to seal the deal, then?" His voice was low, next to her ear. The timbre resonated inside, sending a thrill down her spine. It was impossible to let him go, even when someone said, "Well, now, we have made some progress on the feud between neighbors, haven't we?"

Clay's sigh ruffled the loose hairs at her nape but he didn't let Jordan go. "Beat it, Matt. No one called for a little brother."

The picnic table shook as Clay's youngest brother sat down across from them. "I love to be a happy surprise." She'd met all the Armstrong brothers at one time or another, but she'd never gotten used to how good-looking every single one of them was.

Clay squeezed Jordan tighter to his chest before moving away.

In her head, she would call it "regretfully," the way he scooted back across the bench. Or was it a "lingering" move or… The fact that she couldn't decide on the correct and most romantic way to say that Clay enjoyed holding her and didn't want to let go worried Jordan.

But not as much as the coldness that settled over her when Clay was no longer touching her.

If she got used to that warmth, the comfort in his arms, it would hurt when she left. Or when he did. One of them was most definitely leaving Prospect soon and her arms would be empty.

"What did you want, Matt?" Clay asked. Before he answered, a guitar played the first notes of a country song that Jordan recognized but couldn't name. The crowd applauded wildly and couples moved to the open area in the center of the picnic tables.

"A dance partner?" Matt asked and held out his hand to Jordan.

Before she'd fully made her decision to dance, he tugged her up from the bench and guided her to join the other dancers. For the first half of the song, he showed her the steps patiently while Jordan stepped on his boots, but eventually, she caught on.

As they danced, Jordan stared over Matt's shoulder at Clay, who was frowning as he watched them. "Wes told me that you might be needing traps over at the Majestic. I do not do pest control myself," Matt said as he spun her away and then back. Clay frowned more. "But I have humane traps that I can loan you if you want to try to catch your kitchen raccoon or whatever it is that's rattling the pots and pans."

"That might be a figment of Sarah's imagination. I haven't heard anything suspicious." Jordan pointed at Clay over her shoulder. "Neither of us discovered any 'sign.'" She waggled her eyebrows at Clay's brother, Prospect's veterinarian. "Is there any kind of animal that smells like vanilla?"

Jordan was afraid she'd never be a great two-stepper. LA's night clubs required less skill than Prospect's pop-up dance floor, but she'd never enjoyed dancing as much as she did this cool night under the stars. Only one thing could have made the dance any better.

Only one man could have made it better.

If she was here for Prospect's next food truck night, she'd have to try her luck and lure Clay to the dance floor. Why did that sound like the perfect way to spend a pretty October night?

"Vanilla? Never heard that before, no." Matt sniffed. "No feces, you say." He tapped his chin. "No food ruined, or chewing on any of the furniture, either?" He paused. "We can set the traps and see. If we find any varmint that smells like cinnamon or spices, we might make a fortune." He winked at Jordan and the impact was immediate. Her smile bloomed of its own volition.

When the first song ended, Matt led her back to the picnic table. Clay's eyes were narrowed and locked on Matt's hand holding hers.

"I'll drop the traps by the lodge this week. Better decide how you feel about double weddings, Jordan." Matt made a show of removing his hand carefully. "Is it double cousins when brothers marry sisters? I think that's what the kids say." He was whistling as he walked away. Two women immediately waved at him from opposite sides of the large crowd.

"It takes some getting used to, the way people in Prospect hear wedding bells whenever you spend any longer than three seconds together, but your brother is charming." Jordan picked one of the remaining strawberries off her nachos.

Then she registered his silence. When she noticed his narrowed eyes were now locked on her, she said, "What did I do?"

"Flirting with my brother is one thing." Clay bent forward to speak quietly next to her ear, sending that shiver down her spine again. "Telling my mother about a kiss between us is like waving a red flag in front of a bull. We're both in the center of the ring now."

Oh, that. Jordan had done her best to forget her misstep. "So are we both matadors? I'm losing the analogy."

This close, she could see the glint of gold in his hazel eyes.

She wished she didn't know about that glint.

She opted to explain to try to distract herself. "I thought, from what she said, that she already knew. Was your mother a spy? Trained in interrogation techniques? Because I never intended to tell anyone about that and it slipped out." That much was true.

Clay shook his head. "No CIA background, so it must be natural skill that she honed raising five boys."

"Could be. Was it terrible? The questioning?" Jordan wasn't sure what the atmosphere was between herself and Clay just then. Something had changed, but she was enjoying herself.

"Uh, no, I was in a hurry to talk to you." Clay straightened. "About the roof. And the plan. The exchange. That's why I was in such a hurry."

Jordan did her best to keep a straight face, but he was giving away more than he intended to by using too many words. "Aw. You missed me."

She giggled at the way he scowled. Neither one of them wanted to feel this way, but it had a life of its own.

Sort of the same way their connection had grown that first summer. Knowing that they'd been in the same boat back then dramatically changed how she felt about their first kiss.

"I missed you, too," Jordan said softly. If they were going to sink, they might as well sink together. Maybe if they were both aware of the danger, they could help each other make it safely to the other side.

"Your life is a whole collection of question marks right now." He spoke softly, acknowledging her truth.

"And you have all the answers for your next five-year plan lined up. None of them match any of my options," she added, just to make sure that he understood the problems lying in wait for them.

He held his breath before letting it out slowly.

Any minute now, he'd start counting to ten to go with it.

"Right. That was our problem then. Different lives. Nothing has changed." Clay's tone was firm. Was he convincing her or himself? "Why do we feel inevitable then, Jordan?"

Jordan's mouth was dry as she searched for a funny response, something to break them free of the moment.

"Faye told me I'd find you both down here." Wes had stopped at the end of the table while they were frozen. "She never leaves the Ace, but she's got an impressive amount of information."

Jordan blinked first. "That is good to know. Clay was giving me the details of the plan for the roof. Roofs. Rooves?" Why could she not find the plural of roof at this second? Her brain was scrambled.

"Great. We appreciate the space. It's going to make everyone more comfortable." Wes tipped his cowboy hat up. "But I wanted to let you know that Erin Chang called this afternoon. She has an interested couple who will be here Monday to tour the Majestic."

As Jordan absorbed the news, she was

aware that both Armstrongs were watching her closely.

She grabbed her water bottle for a sip to stall for the answer of how to respond.

Eventually, she said, "That's great timing, Wes. We won't have to worry about the crew's sleeping bags and other stuff. Plus, I've been cleaning like I enjoy it or something. Sarah would be impressed. And the leaves. The lake has never been more beautiful. If we want them to see the potential of this place, this is the perfect moment."

Both Armstrongs had *concern* written all over their faces, but Jordan didn't want to take this any further, so she picked up her trash, ready to be alone with all the thoughts tumbling around in her brain. "Can you let me know the time they'll be in on Monday?"

Wes nodded. "Erin is going to call when they leave Denver. I'll let you know. Will you join us for the tour?"

Jordan rubbed the ache in the center of her chest as she tried to decide.

"She'll let you know on Monday," Clay said as he reached to take the trash out of her hands. "I'll walk you back to your car."

When she raised a hand to wave him off,

he bent his head down to catch her eyes. "I'll walk you back to your car."

Jordan nodded. "Thanks, Wes." She should say more because they were both doing so much to help her, but she couldn't right now.

Clay threw their trash away and then put his hand on the small of her back to guide her through the noisy crowd. They were silent as they walked toward the Homestead Market. Jordan wanted to chatter to fill the space between them, but she couldn't figure out how to make it clear that everything was okay. She was fine.

Wes's news was the result they'd all been hoping for, the opportunity she'd been wearing herself out to prepare the Majestic for. Jordan realized that she'd begun to believe a sale wasn't ever going to happen.

She'd been getting ready to offer herself as the last option, a way to keep the Majestic intact by reopening it.

When she and Clay stopped next to her car, it was easy to see the giant mums looming in the back seat.

"I see you fell for the Homestead's mum display." Clay leaned against the car door as if he had unlimited time for idle conversation.

"They were too pretty to pass up. The cashier warned me I'd have to watch for frost. I may put them on the check-in counter in the lobby. To brighten up the place." Then she remembered Sadie's painting that Sarah had brought with her from LA, the one Sadie had loved so much. It featured the Rocky Mountains and reminded her of Prospect. "Could you help me hang the painting before the tour?" Then she realized how silly that would be. "Never mind. We'll have to take it down again when we sell."

Clay crossed one ankle over the other. "When? Or if?"

She moved to rest next to him. "This is good. These possible buyers will help us all decide, right? If they love the spot and make an offer, Sarah, Brooke and I will talk it over. There will be a real option on the table."

He nodded. "Then you and I can argue over whether we work in Prospect or LA or the moon." His drawl helped ease the pressure in her chest.

Until she understood what he was implying.

Location didn't matter to him. Was he saying he could be home in LA or Prospect?

She peeked up at his face to see that he was waiting and watching her, as he often did.

"Are you saying that you want to...?" What? How did she fill in the blank?

"I have one important question before we make this choice at the crossroads."

Jordan had tons of questions. They might as well knock his single question out first.

"Did *you* kiss *me* when we were kids? Or did *I* kiss *you*?" His lips curled slowly.

Jordan gulped. The emotional rollercoaster precipitated by dessert nachos was totally out of control. "Yes?"

He chuckled. "Okay, that's clear."

"I thought I was on my own with that kiss, that I had embarrassed us both by kissing my *boss*, who was only being a nice guy to me all summer, and wasn't flirting. I had mistaken niceness for romantic interest and then made a fool of myself. At sixteen, that's nearly fatal. After sobbing about how you were going to pity me and my silly little crush on you, Sadie gave up and gave in. That kiss accomplished what my angry sulking and mean expressions couldn't. I got to go home, but if I'd known then what I know now, I would have rewound that day. If I could." Jordan covered her hot cheeks with both hands. "The embarrassment has lingered. Meeting you at breakfast that first week back in Prospect… Could you hear the pounding of my heart? All shame and embarrassment coursing through my veins. I wanted to avoid you, but you wouldn't leave my side."

"I had my own regrets that I'd been living with, and I was afraid you'd never reappear to let me make amends." Clay rested a hand at her nape. "Then you left so suddenly, didn't let me apologize for scaring you away."

She wrinkled her nose. "Sorry?" Then, before she could admit there was an alarm ringing in her head, Jordan stretched up tentatively to press her lips to his. When his hand moved down her back to urge her closer, she shivered and pressed her hands against his chest. She could feel his smile on her lips and the kiss was so sweet. There were no doubts between them here.

The happy shouts of children blocks away penetrated the haze, and Jordan stepped back. Clay's hands slipped off her hips as he reached to open her car door.

Jordan was dazed as she slid into the driver's seat. He sighed. "I don't want to fight right now, so I won't insist on escorting you home, but…" He bent down and pressed another hard kiss on her lips before brushing her bangs out of her eyes. "Please text me when you're at the lodge, so I know you made it safely home."

Words seemed impossible, so she nodded when he shut the car door. She carefully pulled out of the parking spot as Clay watched her leave. She made the familiar drive back to the Majestic but could only think of how the whole world had changed.

She'd promised herself at sixteen that she wouldn't let anyone else make decisions for her.

It was time for Jordan to fulfil that vow again.

CHAPTER TEN

ON SATURDAY MORNING, Clay winced as he rolled over in the sleeping bag in the middle of the ranch house living room. Every morning since he and Jordan had discussed his crew staying at the lodge, he'd woken up determined that he'd spent his last night at the Rocking A until all the bedrooms were finished. Painted. With real beds.

Then he'd remember how much he thought about Jordan and he'd convince himself that a crick in his neck bothered him less than watching her run back to LA.

Clay wasn't sure whether he was protecting her or himself, but every night, he found a clear spot, unrolled his sleeping bag and tried to sleep. The restless nights were piling up and his normal, even disposition was fading. His job site did not need three Armstrongs with the personalities of bighorn sheep, always tangling horns.

He shoved Grant's boots over with his foot as he stood to stretch.

"Morning, sunshine," Wes said as he offered a cup of coffee. "I wasn't sure you were ever getting up."

Clay peered out the window. "Yeah, it must be all of…six in the morning?" He rubbed the sleep out of his eyes and took a bracing sip of the hot coffee. Wes brewed it strong enough to wake him up three days into the future. It was exactly what he needed.

"Yeah. Travis has headed out to the barn. He wanted to check on the cows up in the pass." Wes sighed.

"And he wanted to get away from hammering for a while?" Clay shook his head. "I understand the urge."

Wes motioned with his head. "Grant's painting the new Sheetrock in the old bedrooms." They communicated with raised eyebrows.

"I guess tearing out the kitchen helped somehow? Got out some of the big feelings?" Clay had been amazed at how quickly the old cabinets had disappeared from the kitchen. The appliances had been moved out to the porch, and only the coffeepot and the microwave remained, sitting on the boxes of stored food that had once filled the old cabinets. When Carlos arrived with his team, his trailers and the navy cabinets, Clay could move inside with Grant and they could make serious progress in the kitchen. Finally.

"I'm gonna ask Dad to head into Fairplay to rent a floor sander." Clay had tried to optimize the crew and the time he had. Floors should be the last task, but they might be able to work around some of the other jobs. Staining the floors could take place while he was comfortably sleeping at the Majestic.

"I like that idea." Walt stuck his head around the corner from the kitchen. "You make those changes to the layout in here, like I asked? I can get any of the necessities while I'm out, you know." He raised his eyebrows.

Clay grunted. "Unless you want your soaking tub sitting out in the yard, we better wait a minute on that."

Wes whistled. "A fancy tub? In this house. I never would have believed it. When the pipes froze that time, you tried to convince us you bathed in a horse trough growing up."

"And that you liked it," Clay added in his best attempt at impersonating his father's delivery.

Walt ran a hand over his mouth. "Don't tell your mama about the tub."

Wes buttoned his lip and raised his coffee mug. Clay knew Wes would be asking for details later.

"Since we can wait on that, you might see if Mom would like to tag along, Dad. You two can pick out the new stain for the floors together. Do some rug shopping? She had a suggestion for one under the kitchen table. Sure would be nice to have her input with it." Clay could feel the weight of Wes's eyes on the side of his face, but he didn't dare make eye contact.

"What about the store?" Walt raised a brow. "Hers. The boys can handle the hardware store. Should be a busy day in town with the leaves the way they are. Prue won't want to miss her customers." He stared at the place where the refrigerator had been as if he were weighing his options.

"When I was in Handmade, she mentioned Rose had offered to stay with the store if she wanted to get away." Clay knew he had to be careful here. Making it seem like Walt's idea was the key to success. "And she was open to it. There won't be too many pretty days like this left before everything's covered in snow."

Clay knew it would work if they let off the gas at the right time, so he sipped his coffee.

Walt scowled down at his jeans. "I better change my pants. These have paint on them." Clay did his best to maintain a poker face, but Walt shook his finger at both of them as he hurried by. "I don't want to hear it out of either of you. You wait until a woman has you so tied up you don't know whether you're coming or going." He was still muttering as he turned the corner to his bedroom.

"Good work, little brother." Wes clamped a hand on his shoulder. "Now we have to wait to see if he can put off arriving at Handmade until a reasonable hour, instead of interrupting Mama's beauty sleep. Tell me about the tub. I am intrigued."

"Don't know how he managed it, but Dad found a small pot of gold and gave it to me with only two requests." He held out two fingers. "The tub, which will go in the bathroom in his new apartment." He and Wes both nodded. "And a pot filler."

His brother's blank expression made sense. They definitely weren't standard issue in Colorado ranch houses. "It's a kind of faucet on a long arm that you put over the stove." Clay moved his arm to show Wes how it worked. "To fill your tall pots with water." Before Wes could make the valid criticism Clay could read on his lips, Clay warned him off. "Doesn't matter how often she would use it. She wanted one, and we seem to have entered a phase where he is all about getting Mom what she wants."

Wes whistled. "That is something different. Used to, he'd tell us how many cows he could buy for a soaking tub."

Clay said, "He's planning surprises now. We better hope Mom and Dad make it back from wherever they end up going in one piece and in the same vehicle, or we will have wasted a small pot of gold that could have bought cows."

Their chuckles attracted Grant's attention. "You didn't tell me the coffee was ready." He frowned as he passed by them. "And what's so funny?"

Clay shot Wes a look. So Grant's work ethic had always been strong, and his mood had improved, but he hadn't had a whole transformation obviously. "Clay finagled Dad into taking Mom on a date, a shopping trip into the city."

Grant froze. An unfamiliar smile turned up his lips and he offered Clay his hand for a high five. "Nice work. I love it when you two put your brains to good use."

Then he disappeared into the kitchen.

"Was that a compliment or an insult?" Wes asked. "Like we don't always use our brains?"

Clay shook his head and bent down to grab his sleeping bag. Instead of rolling it, he folded it and thumped it down on the duffel he'd been living out of while he was home.

"Count it as a win and keep moving."

"Good advice." Wes stared at the living room. "What's first on the list? Cover up the furniture, take everything off the walls and start painting? No primer?"

Clay understood Wes's up-and-at-'em readiness, even if he would rather start off with a big breakfast and a hot shower. "The paint includes the primer. Let's do ceiling and trim. We need to keep the floor clear until the bedrooms are all painted so we have some place to sleep."

Wes had turned to study the line of photos that covered the hallway from the entry to the kitchen doorway. "What are we going to do with these?"

Clay joined him, propping his hands on his hips. In the first picture, he and Wes were around fourteen and covered in mud, head to toe. It wasn't the normal graduation or sports team picture he'd seen parents hang in his friends' homes, but they had their arms propped up on each other's shoulders and big happy grins on their faces. It was a good memory, but they were grown. No one wanted to be reminded of their lengthy awkward phase for the rest of their life.

"Besides having to take them down…" He pondered his options. "We can deliver them to Mom in town, but where would she put them all up in her apartment?"

"Handmade has lots of empty wall space," Wes mused.

"If she dared hang these in the store, we'd all have to leave town forever." Clay would find some way to add on to the apartment she was renting to avoid that fate.

Wes grimaced. "Yeah, we lived through puberty. No one needs to be reminded of it."

"They are not going back up in here. If Travis gets his way, there will be new kids running through these doors. We don't want them to have this type of ammunition against us, either." Boxing them up and moving them into a closet somewhere would be easy enough.

Wes shuddered. "No way. Kids are ruthless." He brightened. "I got it. We should have them scanned, and get Mom and Dad both one of those picture frames. You know, the kind you can plug in and they play a slideshow? Good for small spaces and Dad would never, ever remember to even turn the thing on. Problem solved."

"I like it." Clay turned to his brother. "I'll get the frames. You handle the rest." He thought Wes was going to argue, but instead, he grinned.

"Doesn't Jordan do something with computers?" Wes asked innocently. Too innocently. "She might be able to knock the whole project out in no time, especially if she had a helper. Who could we ask to sit next to Jordan and steer this project?"

Clay was already digging through his clothes for his phone to give her a call. Did they need her for this project? Not really. He and Wes could take care of it eventually, but he wouldn't mind being Jordan's assistant.

Then he saw what time it was, as if his

phone were flashing a warning about not calling normal people at this early hour. He was
as bad as Walt, which meant he might already
have it as bad for Jordan as his father did for
his mother. Heartbreak was already on the
table. He needed to take a minute.

"Go on, you can handle it, big brother."
Clay ignored the big question mark over Wes's
head as he changed his mind and direction.
While he brushed his teeth, he reminded himself that absolutely nothing was settled for either himself or Jordan. Getting more tangled
up with her before she was on the same page
was too dangerous to his heart. Space and
time apart would be a good thing.

JORDAN WASHED HER cereal bowl Saturday
morning and realized making the trip into
Prospect had improved her mood. She had
been an all-work, no-play grump for weeks,
and there was no fairy godmother with a
magic wand in sight to change things. A kiss
or two from a flanneled prince in work boots
and a healthy dose of dessert nachos had her
feeling more like herself. What kind of sad
princess was she?

"Jordan, you are losing touch with reality,"

she muttered to herself as she watched the late morning sun shift over the mountains rising up behind the lodge. The scrubbing, which she had done all by herself, no forest animal assistance, was destroying her brain as well as her manicure.

"Time to get yourself together." She pointed at the faint outline of her reflection before shaking her head and moving back to the island, where she'd plugged in her laptop and phone to charge. Jordan hadn't been able to sleep after The Kiss, Part Two, so she'd worked on lists. Her older sister would be so proud.

So far, she had "Reasons to Sell the Majestic." It was short, with one entry only: dollar signs.

"Why Jordan Should Reopen the Lodge Herself" was longer. At the top of that one, she'd put Sadie's name to try to capture what the place meant to her and the whole family. Sarah would understand. There were other entries of varying degrees of importance, such as Jordan's need for a job, the impact the lodge would have on Prospect as a tourist destination, Sarah having a place to stay until the inevitable happened with Wes and "historical significance," which she'd added in a late-night fit of inspiration. She wasn't sure any of these outweighed the dollar signs on the first list. Should she add that they could attach the Cookie Queen museum somehow? Maybe displays in the lobby and restaurant? Jordan typed it but then deleted it. That was Sarah's thing. She would see the possibilities better than any of them.

The third list needed more work. "Other Jobs for Jordan." If she were honest with herself, she'd been content in LA. After half an hour of searching her usual job sites, Jordan had applied for a few positions that matched the one she'd walked away from. Then she realized that might be a mistake. She'd hated that job, except for the paycheck, so that would make it easier to pick the Majestic. Sarah would call her on that, too.

"If you could do anything, what would you do?" Jordan asked herself as she removed the job title from the search and told the program to match her skills to what was available. When the results loaded, Jordan wasn't sure if she was happy or sad that the top positions were the listings she'd already applied for, but she scrolled until the heading "Film Production Project Management" caught her eye. The requirements included "love of the movies" and "ability to travel as needed," so Jordan applied even though she didn't have all the qualifications listed. Finding something that sparked her interest strengthened the third list, demonstrating that Jordan was putting in the effort to figure out what should come next.

Would Sarah be satisfied with that? Was that what mattered most?

Jordan had decided that the way to approach this pitch to reopen the Majestic under Hearst ownership was to convince Sarah first. Her older sister already had one foot in Prospect, thanks to Wes. Jordan wouldn't have to tug hard to pull her into the idea of the lodge being put to use again.

With lists at the ready, Jordan couldn't put off calling her older sister any longer. Brooke had asked her to do it. If she delayed too long, her window of opportunity to break the news about Brooke's divorce would close and both sisters would be angry with her.

She decided to stroll over to the marina dock to make the call. It was a beautiful sunny day. There might not be many left where it was warm enough to sit by the water, so she should take advantage of it. When she was seated cross-legged at the end of the dock, she propped her phone up on her laptop and called her sister.

"Video?" Sarah said as she appeared. Jordan wasn't sure the phone had even rung once fully before Sarah answered. "I was beginning to wonder if the kitchen ghost had gotten you." She bent closer to the screen. "It has been too long, Jordan Marie Hearst, so I'm relieved to find you in one piece." Then she frowned. "You look tired."

"Uh-oh, she's pulling out the full name," Jordan muttered as she rolled her eyes at her sister. "I am tired. I've been busy here. I'm sure you have, too. Everything is fine. It's no biggie. We can go a few days without talking. Besides that, I know that there's an informant living at this ranch next door who keeps you up-to-date on current events." When they were both in LA, the time between their calls could easily stretch to a week. One or the other would call on the weekend, then they would connect with Brooke. After a quick round of updates, they would return to their own lives and concerns. Now that they shared the Majestic, they were all tangled back up again.

Jordan wasn't complaining. She'd missed time with Sarah and Brooke.

"O-kay." Sarah drew out the word to show her dissatisfaction with that answer. "I guess I'm as guilty as you are."

"Phones work both ways, big sister." Jordan stretched her legs out, relieved that the first hurdle of the conversation had been cleared.

"Should we get Brooke on this call, too?" Sarah asked, already reaching for her phone to do that.

"Let's wait. I want to talk to you about something first."

"Is it about the lodge?" Sarah shoved her hair behind one ear. "Wes called me yesterday to tell me that Erin had a possibly interested buyer."

She'd expected the conversation to go in many different directions. This was one she wasn't ready to tackle yet. It made more sense to cover Brooke's news first. "Yes, that's right. He's going to call me on Monday to let me know when they're on the way to take a look at the place." She brushed her hair over her shoulder. "It's good timing. Last week,

I was wondering if I should send Erin some new pictures, now that I've uncovered all the windows. I'd forgotten how it feels as if the lodge is sitting right on the edge of the lake on days like today."

Sarah asked, "Have you been wearing yourself out cleaning it up, Jordie? There's no reason to do that. These buyers can see the potential under dust and cobwebs."

Jordan adjusted the laptop. "I have worked hard. You would be impressed. I even had to go into Prospect to buy a new vacuum. Brooke and I had a good laugh about that when I told her I was cleaning. How Mom would have thought that was hilarious."

Sarah grumbled, "You never did want to fold laundry, but leave you with cobwebs, dust and a ghost, and you're all in."

"No ghost. No sightings. No rattling chains. Vanilla sometimes seems to waft in the air but… You made it up, didn't you? This is a prank, a long-running joke you're playing on your poor little sister." Jordan tried her mean face, but she'd never been great at intimidating Sarah.

"Could it have been a hallucination?" Sarah sounded confused and a wrinkle marred her forehead. "You heard it. On the call. We both heard it!" Then she waved her hands. "Never mind about that. Don't distract me. Why are you pushing so hard out there?"

Jordan wished for something to drink. Her mouth was so dry in that instant. "We know finding a buyer who will keep Sadie's version of the Majestic is a long shot. The three of us have talked more than once about how it will feel to see the place knocked down. If I can put in some effort, add a bit of shine, to influence the decision to make repairs instead of annihilating it, I want to do that." She wrapped her arms around her knees. "There might be something…healing about it, too. It's scary to face a world without Sadie. When I uncover something here that reminds me of her, I realize she hasn't left us completely." Not yet. Jordan inhaled slowly and forced herself to stop talking.

Sarah opened her mouth but changed her mind and closed it again.

The second time she did it, Jordan huffed out a breath. "What? Say it."

"I wish I was sitting next to you on the dock," Sarah said. "You've been waffling back and forth on staking a claim on the lodge, have been ever since we found out we inherited it, always making sure that we keep our options open. Brooke can see it, too. She's sent me more than one text warning me not to let you talk me into taking it on for you. It isn't like you to hesitate, Jordie, so don't 'what?' me. I'll just 'what?' you back."

Jordan knew it was true. None of them were pushovers.

"What are you afraid of?" Sarah asked.

That was the real question, wasn't it?

"If I say, 'Let me run the Majestic, and give me all the money we got from selling that chunk of land to the Rocking A, plus anything you can spare from Sadie's estate when it settles,' and I somehow convince both of you to go along with me," Jordan said, "what happens when..." She stared out over the water. Was she actually going to say it?

Sarah crossed her arms, patiently waiting.

"What happens when I have a mess I can't fix and I want to run away from it? What will you and Brooke lose that you might not get back?" Jordan rubbed her nose to chase the sting of tears away. "I can be unpredictable, you know."

"I had no idea," Sarah drawled.

At her sister's sarcastic answer, Jordan relaxed. She'd admitted her fear out loud. She didn't have to carry it alone anymore.

"A rational woman once told me I didn't have much to lose if the Cookie Queen museum failed, even if it cost a bunch of money." She tapped her lips. "Who was that? I can see a face, but the name escapes me."

Jordan hadn't expected Sarah to throw her own words back at her, but she totally should have. That ability was a Hearst family heirloom.

"If we're careful with the investment in the place, we give it a shot and it doesn't work," Sarah said, "we've lost some cash, but we still have the lodge, the lakefront and the marina. We close up, sell it knowing full well a beautiful luxury home will take its place, and we don't have any doubts because we did our best to hold on to the Majestic." She shrugged. "You don't have much to lose here."

Jordan closed her eyes. "If you knew this all along, why didn't you tell me it was time for me to learn how to run a fishing lodge?"

Sarah chuckled. "Because it's not a small step, Jordie. If this isn't what you want, you won't be happy. What about LA and your friends? Your career and the freedom to choose? All of that goes away and you're left with Prospect and a run-down old building to show for it."

Jordan nodded as she watched the slow waves ripple across the lake. "I made lists."

Sarah gasped and covered her heart. "I knew I could be a good influence."

"I thought you would make me jump through all these hoops before I could tell you I wanted to do this, like apply for jobs in LA, come up with a business plan and a budget." Jordan twiddled the pen in her fingers. "I haven't done that last part. It's a lot of work to put in if I couldn't get anyone to listen to me in the end."

Sarah snorted. "Smart girl, but I don't think you can put it off. Before we speak to Brooke, we need to meet with these buyers, and it would be helpful to have a ballpark number for what it would take to get the lodge doors open before Western Days in the spring." She held up a finger. "The biggest tourist weekend in Prospect and the beginning of lake season, so it's a good deadline."

Jordan narrowed her eyes. "Admit it. You've

already started the business plan and the budget."

"Guilty." Sarah grimaced. "I like a good spreadsheet, you know?"

"And you love your sister and are in tune with when she needs your assistance," Jordan added.

"You don't have to do any of this alone, but you do have to decide whether you want to make big sacrifices." She sobered. "And whether you want to take the gamble if these buyers are all in on running Sadie's place as it is."

Jordan frowned. That might be the hardest part of the decision. If it weren't all or nothing with the Majestic, if they could hold on to a piece of Sadie without dragging the three Hearst sisters into the fishing lodge business, what then?

"What did you want to talk about if it's not the Majestic?" Sarah asked.

"I wanted to ease into this but I can't figure out a way." Jordan picked up her phone and fell back to stretch out on the dock. "Brooke called me to let me know she and Paul are divorced. It was final this week."

Jordan turned on her side and propped her

head on her hand as she waited for Sarah to absorb that.

"Wow," Sarah said in a small voice. "I hate that for her, but we were afraid something was going on. When she was in LA, she seemed... tense."

"Good thing you didn't let me push her out of the car for being a broken record about how she had to get back to New York. It makes so much sense now. Paul is not making this easy for her."

Sarah cleared her throat. "Why didn't she call me to tell me herself? We didn't even know she was in trouble for sure." This was the question Jordan had dreaded the most. Hurt was easy to hear in Sarah's voice. "I would have booked a flight. Dropped everything. She shouldn't be on her own now."

Jordan smiled at her older sister. "That's why, Sarah. Brooke knows you've got a life. She promised she would call when she's ready to move out of their apartment. You can wheel my passed-out body through the airport, strap me into an airplane seat and when I wake up, I'll be ready to carry a sofa down the stairs. I promise."

When Sarah snorted a laugh, Jordan was

relieved. All three of them had their roles. Brooke was the baby. She depended on them for advice, and Sarah was the mothering type, always ready with a hug or a plane ticket.

Jordan was the comic relief, the one who evened out the surface, so they could handle whatever came next.

"You really have been working out if you think we can manage a sofa." Sarah shook out her arms. "Okay, so when we talk to Brooke next, we're all going to be our normal selves. Practical. No tears. No emotional vows of undying sisterly love. And Brooke will be able to keep her chin up, look herself in the mirror." She nodded. "Because she asked you to call me and tell me, so she didn't have to."

Jordan didn't respond to that. It was true, but that wouldn't make Sarah like it any more.

"The only time you two ever get along is when you're managing me. How does that happen?" Sarah asked.

Jordan cleared her throat. "How's Sadie's collection going?"

Sarah stared hard into the screen to let Jordan know she was aware that she was trying to change the subject, then she let it go. "Good. Michael and the board are satisfied with the mementos and memorabilia I've chosen for headquarters, and he had a meeting set up last week with the company that's going to assemble the display cases in the lobby." Sarah sighed. "There's so much I didn't know that I didn't know about archiving things so that they're protected, and the best storage techniques, how to track items in inventory. When we were discussing a museum, I only had in mind the adorable displays I could put together, but there's so much more to it, especially if we can roll Sadie's life into a wider history of Prospect."

"I get that." Jordan had felt the same way about everything happening at the Majestic. "Like how I never knew there was an actual gas tubey-thing, a pilot light, inside the oven that makes it heat up, so if it's not working, check it. Clay taught me that." Remembering how patiently Clay had repositioned the flashlight while she was his assistant made her happy. He'd always been a good teacher.

Sarah's silence got Jordan's attention. "What?"

"Roping Clay into your plot to sidestep your promise about not making repairs to the lodge was clever," Sarah huffed. "But you and Clay don't like each other."

Jordan realized then that whatever she'd confessed to Prue Armstrong hadn't made it through the Armstrong grapevine to Sarah. Yet. If Wes had heard the story, her older sister would have, too. "Actually, we were friends when we both worked at the marina during the Summer of Exile."

Sarah rolled her eyes. "You're so dramatic. It was never exile. Can't be the end of the story, though, so keep going." She widened her eyes in expectation.

"There was a kiss." Jordan shook her head as her sister whooped loudly into the phone. "He thought he'd scared me away, and I was sure I'd embarrassed myself with this guy I had a crush on. Fast forward all these years and…" Fanning her face was a distinct tell, but the flush was coming no matter what.

"And?" Sarah drew out the word. She knew there had been a new chapter somehow.

"I kissed him again last night." Jordan covered her mouth. "And then he kissed me."

Sarah's eyes were huge as she yanked up the telephone. "Jordan. Two more kisses. It was that porch swing, wasn't it? It's dangerous. We have to get one at the lodge."

Jordan giggled as she watched her sister's

wild victory lap on the screen and wondered if Sarah understood how she was making plans that involved the Majestic continuing on. Adding a porch swing would be an investment in the future.

And it would also present the Hearst sisters with plenty of dangerous kissing opportunities.

Even if she and Clay had managed to make their own opportunities, using the dock and the parking lot in front of the Homestead Market so far.

As she thought about that, she realized she and Clay might need to examine the romance in their relationship.

When Sarah settled down, she asked, "So what now?"

Jordan knew she meant with Clay. "We'll see what the buyers say, I guess."

Sarah studied her face. Was she going to insist on pushing the love question? Eventually, she nodded. "Okay, we figure out the lodge question first. Then we'll tackle the love."

Jordan sighed. "I don't know which one is more confusing right now, honestly."

"I would say—" Sarah paused as she seemed

to choose her words carefully "—we've got to watch out for Brooke. She's not here, so it's important to keep her in mind."

Jordan nodded. That was true. Neither one of them had any doubt that Brooke was ready to sell. With a divorce and the need to make a new home for herself in New York, money would be a blessing.

"But…" Sarah waited for Jordan to turn back to the phone. "If I knew someone who had thrown herself into cleaning up a lodge, to the extent that she was beating mattresses to try to salvage them, and she wanted to re-open the lodge herself…" Sarah shrugged. "I hope there's a way to make that a success."

Jordan smiled. "You're a great big sister, did you know that?"

"I do know it. The two of you ganging up on me…" Sarah tsked. "Almost makes me sorry I sent you a wonderful care package." Her sly grin was cute.

Jordan tried to guess what might be in the care package, but eventually gave in and said, "I can't wait to get it."

CHAPTER ELEVEN

LATE SUNDAY MORNING, Clay shoved his phone in his pocket and grabbed the end of the sofa that Wes was waiting patiently for him to lift. He'd developed a bad habit of checking to see if Jordan had called. Did that make sense since the phone was in his back pocket and he definitely would hear it ring? On the second day of no contact with Jordan, "making sense" was less important than he liked.

He'd decided Jordan didn't need any more projects, especially not Wes's photo frame. There would be plenty of time to sort that out after the house was settled.

Clay had lost count of how many times they had moved the massive brown couch to finish two coats of paint, but the ceiling and trim were finally done. Instead of scooting it across the floors he planned to sand and refinish, Wes insisted on picking up and moving it. To be fair, Clay could still remember the way their mother had yelled the winter they'd decided to move all the furniture out of the way to play indoor hockey, using socks as skates, an assortment of broom and mop handles as sticks, and one of her old slippers as the puck.

If he squinted, he could still see the scrape they'd left when they'd gotten into a fight about a nonexistent icing call.

"You know, Mom must have nerves of steel," he said as he set his end down carefully to avoid a loud thump.

"I'm not sure anyone should have made it through having all of us cooped up in this old house for winter days. She should have shut us out in the barn," Wes agreed. "You hear anything from Dad about how the day went yesterday?"

Clay rubbed at a dried smudge of paint on his hand. "No. Where is he?" They might have been lifting instead of scooting furniture across the floor, but the grunts of effort should have precipitated some commentary about lifting with their legs or working smarter, not harder.

Wes shook his head. "I haven't seen him. He must have left before dawn this morning."

Clay wrapped the tarp they'd slung over the couch tighter and then straightened. A suspicion about his father's absence flashed in his mind. "You don't think…"

Wes frowned at him as he set the recliner down; it was also brown. In a feat of strength, he'd hefted it by himself. "What?"

The deep brown couch, the lighter brown recliner, a love seat that used to be tan if he recalled correctly but had…darkened to brown and two hunter green armchairs were stacked against the wall in a jagged pile that was giving "dead leaves." Everything had exceeded the normal life expectancy in a houseful of active kids. He pulled out his phone, temporarily removed the tarp, took a quick photo and texted it to Chaney. No message would be required. She would understand it was a cry for professional interior design help.

Clay didn't want to voice his question. Once the words were spoken out loud, he could never unhear them. "Never mind." Instead of explaining, he rolled up the tan rug that covered the center of the living room and dropped it on top of the couch.

Wes scowled at him. "You had to go and ask the question, didn't you?"

"I didn't say a word." Clay held his hands out to show that he was completely innocent.

They stared at each other for a long moment until Travis came in from the barn. He stomped his boots inside the door. "Did Dad spend the night in town at Mama's place?"

Their loud groans brought Grant running. "What? What is it?"

Travis was laughing at the reaction he'd stirred up. "Wes and Clay are easily shocked, that's all. They think our parents slept in separate beds."

Grant propped his shoulder against the wall and immediately straightened to check for paint on his shoulder. Not that it would have mattered, since he was covered head to toe in a mixture of prior paint choices. Chaney had chosen white for all the trim, but the old bedrooms were all a soft blue-gray. Clay wanted this done, so he would accept whatever color he got.

"Guessing you're talking about how Dad didn't sleep in his own bed last night," Grant said.

Before they could all groan again, Clay heard truck tires on gravel, so he opened the front door. "Speak of the devil," he called over his shoulder. "And he's got an angel in the passenger seat."

They filed out onto the long porch that covered the front of the house.

"Come grab a load," their father yelled. "We brought food. Been cooking all morning."

That changed things. Clay had been prepared to stand there, tapping his boot the way his father had when he'd come home past curfew as a kid. But they had brought lunch. Now was not the time to quibble. The four brothers lined up in the yard to bring the dishes in, assembly-line-style.

"Where are we going to put it all?" Travis asked as he turned to go inside. "Everything is a mess."

"Put it on the kitchen table," his mother said as if the answer were simple. She pointed at it sitting on the porch where they'd moved it to keep it safe while they tore out the cabinets. They deposited all the bundles and stepped back for her to do the unveiling. When a large pot of beef stew was uncovered, every man in attendance stood straighter.

Their mother had also delivered one of Sadie Hearst's chocolate sheet cakes, one of the first things she'd learned to cook. Dad told the story of how she'd surprised him on their six-month anniversary with that cake and it had been his favorite ever since.

"Now, go find the bowls and some silverware." She hurried over to the refrigerator, conveniently plugged in and running right there on the porch, to pull out butter. "I've got corn bread, too."

Clay was about to elbow Wes out of the way to follow his mother's orders when Grant stepped outside with the necessary items. Travis grabbed sodas and passed them around, while their mother dished out the stew. No one said a word until they'd all claimed a post or a railing to lean against, bowl in hand.

Clay observed how his parents had each claimed one side of the top step. They weren't exactly touching, but it was hard to name the atmosphere between them. Whatever it was, Clay decided they were adults and he did not need to be involved in that conversation. He shared a side-eyed glance with Wes and then they both focused on their meals.

"I don't want to go inside. This is your project in your house, after all." His mother studied his father for a long minute before beaming at them all. "But from the state of things, you boys are getting a lot of work done." She reached over to pat Travis on the back. "This is going to be exactly what you all needed, Trav."

Clay inhaled and exhaled slowly as he realized he was pretty close to agreeing with her. It had gotten easier for him to see the end product thanks to his years of renovating and flipping houses. Right now they had plenty of mess still, but if they stayed on schedule, in a little over a week—possibly less now that Carlos was on the way—they would have a beautiful home to open up to the caseworker when she returned.

Building the sort of large development he imagined and drafted up on paper was exciting, but taking this place that had been loved and giving it new life was genuinely satisfying.

"Couldn't have done any of this without Clay." Travis turned in a slow circle. "Well, without any of you guys."

"Except Matt," Grant muttered, "who is absent again."

Amused, Clay relaxed into the lunch break.

"Last I saw him, he was sleeping on a secondhand couch he picked up for his office in town, so you might all remember that he's making contributions, too." Their mother sniffed and Clay ducked his head to contain his laughter.

"So, is that the floor sander in the back of your truck?" Grant asked innocently. "Was it too heavy to unload last night? And then you had to carry it back into town when you went to help Mom cook, I guess."

If Clay could have covered his head with his bowl, he would have. The answer, no matter what it was, was going to be awkward.

"We got caught in traffic yesterday and it was very late when we made it back to town," his mother said primly. "I didn't want your father to drive all the way out here in the dark." Then she took a dainty bite of her corn bread. Clay waited to see what Grant might do. Of the four of them, he'd always been the one to push his luck.

Today? He flattened his lips into a straight line and chose silence. Was that a sign of growth?

No one stepped into the conversation, so peace settled over the porch again.

"Clay, I was hoping you would take some of this over to Jordan. Your father said she's been working herself to the bone cleaning that place up. If you weren't so busy here, I'd tell all four of you to get over there and help her." His mother motioned over her shoulder with her spoon. "Jordan has her own container of stew."

"I'd be happy to, Mama," Clay said as he reached into his pocket to check his phone. He'd tried to call Jordan three times with no return call. "I'm not sure we're still talking to each other. Anybody hear the screeching tires of Jordan Hearst peeling out of Prospect on her way back to LA?"

His mother raised her eyebrows. "What did you do?"

Wes laughed as Clay shot him an aggrieved look. "Why would you assume he did something?"

She snorted a laugh. "Because I know you boys. Not a romantic bone in any of these bodies, so tell me what you did."

Wes grinned. "He kissed her. Again. That chased her away from Prospect the first time, so he's wondering if it had the same effect now. Clay might need some practice."

Clay glared at his brother. "I learned a couple nights ago that I wasn't all alone that first time. She kissed me, too."

His mother had that "gotcha" gleam in her eyes. He was a goner.

"But you did it again? Since she's back in town, you kissed her again?"

Clay glared harder at his brother. "How did you know that, anyway? Were you trailing us?"

Wes shrugged. "I didn't need to. The idea of the next kiss was written all over your face when you followed her out of the Garage. I'd be more shocked to find out you didn't kiss her." He bent closer to Clay. "And I know how that goes."

Clay blinked as he and Wes were caught in a stare down. Then he sighed.

"I should have skipped the calls and gone over there yesterday," Clay mumbled as he set his soup bowl down. He might have if he could have convinced himself to make a stronger argument about jumping into this thing between them with both feet. He'd tried being prudent, opting for the smart option of more space and time apart, but his heart wasn't interested in intelligent decisions.

And it wasn't like Jordan to hesitate, so this lack of communication seemed like an answer in itself.

"I've given you the perfect opening, Clay," his mother said sweetly but firmly. "I hope no one here believes that one of my meals, hand delivered, would ever fail in courting."

Courting.

Was that what he was doing? Investing time in something that could turn into forever?

When the suggestion didn't fill him with panic, Clay said, "No, ma'am. If there is anything that could convince Jordan Hearst to go all in with me, it would be the promise of a lifetime of your biscuits and corn bread."

"She's had the biscuits." Walt stood as he reminded them all of the business meeting Wes had called when the Hearsts first came to prospect. "Corn bread will be better than a bouquet of flowers."

His mother held her hands in front of her, pretending to weigh one against the other. "Could be roughly equal. Why don't you saddle up Starla and invite Jordan for a ride? Take her mind off the lodge so she can focus on you." She waggled her eyebrows. "Bet there would be a kiss in it."

Wes grunted. "Not if he shows up with a horse."

Clay held up a hand to make sure his mother didn't overreact. "Jordan is afraid of horses."

Since his mother loved her horse, Lady, as much or more than her sons, he knew this could be a deal breaker for her. They all watched her inhale and exhale slowly. "Okay. This is a shock, but I will always be open-minded toward people who are different than we are."

Walt wrapped his arm around her shoulder, there to comfort her in her troubles.

"I…" Was his mother at a loss for words? "I don't know how to help here, not after that revelation."

"It's a challenge," Clay agreed. "When we were young, she desperately wanted to see the ghost town, but Sadie wouldn't let any of them go up there. I might be able to tempt her out of the lodge with a quick tour of Sullivan's Post." He turned to Wes. "Will the truck make it up there?"

Wes was shaking his head sadly when Travis stuck his nose into the conversation. "Take the side-by-side. Let her drive. Jordan seems like the type who likes to take charge. Adventure should be better than roses, for sure."

Clay studied his brother with newfound

respect. It was easy to imagine Jordan driving the UTV aggressively around the Majestic property. He offered his brother his hand to shake. "We have a winner here, lady and gentlemen. I am taking the afternoon off so I can deliver a meal to our neighbor, but don't let me stop the work from happening. Still plenty of painting to do before we tackle the kitchen."

They were chattering when he ran inside to grab his hat and light jacket. They cheered when he ran back out to leap off the porch.

And they guffawed when his mother yelled at him to come back because he was forgetting the food—the whole reason for the visit.

By the time Clay settled behind the steering wheel of the side-by-side, he was out of breath. His heart was slamming in his chest, and he realized he'd better calm down before he putt-putted up beside the lodge with corn bread and stew or Jordan would be worried.

Determined to enjoy the ride, Clay headed across the pasture toward the fence that joined the ranch and Sadie's land. The only thing better than skipping out of an afternoon of work by driving away would be by riding Charlie, his favorite of the Rocking A's quarter horses. He was almost relaxed by the time he got through the gate and shut it behind him. Then, when he parked in front of the lodge, he realized his pulse had sped up again.

There might not be much he could do about that. Jordan had always been able to add that zing to his days.

Clay grabbed the food container and tried the front door. He wasn't happy to see that it opened easily. Was she out here by herself every day with all the doors open?

He filed the tidbit in the back of his brain to discuss with her some other time. The last thing he wanted now was a debate.

"Jordan?" he called as he stopped inside the lobby. If he'd wondered what she'd been doing since he last talked to her, the state of this large open room answered at least part of the question. The floors were clean. So was the long desk at the front. Cobwebs within reach were gone, and an oval rug in sunny yellows, oranges and reds had been rolled out in the center of the room. The mums he'd last seen huddled in her back seat marked the ends of the check-in desk, and she'd removed the cover from Sadie's mountain landscape.

He was happy to see the big painting was

still against the wall. He wouldn't put it past her to try to hang the giant thing all by herself somehow.

Clay set the container on the desk and listened. Faint thumps were his answer, but he wasn't sure which direction they came from. He went toward Sadie's apartment first and stuck his head inside the open doorway. "Jordan? Are you here?"

Her cell phone was on the kitchen island, which might explain why she hadn't responded to his calls.

Clay stepped outside. Her car was parked in its usual spot. White…something was hanging on the line. It could be fitted sheets, but he wasn't sure. After satisfying himself that she wasn't on that side of the lodge, he moved back through the lobby toward the opposite side. No overhead lights were on in the restaurant or in the kitchen, but he checked it, too, just in case. No Jordan. The sugary cookie smell was there for an instant and then gone, so Clay meandered slowly back out into the dining room. When he picked up the scent again, faintly, he turned in a slow circle. Then he spotted a door he'd missed during their appliance tour. Faint thumps convinced him Jordan would be there.

He moved behind the host station against the wall that opened to the lobby. When he turned, he saw light spilling out under the door.

"Jordan?" he called, hoping to warn her he was there.

"Clay? Is that you? I need help!" Jordan yelled, so he hurried inside a large storage room that was packed with…stuff. There were so many piles and large shapes covered in dust sheets. Boxes on shelves. Linens stacked up. Two large washing machines and a massive old dryer.

And Jordan, who was twisted between what might be two armchairs, judging by the size of the lumps. She was holding an end table above her head.

"If you let go of the table, you could probably free yourself," Clay said as he stepped up behind her.

"But you're here to save us both." Jordan laughed as he wrapped his hands over her hips and tugged her closer to pull her out from between the furniture. When she was free, she put the table down and did a celebratory dance. It would have been cute if she hadn't had him convinced that he was calling the sheriff and organizing search parties. Instead of joining her, he tugged off his cap before yanking it back down on his head. "What are you doing?" He had been more worried than he'd realized.

She smoothed the loose hair off her face. "You saw the fixed-up lobby, right? That's what I'm doing."

Clay knew he'd better dial back the nerves and the irritated tone that would come with them if he wanted to keep this meeting on an even note.

"Decorating?" he drawled. "And scaring me to death?"

She wrinkled her nose. "I guess it was weird when you couldn't find me. I heard you calling but I couldn't yell loudly enough for you to hear me. Sorry about that." She patted his shoulder and then waved her hand broadly. "Can you believe all this stuff is still here? It's in great shape, too." Her face glowed as if she'd discovered a stash of gold instead of...whatever it was.

"I was trying to make the place nice for you and Carlos and his crew. I wanted to put covers on those mattresses, in case vacuuming and whacking them with a tennis racket didn't get rid of all the dust. I washed the sheets earlier." She fanned her hand in front of her face. Her cheeks were flushed and her eyes were shining with excitement. Digging through furniture had made her hot but happy. "I decided to see if the comforters were here. They are!" She pointed at a square stack on top of one of the washing machines. It was wrapped in a dust cloth, too. "But I had to do some digging first, and I found the rug!" She pointed excitedly toward the lobby. "Sarah and I talked about that rug when we got here, and I found it. It's still here."

Clay was doing his best to follow her, but he still wasn't understanding where all the excitement was coming from for old, dusty furniture. Carlos might not even appreciate the decorated lobby.

His confusion was obvious to Jordan.

She moved closer and wrapped her hands around his arms, squeezing to make sure he was paying attention.

He would never be able to look away from this woman when she was this passionate about anything. Pleasure and happiness and so much energy radiated from her. Jordan was magnetic.

"To me," she said as she braced one hand on her chest, "the way all this was packed up so deliberately and carefully to preserve it…" She spun in a circle. "Sadie never meant to leave this place closed. The kitchen is spotless. These linens have been stored with care, so that when it was time, they could be washed and used. The furniture is locked up in here, so that no one would break in to steal it. The marina!" She poked his chest excitedly. "You can't tell me that the way all of that stuff was so carefully boxed and labeled that whoever closed it up didn't have strict orders to protect it. Because she was always planning to come back, to return to the Majestic." She stood on her tiptoes. "Sadie wanted to keep the lodge. She wants us to keep the Majestic. I know it. And this is proof. Sarah and I talked about this…tiny idea that I could reopen the lodge if we don't find a buyer. I was worried she and Brooke would invest and then I'd fail, and we'd have a mess they'd be stuck cleaning up because I would definitely bail, right? But Sadie? She was always right. If she thought we could do it, we can!"

Jordan had found the proof she wanted, but did he dare explain that lots of people, who might even be planning to sell the place, would have protected their investment the same way? Thoughtfully organizing and packing things wasn't a sign of much except that Sarah's planning streak might be genetic.

When Jordan's beautiful smile flashed again, he knew there was no good reason to be too honest here.

He didn't want to be the man responsible for making it disappear or shaking her confidence.

"Want to help me uncover the rest of the furniture?" she asked with a flirty bat of her eyelashes, as if she knew she was offering him his heart's desire.

Clay bent down close to her ear. "Play hooky with me. Forget work for a while." Her reaction to his voice hadn't escaped his notice, and he was definitely not above using it to lure her away from the Majestic for a break.

When Jordan shivered, Clay knew he'd won her over.

"Oh, how the tides have turned, my friend! My conscientious boss has become the slacker."

Jordan tapped her chin. "But I'm weak. You know I'm weak. What did you have in mind?"

"I brought you food." Clay frowned. That hadn't come out as smoothly as he'd expected, although her curiosity immediately transitioned to interest. "My mother sent over stew and corn bread. It's in the lobby."

Jordan gazed longingly over her shoulder at the treasures she still had to uncover there in the storage room. She was about to wriggle right off the hook, so Clay tried again. "I missed you." Her head whipped back around. That got her attention. And it felt so good. "I've been waiting for your call."

She reached in her pocket and then smacked her forehead. "My phone is…" He could see her mentally retracing her steps. "Somewhere else."

"Since yesterday?" Clay asked and offered her the troublesome phone.

"No, I just…" Jordan's shoulders slumped. "I want to leap off the edge with you, Clay, but can you imagine how badly landing will hurt if we're making a mistake? I have Sarah and Brooke on one side, you on the other, and my heart is…"

He nodded slowly. "Since that kiss, I spent

a lot of time staring up at the ceiling, weighing the possible hurt. I was also listening to Grant snore. It was a bad night all the way around." When she laughed and leaned against his chest, he ran his hands over her back, content to have her in his arms. "At least we both know this thing between us could be big. We wouldn't be so scared of falling otherwise. I was afraid you'd disappeared in the middle of the night again."

Jordan frowned at him. "I promised I wouldn't leave without saying goodbye. I don't break my promises, Clay. Sometimes it feels like you know me better than anyone else in the world, but on this, you'll have to take my word. I made you a promise. I'll keep it."

He squeezed her and stepped back. "Good. How about I make good on a promise then? Would you like to ride with me up to see the ghost town? I'll help you make the beds or uncover furniture or practice your tennis serve on mattresses when we get back."

Her lips were twitching. "I have two important questions before we go."

He nodded.

She held up a finger. "Do I have to get on a horse?"

He shook his head. "No, milady, I am aware of your feelings about the noble horse, and you have made yourself clear to my brother, as well. I have another method in mind. You can even drive if you're up for it."

That was all it took. The way her eyes sharpened on his told him she was in.

She held up her second finger. "Do gas dryers also have pilot lights?" Then she motioned with her head. "All this time, I thought it was broken. Then, when I was caught between the rock and the hard place, a stroke of genius hit." She patted his shoulder. "Then you appeared, like every hero in every story, as if I'd called you."

"Like your handy-dandy appliance repair person?" He stepped closer to the dryer. "First thing, let's check the gas valve." He leaned over the dryer and turned the valve to open it. When he moved back, Jordan's eyes snapped up to meet his. The guilty blush on her cheeks made him wonder…

Had she been checking out his jeans? And if so, was she impressed?

She blinked at him in her best attempt at innocence.

"Eyes up here, please," he muttered as he bent over to test the controls on the dryer. Everything was set correctly, so he pushed the start button, then waited as the drum started to tumble.

Jordan casually pulled dust covers off two wooden rocking chairs that would fit perfectly on the rug out in the lobby. The way she danced was impossible to ignore, and he immediately understood how he always ended up fixing whatever might be broken for her. If old furniture and the ability to do laundry put her hips in motion, he wouldn't argue.

If he were lucky enough to be with Jordan Hearst, it should be easy to remember to put her first. His mother's advice had stuck with him.

After the dryer ran for a few minutes, he opened the door. "We may need to test this with a load of laundry, but it's heating up. Seems I may have repaired your dryer, as well."

She clasped her hands under her chin and rapidly batted her lashes. "My hero."

He hooked his fingers through hers and

began tugging her toward the lobby. "The dust is getting to you. You need fresh air. Grab a jacket. The breeze has a cold edge to it today." Before he could tell her he'd pull around back to pick her up, she was skipping down the hallway to the apartment on the back. Skipping. As if she were on the elementary school playground. She'd also scooped up his mother's container on her way.

Clay registered the smell of vanilla again. He wasn't in the kitchen this time. Or the dining room. He wasn't following some paranormal specter to find and rescue Jordan, either.

He studied the lobby. Everything was clean, but the scent wasn't throughout the room. It lingered here behind the check-in desk.

"Well, ghost, thank you for your help. I was starting to worry." Clay moved side to side to see if there was any difference in temperature. Wasn't that the sign of a ghost on TV shows and in the movies? A cold spot. If anything was different, he was warmer. He wasn't sure it was his temperature actually making him hot. Whatever questions he might still have about himself and Jordan... they were going to work out well.

"Ready?" Jordan asked from where she stood in front of him, concern on her face.

"Trying to get a handle on where the vanilla smell is coming from." He offered her his hand and enjoyed how easily she took it.

"I can't smell it." Jordan inhaled deeply. "Nothing here."

Clay scanned the room again before tugging her toward the door. "We better get you out in the fresh air." She was losing her sense of smell somehow.

She laughed and went on ahead of him.

"Are you going to lock up?" he asked before stepping out. "You should keep the doors locked when you're out here working by yourself."

She wrinkled her nose. "Then how will you rescue me when I'm snagged in old furniture and dust covers?"

Clay waited for her to lock the door.

She waited for him to let it go.

Since he was determined to talk with Jordan, not argue, he surrendered and stepped outside to wave grandly at the beat-up ranch side-by-side UTV he'd parked in front of the door. "Your carriage awaits."

Jordan's face was serious as she walked in a

slow circle around it, assessing the UTV with the small bed for hauling things. He knew it wasn't a beautiful chariot. The side-by-side was handy for hauling hay and tools across pastures. The camouflage paint had been scratched in places and completely rubbed off on the front bumper, probably by a too-friendly cow, but it would get them up the mountain to what remained of Sullivan's Post.

"Come on. It has been too long since I was up there. I'm anxious to see what shape it's in." Clay slid into the passenger side and pointed out the key in the ignition. "Quick driving lesson here on the flat road and then we'll go up."

Jordan clapped her hands quickly and slid in beside him. She zipped up her jacket, a men's coat he'd seen on sale the last time he'd wandered into Homestead Market, pushed up the too-long sleeves and turned the key. After sputtering and dying a few times, the engine caught with a rumble.

"Power. I love power!" Her giggle drifted across Clay, and he realized that she had never answered his question about why she hadn't called him back, not really.

Jordan hooted with excitement when the

side-by-side lurched with her foot on the gas pedal, and he decided to let the breeze carry the worry away. Jordan was still in Prospect. She was having the time of her life. And if he was reading her correctly, she was on the verge of answering one of her important questions.

If she chose to stay in Prospect, he didn't have to rush to make his case.

This time together was a gift he wanted to hold on to. When the side-by-side lurched again as Jordan maneuvered through a tight turn, making him clutch the bar in front of him, he realized he'd be smart to get his head back in the game. Life was happening all around him at the moment and he'd better not miss it.

CHAPTER TWELVE

JORDAN HAD NOT known of the existence of side-by-side vehicles like this one before today, but riding across Sadie's land with Clay by her side was a life-changing adventure. Her hair was a mess, there might be bugs smashed to her face and, at some point, she'd lost an earring, but the exhilaration of driving off-road on a beautiful Colorado fall day was satisfying.

"Slow down for a minute. Okay, stop." Clay had to raise his voice to repeat himself, and she realized he meant immediately and put her foot on the brake. "We're going to switch to four-wheel drive to start climbing up." He gripped her arm and waited until she looked at him. "Slow down for now. The steering is harder because all four wheels are getting traction. Right?"

Jordan saluted him, but she wondered if he was going to boot her out of the driver's seat.

Instead, he started counting, each number murmured under his breath.

Recognizing that he was serious about the ride, Jordan nodded again. "I get it, Clay. Safely, safely."

He slowly removed his hand. Then she noticed the other hand was locked around the grip dangling from the bar across the top. Maybe she had been driving a little faster than she realized.

Jordan gently accelerated, testing the steering wheel and how the side-by-side responded as the terrain changed slope, gradually at first and then growing steeper. She followed his directions up into the foothills of the big peaks that ringed Larkspur Pass. She missed the quicker speed, and the moment of hesitation as gravity acted to pull them back but the engine pushed them up was scary yet exciting, too. The fluttering in her abdomen matched soaring in the sky in a roller coaster; she was safe but the danger was right there, in plain sight.

Clay's kiss had given her that same flutter.

That's why she hadn't called him back.

Since she'd also managed to stick out the

sleepless night without running for LA and safety, Jordan had congratulated herself.

She might also have "accidentally" left her phone where she couldn't hear it ringing, but the consequences of that decision had turned out to be fun so far.

The outline of the weathered buildings of the silver boomtown rose up to their left. Jordan craned her head and drove down the middle of what had been the main street through Sullivan's Post one hundred and fifty years ago.

"Amazing." Jordan stopped the side-by-side and set the brake before she pulled the helmet off her head. "Can we get out?" She tapped his white-knuckle grip. "Are you going to need medical assistance to separate your grip from that handle?"

He slowly straightened each finger. Then he shook his hand out dramatically. "When we turned away from the lake, tipping up on two wheels, I was afraid we were both going to need medical assistance, hot rod."

Jordan bit her lip as she slid out. "That is a much better nickname than California. Call me that from now on."

He grunted and came to stand beside her in front of the tallest of the remaining buildings.

"What are we looking at here?" Jordan took her sunglasses off to see better and then remembered the possible bugs on her face and gave her cheeks a quick brush.

Clay propped his sunglasses up on his cap. "My best guess is that it was the hotel. Travelers mention an impressive two-story hotel in the center of Sullivan's Post. The rooms had fine carpets, and the small dining room featured a piano player every night of the week. The rate was one dollar a day. Even with the roof gone, I can make out two floors here." He outlined them with his hands, so Jordan could see them. It was easy to imagine piano music and how the windows would have glowed. In her mind, the building had been painted a dark red.

"When the town outgrew this level space here, they moved everything down to where Prospect is." Clay's eyes swept back and forth over the facade of the building. He was assessing here as he had in each room of the Majestic and the marina, cataloging the details.

It was fun to watch him getting caught up in something he loved.

Jordan studied the street level. At one time, Sullivan's Post had had a wooden boardwalk like the one preserved in Prospect's downtown. She moved closer to brace her foot on one board. "Is it safe to stand on?" She'd be happy to explore with Clay.

Clay frowned. "I wouldn't take a chance, not with you. If I had any spare time, I might grab my equipment, a hard hat and poke around a bit, but it's too far to get help if something bad happens."

"When I convince Sarah we need our own side-by-side, I can come back whenever I want. *Do* whatever I want."

His face had that warning expression, a deadpan stare that told her he was trying to find the right way to convince her, so she added, "Do they sell side-by-sides in pink? Or a pretty blue?" She nodded. "I bet I can find a blue one." As much as she enjoyed teasing him, his concern was real. "I'll order a pink helmet, don't worry. Safety first."

"Jail." Clay pointed at the squat building near the edge of town.

"Do I get one phone call?" Jordan asked

before tangling her fingers through his to pull him in that direction.

"If we're going to explore, let's start there," Clay said slowly. That was his patient voice. "Save the hotel for another day, one when we have better equipment. Today, let's stick with one level."

Jordan wasn't going to celebrate her minor victory, but the way Clay watched her convinced her he expected her to. "Warmly exasperated. That's what I'm going to call that expression."

He pursed his lips as he considered that. "That fits. You've got a way with words."

Jordan was laughing as Clay ducked down through the jail's short door frame. When she followed him inside, she realized her expectations, fueled mainly by Hollywood Westerns, needed to be lowered. The small square room was mainly dark. One corner of the roof had fallen in, but that was the only light inside.

Dark with a side of dust.

"Where are the iron bars that clang shut behind the train robbers?" she asked.

"Movies. TV. Not much of that in the real Western towns." Clay moved debris aside with his boot to show rotting wood in the floor. "See this?" He squatted and lifted one of the boards to show a deep, dark, large hole underneath. "This was the real cell. Not too many criminals enjoyed a stay in the Post's jail, but some of them got to wait for trial down there. The sheriff could keep an eye on them from a seat on top of the trap door. No escape."

"No light, either. We definitely do not want to find any ghosts in here." Jordan shivered as she imagined that. "No wonder they don't show this in the movies."

"Right. And people who don't know any better might step on the boards expecting floor instead of a fall." Clay raised his eyebrows to make sure she was getting his message.

Jordan took his hand and followed him out into the sunlight. "Okay, okay, I get it. I'd much rather have my own personal handsome cowboy give me the tour of Sullivan's Post. I'm scared straight. I won't explore on my own."

Clay squeezed her hand tightly. "I don't know what I'd do if anything happened to you, Jordan, so I appreciate that concession."

The breathless pleasure that swept over her

at hearing him confess his feelings for her made her nervous. Time for a distraction.

"When you were doing research, what other buildings did you discover?"

The way his eyes lit up as he walked down the open grassy area between the buildings was proof that Clay Armstrong was a major fan of construction and engineering and how humans used both in everyday life. She asked questions about the bank and where the saloon might have been. She studied the squat post office, noticed the planing of the logs and how they joined, as he explained how that had made it so much sturdier to successfully withstand the test of time.

Sometime around a discussion of the window glass and how the second floor of the hotel was ventilated, her eyes might have glazed over because he said, "I'm boring you. Sorry."

"Not one bit. Do you know how long I've wanted to see this place?" Jordan asked. "Sadie was right to keep us away, though. Without you, we might have gotten into something we shouldn't have." She wanted to step up on the boardwalk, but she knew the ride back to the Majestic with a broken leg would be excruciating, especially since Clay would be saying, "I told you so," and driving slowly the whole way. It would be prudent to follow his warnings.

"I love to imagine how it might have looked back in the day when there were people still living here," Clay said.

"Did you find histories of any of the people? Town preacher? Famous outlaws from Sullivan's Post?" She stood on her tiptoes to get closer. "Are any of them still here, haunting unwary visitors?"

His slow smile made her heart skip a beat.

"Not that I know of, but we can't rule it out. Cemetery is that direction." Clay motioned over his shoulder with his thumb. "Want to see if we can find the kitchen ghost some company? A grizzled miner ghost would add some interest to the Majestic."

"Let's wait until we have our helmets. I don't want us to become the latest people haunting Sullivan's Post. Safety always, Clay." Her lips were twitching as he huffed out a laugh.

"In the movies, the center of town is always dirt." Jordan kicked at a clump of grass. "Isn't it?"

He nodded. "Here, too. Lots of people on horses must have been coming and going. Grass will always find a way to thrive, though."

At the suggestion of all those horses, Jordan shivered. "I like UTVs better."

"What is your deal with horses? Did one steal your boyfriend?" Clay asked as he offered her his arm, as if they were on a promenade down the middle of Sullivan's Post, genteel citizens on a leisurely stroll.

Jordan hoped the ghosts were enjoying the show.

"No. It's the teeth. They're too big."

The way he blinked at her.

As if all the words in the world had never combined together like that before. "You know, some days you fit in here like you're a part of the mountains, just natural. And then you say something like that, and I remember you're from LA."

Jordan laughed. "Unhappily raised in the big city, and Denver might as well be California, I know, I know. I wasn't born in a saddle like you were."

"Would you believe that I, too, was born in a Denver hospital? Lived there, bounced around a little before I landed with my foster mother. My first home was an apartment complex in the big city. Can you imagine?" he asked.

Regret swamped her immediately. "Clay, I am so sorry. I forgot. I just… You really are a part of this place, so it slips my mind. I want to take that all back." The hollow spot in her chest made her stop until he caught her eyes and waited for her attention.

"I get it. I accept your apology. It's not a painful reminder now because you are right. This is where I belong, always have." He tugged her closer. "I get it that you don't love horses. I guess. Although, it did shake my mother's faith in how perfect a match the two of us make."

Surprised, Jordan jerked to a stop. "A match? Between us?" Perfection? Did Prue Armstrong truly believe they were perfect together?

He nodded. "Uh, yeah, after you told her about the kiss, you should have been ready to face tactical maneuvers from my mother. She wants all of us married and settled nearby. She loves your sister, and in her mind, there's going to be a big ol' Hearst-Armstrong conglomeration spread out through Larkspur Pass for years into the future."

"But I don't like horses. I don't live in Prospect." Jordan walked on. "When I was a kid, I didn't understand how anyone could live in such a small place. I'm not sure I understand it now. No way is your mother plotting to put us together."

He stepped closer, until his boots nudged her sneakers. "She made up a special container of her stew and corn bread so that she could send me over with it." Clay tipped his hat back. "That was before the revelation about you and horses, but she didn't scrap the plan after she knew the truth."

The flutter of nerves in her stomach distracted her from how he caught up to her so quickly. When she slowed, his hand brushed her hair off her cheek.

"You're going to have to talk to me sometime, Jordan. That last conversation we had, where I laid it all out on the line, put myself out there and you…didn't. That was mature Clay, trying to make sure I had your permission." Clay sighed. "I don't want to kiss you if you've decided it doesn't make sense to give us a shot." His lips curled. "But I do want to kiss you. I forced myself to stay busy yesterday because you never called me—"

Jordan stood up on her tiptoes and pressed her lips to his, so he would stop talking and because she wasn't any clearer on what to do about them or their future. But she was certain that if Clay Armstrong was within kissing range and willing, she wasn't going to waste her opportunity.

When he squeezed her to his chest, Jordan relaxed against him.

She lost track of how long they stood there.

Then the flood of questions that had kept her awake crowded back in.

"Did you mention LA the other night? As if that was an option for us?" Jordan stepped back. "You would absolutely hate living in LA, Clay. Traffic. Smog. There's almost no one wearing flannel. You belong right here in Colorado."

He frowned. "That might be true, but I lived in Denver for years as an adult."

She sighed. "No matter what the mountain dwellers believe, Denver isn't much like California."

He nodded. "No ocean."

Jordan laughed. "Among other things."

"What about your business?" Jordan asked. "The one you've been building in Colorado.

Is it so easy to move all that? What about your business partner? What will they do? Your employees that live here and depend on jobs here?"

"I…" Clay closed his mouth as if he couldn't find the words, but Jordan waited patiently. "This business is important to me. Ever since I was a kid, growing up in the apartment complex and then here with Prue and Walt, I wanted to build something of my own. I'm good at this and I've put all of me into it. Chaney is as rooted in Colorado as I am, but I can't imagine letting distance be the deciding factor that convinces me to let you go. Not again, Jordan."

Jordan couldn't imagine letting him make such a sacrifice for them to stay together, not when his passion was so clear. But life was short, and she was going to take the step she could see today.

"Here's what I want." Jordan pressed another quick kiss to his lips for her own satisfaction. Whatever pain that came tomorrow or later would be worth it. "Today, I want you to kiss me whenever you like."

His smile didn't reach his eyes. "What about the next day and the day after that?"

"I promise I won't leave without telling you." She paused to rearrange the jumble of thoughts in her head. "Tomorrow is too big today." She searched his eyes. "Does that make sense? I just know today. And today, I've had the best day of my life." Jordan gazed at the sky. Did she mean that? The longer she stood there, in his arms, absorbing the emotions that were bubbling but without threatening to overwhelm her, she knew. "Of my entire life, Clay. And I won't leave without telling you I'm going. I am certain of that. Everything else is too uncertain, but I'm okay with that."

Clay tugged his cap down. "I've spent the last years struggling to keep my business profitable, worried about my mom and dad and sometimes my brothers, and you weren't even on the radar. Meeting you here, in this spot and time, feels like it was fate." He shook his head. "I don't even trust fate, but I trust this."

Always she'd struggled to find her place.

She realized she knew exactly what he meant.

Whatever happened tomorrow or next month, she was exactly where she needed to be right in this moment.

"Come back to the Majestic with me. Help me hunt for more dusty treasure." She grinned at the way he groaned.

He was grumbling something about hoping to find a quiet place for a nap when they slid back into the side-by-side. "Would you like to drive us home, Captain Safety?" Jordan turned the ignition and then slipped the helmet back on over her messy hair.

"I would never deprive you of the joy, hot rod." Clay made a big show of gripping the safety bar and pointed down the hill. "Keep it in four-wheel drive until the slope levels out."

"Got it." Jordan maneuvered down the hills until she stopped close to Key Lake to change back to two-wheel drive. It was such a gorgeous day on the lake. It still amazed her that the boating traffic was so low. "Would reopening the marina draw more people to this end of Key Lake?" she murmured as she drove sedately back toward the lodge.

He surveyed the lakeshore. "I think so. Reopening the lodge, running some advertising would do a lot to remind everyone about the boat ramp up here."

"So much traffic that Prospect is missing out on because the lodge closed." She wasn't sure what the observation led to but it was something to add to her lists.

As she pulled up to the lodge, she could see an SUV parked in front that hadn't been there when they left.

"You have company." Clay pointed and said, "That's why you need to keep the doors locked while you're out here all alone. You never know who might show up."

Getting close enough to see the man in the driver's seat cleared up her concern. "That is very true, but I know him."

Clay must have heard something in her voice. "Who is it?"

Jordan put the brake on and pulled off her helmet, as the driver opened the car door. "That is my father."

She didn't have time to see how Clay accepted that because she put her hand up over her eyes to cover the glare. "Daddy, is that you?"

Her father held his arms open wide and she moved closer to slip her arms around his waist in a hug. The way he immediately gripped her tightly and squeezed her close was familiar. He had always been the best hugger. "What are you doing here?" Then she remembered Sarah saying something about a care package. "Did Sarah wrap you up in a bow and send you here?"

"In a way. She filled the back of my SUV with boxes. Some are marked Jordan, one is for the Majestic lobby and the rest say Do Not Open in mean, bold, block letters." Her father ran his hand through his thinning hair. "Guessing that would be Sarah's stuff."

Jordan nodded. "Yeah, she had the same sign on her bedroom door, if I remember correctly."

Her father's attention was locked on what was over her left shoulder. Jordan didn't have to wonder who he was staring at.

"Dad, come meet Clay Armstrong," she said as she led him over. Had she ever been in this awkward spot before? Jordan couldn't remember introducing her father to any other man she'd kissed in her lifetime, let alone the boy who kissed her first and the man who kissed her best.

"Clay, this is my father, Patrick Hearst." The urge to fill in the awkward silence with chatter was strong. Jordan tangled her fingers together and contemplated ways to torment

Sarah as payback for not warning her that her father was coming.

It wasn't that she didn't love her dad.

She didn't want to deal with all the old and new emotions seeing him here at the Majestic stirred up. Forgiving him for sending her away that summer had taken a long time and coaching from Sadie. Jordan had managed it, but the Majestic and Clay... And then there were all these new feelings.

"Mr. Hearst, it's a pleasure to meet you." Clay shook her father's hand and pointed at the side-by-side. "We took a field trip up to see what remains of Sullivan's Post."

"And Jordan was driving." Her father shook his head. "That doesn't surprise me in the least. Growing up, she was my shadow, stepping on my heels wherever I went. When we'd stay here during the summers, she did not let up about driving the boat out on the lake." He shot Jordan a glance. "It's a good thing it was a small boat and the marina had a sturdy dock, isn't it, Jordie?"

Clay's lips were twitching as his eyes met hers. Jordan wasn't sure if it was because of the mention of the sturdy dock or because she drove with confidence and speed, no matter how old she was. But she ignored all that. "I'm an excellent driver."

"She is," Clay agreed gallantly. "If I had a boat, I'd trust her as the captain."

Her father nodded.

Jordan squeezed Clay's hand as her father turned to face the lake. "This place…" When he turned back, he said, "I was sure I remembered how beautiful it is, but standing here, I see that the colors had faded in my memory. Days like today makes me itch for my easel and paints or chalks. It has been a long time since I experienced that."

They were quiet as her father soaked in the idyllic surroundings.

"How long are you staying, Mr. Hearst? If you ride horses, I hope you'll stop next door at the Rocking A. I'll ride out with you through the pass so you can see the fall colors. You came at exactly the right time. We'll be seeing snow flurries before too soon."

Impressed with how…formal and…gentlemanly Clay acted, Jordan waited for her father's answer. She and Sarah had already discussed Wes Armstrong's old-school chivalry. It wasn't harsh, over-protective bossiness, but the care and kindness of a decent man who always acted when he could help. Strength and compassion were at the center. Clay had it, too. This was part of Walt Armstrong's legacy, no doubt.

It was so much hotter than she ever expected.

"I'm not sure. I closed up my shop for at least a week."

"Have you ever closed your art supply shop before, Dad?" Jordan asked.

"No. Fairly sure that's a mistake, but it's not too late to fix it. So, here I am. Sarah told me how much work you're doing around here to make sure the lodge shows well. I wanted to help."

Jordan knew the softening around her heart was a good thing.

"Good timing, Dad. We have people coming to stay tomorrow, including Clay. He's doing renovations on his family's ranch house next door, and his crew isn't too fussy on where they sleep, so…" Jordan waved a hand at the Majestic. "I have clean linen enough for all of us, if you want to make beds. I also have a running dryer, thanks to Clay, so the possibilities are endless."

Her father braced his hands on his hips.

"Well, now, I know how to make a bed. First, I'm going to grab one of these Jordan-marked boxes and carry it inside in case you need a private minute to say goodbye to your…Clay." He nodded courteously on his way into the lodge. "Nice to meet you."

Once her father was gone, Jordan exchanged a long look with Clay until she finally laughed. "This is Sarah's revenge for something I did while she and Wes were all flirty, I know it."

"Does your sister know we're getting flirty, too?" Clay asked.

Jordan frowned as she tried to remember exactly what she'd told Sarah, then she shrugged because it didn't matter. "Sarah knows everything Wes knows. I'm sure of that."

He nodded and pressed a kiss to her lips. "May I be excused this afternoon? Now that you have a helper, I should return to see if there's been any progress on the paint in the ranch living room."

"Are you avoiding time with my father?" Jordan teased and then realized she didn't blame him.

"I can stay if you need me," Clay said.

"You've already been my hero for the day."

Jordan moved toward the back of the SUV. "I'm glad you were here to save me this afternoon. I'm glad you missed me and your mother sent food."

He was laughing as he slid behind the wheel of the side-by-side. "When I call you later, will you answer?"

Jordan's heart thumped as if she was sixteen all over again.

"I promise you I will answer when you call," she said softly.

The soft glow in his eyes lit the answering warmth around her heart. "And you always keep your promises." Clay waited until she reached the lodge's front doors. Getting through this visit with her father would be challenging, but she had her next conversation with Clay to look forward to. Jordan wrapped her hand tightly around the phone in her pocket as she went inside.

CHAPTER THIRTEEN

ON MONDAY AFTERNOON, Clay was so pleased with how much work had been completed by Carlos and his crew on the Rocking A's roof that he was almost light-headed. The new addition should be ready by deadline. Ever since two trucks pulling trailers had rolled up to the ranch before nine o'clock that morning, Clay had almost made a cheering section of one. Instead of clapping wildly, he'd roused every Armstrong in the place to help unload the kitchen cabinets and fixtures quickly before they prepped the roofing materials and got started.

Carlos had put them all to work. He wasn't related to Travis, Grant or Wes, so they had listened carefully and followed his directions to the letter. Clay would complain about that to his brothers later.

Much, much later. Years later, most likely.

The trusses went up so smoothly. The rafters were a breeze. And they'd moved into adding the sheathing ahead of schedule. Clay had hated blowing the budget. Making this call had been a big swing and they'd knocked it out of the park. The return on this investment was already paying dividends as he heard Travis and Grant laughing at something Carlos said.

The sun was setting when Wes stepped out of the fully framed doorway that marked the end of the hallway in the addition. He and Walt had been working with some of Carlos's crew to complete all the interior insulation and sheetrock and the new bedrooms.

"We may have a completed roof this time tomorrow," Wes said. "The difference between the amateurs and the big leagues is drastic. It's hard for a man to realize how poor his construction skills are, but I am ecstatic your pros could ride to the rescue. Left to us, we might not have had a roof come springtime."

That might have been a slight exaggeration, but Wes was right about the difference in watching experts do their thing.

"Time to head over to the Majestic?" Clay asked Wes and climbed down the ladder.

Clay had tried to stay focused all day long,

but he knew he'd been close to pulling a Wes by dropping his hammer on his own hand more than once. Half of his brain was there, locked on the job and the next part of the project; the other half was wondering how Jordan and her father were getting along.

He and Wes had discussed whether Clay should make an appearance for the real estate showing or not. Neither one of them was certain Jordan would appreciate it if he tagged along, and there was still more work to do around the Rocking A before the sun set fully.

Then the interested buyers, Jen and Dwayne Humphrey of Chicago, had a late arrival due to a delayed flight, and they'd stopped to see another property on the way to Prospect. So the midday showing had been bumped to late afternoon and that made Clay's decision easy.

"Carlos, you and the crew head into town for dinner. Faye at the Ace High knows you're on the way. After, we'll get you set up for the night over at the lodge." Clay pointed in the direction of the Majestic. He'd explained how close the lodge was, a couple of miles past the turnoff to the ranch. Carlos gave a thumbs-up and whistled loudly to signal quitting time. Clay yanked off the coveralls he'd thrown on to help battle the chilly wind that had whistled across his back while he'd been up on the roof.

He wanted to see Jordan. He'd missed her all day. Was that going to be his life, pining for her whenever they spent hours apart like this?

Wes exhaled loudly. "Let's get moving. But stay out of the way if you get the feeling the buyers aren't interested in your opinion."

Clay nodded firmly. He could totally handle those orders. "I'm not dressed for negotiations at this point, anyway."

Wes grumbled on the way to his truck. "I'm driving."

When they pulled up in front of the Majestic, Jordan's father stepped outside to greet them. He raised a hand and Clay shot a look over at Wes. "Now the tie makes sense. You're about to meet your future father-in-law. Show me how it's done, big brother."

Wes muttered something but pasted on a smile and hopped out of the truck. Clay watched Wes cross the bridge that led up to the Majestic with his hand held out to shake. Then Clay realized he was going to be facing Patrick Hearst again, too.

By the time Clay followed Wes, Jordan had

also stepped outside. When her eyes locked with his, he saw gratitude. Clay understood she was anxious about how this showing would go, but had her father's visit complicated things?

She waved at Wes before making a straight line for Clay. Her arms were wrapped around his waist and her face was pressed against his chest as he made awkward eye contact with her father. Clay turned them both and urged her to move closer to the lake. He bent his head to murmur, "You okay?"

She sniffed as if she was on the verge of tears.

That scared him.

"What happened?" Clay bent down to stare into her face.

She rolled her eyes and scrubbed her hands down her cheeks. "Nothing. Nothing happened. I just…" She groaned. "I was glad to see you. I didn't know I needed you here today. I was sure I didn't need anyone until I saw you standing there. Then I crumpled like tissue paper. You believe in me. For better or worse, Clay Armstrong believes in me."

Clay pulled her close again, relieved that he'd made the right guess. Jordan might always be hard to read, but he was learning to navigate that. If he remembered to put her first, the decision got so much easier. For the second time, he'd have to thank his mother for that advice without letting her know she'd been right again.

"I do believe in you, but you don't have to sell the place, hot rod. Just be on hand if there are any questions the buyers need answered. Erin Chang has the hard job. She should be nervous, not you."

Jordan nodded. "Right. But I want everyone else to love the Majestic like I do, and I want the buyers to want this lodge, even if I've been imagining her as mine for days." She exhaled slowly. "Even if they have a big fat check in their hands, Sarah and Brooke still have to sign off on a sale. Nothing is final today. That's the part that I've been repeating to myself."

The sound of tires on gravel drifted up the road, so Clay knew their time alone was running short. "How is the visit with your dad going?"

"Fine? I mean, my dad is…" Jordan hunched her shoulders. "He's never been the authority figure." Her tone was uncertain as she untangled her answer. "He does the jobs I point out to him, and he makes jokes, but…"

"There's a lot of history here, and the two of you haven't had a chance to discuss it yet." Clay squeezed her shoulders. "Give it some time. I'm sure you've been working your fingers and his to the bone."

She pursed her lips. "I have. You're right. For some reason, the Summer of Exile has faded a bit in my memory. Batting mattresses with tennis rackets and watching my dad mop every floor in the place might be exactly what I needed to heal." Their laughter must have smoothed her jarred feelings because the smile stayed on her lips. She stepped back. "Sorry. I was losing the threads that keep all these big emotions tied together. Tears? How embarrassing, but I didn't know what I was feeling until I saw you standing there."

Clay entwined her fingers with his. "No apology needed. It's between you and me. No embarrassment at all. Your secrets go with me to the grave." He waggled his eyebrows. "Is that dramatic enough?"

"It's so funny how you have always been the one who could take the mess of this…stuff—" she held her fist over her heart "—and calmly untangle it all. You're like my weighted blanket in human form."

Clay frowned. "That is not sexy. At all."

"Oh, you know you're sexy. All flanneled up and strong and robust from being outdoors all the time." She traced a finger down the line of buttons on his shirt, and Clay was sorry this conversation had started in front of an audience. "It's the emotional support that comes with you that makes you devastating to me." Jordan bumped his shoulder with hers and then marched toward Erin Chang, who was introducing a nicely dressed older couple to Jordan's dad and Wes. Clay knew from Jordan's expression that she had assumed her business persona. All emotions back under tight control.

Mindful of his promise to stay out of the way, Clay loitered behind and tried to come to terms with being called sexy and devastating like that.

A man would never forget hearing those particular words from Jordan Hearst.

She was the kind of woman who made an impact. In the best possible way. He was more certain than ever that she was what he needed and wanted, even if it was like lassoing a runaway mustang. He'd never be able to predict where she was headed, but as long as she slowed down now and then to let him catch up, it would be the adventure of a lifetime.

When he joined the group inside the lobby, it was immediately clear that Jordan had been running a tight crew of two. She and her father must have worked nonstop after he'd left them because they had created something impressive inside. The lobby floors still needed to be refinished, but they gleamed in the fading sunshine coming in through clean windows lining the front wall. The rocking chairs and the table that had snagged Jordan were arranged in the center of the room in a welcoming group on top of the faded but beautiful rug. Sadie's painting was uncovered and drew all eyes in the room.

As her father stepped closer to him, Clay offered the man a hand to shake. "I can tell you have had a busy day today."

Her father sighed. "A man with three daughters learns early on how to keep his head down and trouble to a minimum. All three of mine like to run the plays, you know? Jordan might have taken that to new heights in her determination to get this place ready."

Clay nodded at Patrick Hearst. "I've met Sarah. I've known Jordan ever since we worked at the marina. The only unknown in this equation is Brooke, but I have a feeling I would not want to cross her, either."

"I'd like to blame Sadie for that, but as much as I owe her for getting them to adulthood in one piece, it's hard to argue with her methods or success."

Clay wanted to agree, but before he could, Jordan called out, "Hey, Dad, do you know the artist of Sadie's landscape? The Humphreys are impressed. I told them we couldn't possibly sell it but there might be others out there."

Patrick Hearst ran his hand down his nape. "Uh, no, that's a one of a kind."

Jordan smiled awkwardly at the Humphreys, obviously confused by his answer.

"I painted it." Patrick cleared his throat. Clay wasn't sure but there might've been pink in his cheeks. "Haven't done anything since, certainly nothing that size."

Erin Chang said, "Maybe you should reconsider that, Patrick. It's a lovely landscape." Then she shepherded the group toward the restaurant.

Clay trailed behind them. If Erin Chang had done anything to point out the stains coming from roof damage, he'd missed it. He'd intended to chime in that they were planning to take care of any preventive maintenance before the weather changed.

"I meant to ask…" Her father paused inside the doorway to the restaurant. "That summer, when Sadie showed up at my house with my daughter in her car two full weeks before she was expected, all she ever told me was that there was a boy involved. Jordan had stopped crying by that point, but the tears showed on her face." Her father looked at him suspiciously. "You wouldn't have any information on who that boy was or what he did, would you?"

Clay started to answer, but there was a loud clatter, metal clanging as if it had fallen.

"What was that?" her father mouthed.

From the way Wes and Jordan exchanged a look, Clay was almost certain that the ghost was visiting again.

"I, uh…" Erin Chang pointed to the kitchen. "Maybe pots in the kitchen?"

The Humphreys pushed the swinging door open and everyone filed in behind them. Wes flipped on the overhead lights. The floor and counters were empty.

"It had to have come from in here, didn't it?" Jordan's father was obviously puzzled. Clay could understand that because there was nothing inside that could have made that clatter.

Erin coughed. "That is a mystery. We will definitely have to do an investigation, but let's finish the tour so that you still have daylight to explore the exterior. This lodge is situated beautifully to take advantage of the views but it also blends perfectly with the scenery."

Jen Humphrey nodded. "A little paint, possibly a new metal roof, this place could shine."

Erin hooted with excitement, and the women began talking design possibilities as they moved back into the lobby.

Jordan stepped closer to Clay and her dad. "That was the noise. The one I heard when Sarah was first exploring the day she arrived. What is it?"

They both shook their heads.

"Does this part of the lodge have an attic? Overhead storage?" Wes asked. Clay studied the height of the ceiling and realized that it opened up more options for the location of whatever critter was rattling around.

"When Carlos climbs up to examine the roof, I'll ask him his opinion." Then it occurred to him where the attic access would have to be indoors—in the storage closet where he'd found Jordan wedged into the furniture and celebrating all the treasures she'd discovered. "We'll climb up and investigate after everyone leaves."

Wes nodded and they all rejoined the tour. Jen Humphrey was doing a slow circle inside Sadie's small personal kitchen. Clay was reading the downturn of her lips as the first clue that the property didn't fit all of her expectations. "This is much smaller than I was hoping. Two bedrooms, you said?" She tapped her chin. "And of course everything would need to be torn out and replaced."

Clay studied the cabinets and realized he'd always thought they fit the vibe of the lodge itself. Some people would embrace the aesthetic, call it kitschy or vintage. This woman was not a fan of the retro decor.

It was impossible to tell what Jordan thought about Jen Humphrey's judgment as they filed out the back door to the parking area behind the lodge. The sun was setting, leaving a golden glow in the distance, but they were in the shadows as Erin Chang pointed toward the lake.

"Would you like to walk through the marina?" she asked.

When both the wife and husband nodded, Clay decided that could indicate interest. Why go all the way down the rocky path to see another empty building and dock if they weren't seriously evaluating the business opportunities?

Instead of following, Jordan pulled him aside to whisper, "I didn't know there was a storage spot above the restaurant." She grimaced. "How bad will it be if we find a raccoon living up there?"

Clay hoped that was all it was. "Well, it shouldn't be too hard to clean it up and make the repairs if they're going to buy the building with the plan to reopen it. They'll want to do an inspection, which will turn up a list of things that we'll need to fix."

She chewed her lip as she contemplated that.

"Do you want to catch up to them? Hear

whatever they're saying now?" her father asked from behind them.

Jordan shook her head. "No. It's clear to me that they're interested, but they have their own plans for the place. Which is fine. That is what you'd expect." She nodded firmly as if she were agreeing with whoever had said that.

"I didn't know you painted the landscape, Dad." Jordan moved to press her back to Clay's chest and he tangled their fingers together, content to support her that way.

Patrick Hearst hesitated. "No, well, it's not my usual style, but Sadie… You know that question about what do you buy for the woman who has everything? That was Sadie. She made a huge sacrifice to follow us to LA and take care of you girls the way she did." He tugged his sleeves up and then back down. "I only had one way to thank her, so I tried to paint the mountains she loved."

"Why haven't you painted since?" Jordan asked. Clay could feel the tension in her hand.

Patrick motioned over his shoulder. "When I was working on that, losing your mother was still so fresh. I cried every time I picked up a brush and I was always afraid that I'd never stop sobbing." He sighed. "I didn't want you girls to see that. Of course the tears did stop, and I kept painting. I kept that canvas in the new art store until I finished and…when it was done, I was done painting for a while. I didn't expect it to be forever."

The Humphreys were on their way back up to the lodge.

"As you can see, the siding will need to be refinished or replaced," Erin was saying as she pointed out the worn exterior features. The whole group drifted over to stand next to the restaurant's exterior entrance. "New landscaping will brighten up the facade."

"Place is smaller than we imagined. Wanted more rooms like the first place we toured today, so we could be looking at building on and trying to match the original if we choose this one." Dwayne Humphrey had a hand over his eyes as he peered up at the gable over the restaurant. "New roof, I'm betting. That'll be expensive."

Erin nodded but before she could answer, he asked, "What's that? You have mice in the attic?" He pointed up at the gable.

"Oh, no, absolutely not," Erin said, but even as the shadows were growing, it was easy to see something wriggling out of the gable's slats. A mouse or a rat would also be easy enough to take care of. That's what Clay immediately started repeating to himself, because he'd cleaned up a lot of mess due to his house flipping, but he'd never come to terms with the panic large rodents caused when he found them unexpectedly.

He was prepared to handle a rodent problem bravely for Jordan, if necessary.

But when this rodent in question wriggled out and then flew off, a breathless gasp swept through the small crowd. They watched when the first one was followed by another and another and another, until the flapping of wings cleared.

"Bats." Erin pressed a hand over her mouth, stifling her strangled shout. "You have bats in the attic."

Jen Humphrey, their best hope for buying the lodge to reopen with only updates, had knelt down in the grass and wrapped her arms over her head in a defensive posture. Dwayne Humphrey had one hand on his wife's shoulder as he peered anxiously at the sky, as if expecting an imminent attack.

"We aren't going to deal with bats, no ma'am." He cleared his throat. "Rabies. Bites.

Flying. No!" he lamented, a continuously bobbing head saying no-no-no-no to bats.

Clay was sympathetic.

"Hey, good news! None of us will have to face those bats. They are a protected species. You have to hire professionals to clear out bats." Erin did a bad imitation of a carefree laugh. "The pros will even clean up the guano, which is a hazardous material." She said the last part through her clenched jaw and glowered at the building as she helped Jen to stand. The real estate agent tried to brush grass off the woman's slacks until she slapped Erin's hands away. "I'll get Jordan and Wes the names of companies who handle this sort of thing, and they'll get it remediated immediately. You'll never know the bats were there."

Jen and Dwayne continued shaking their heads no-no-no-no.

Erin brightened. "We'll also include a warranty to make sure if they ever come bat…" She gulped. "I mean, if they ever come *back*, we'll take care of that, too."

"Come back?" Jen asked weakly as she craned her neck to study the pink sky overhead. "When are they coming back?"

Clay couldn't understand what Erin said to calm their fears, but she led them to her car and made sure they were safely inside before she hurried back.

"Bats!" Her eyes were huge. "People frown on bats in the businesses they plan to purchase and live in," she snapped and pointed at Wes. "I'll text you the names of those companies. Call them first thing in the morning to get them here. Bats can only be remediated through the end of October, which is next week! Get this taken care of ASAP." Then she pasted on a professional expression, turned and headed back to her car.

Jordan, Wes, Clay and Patrick Hearst stood there as they watched Erin speed away. No one was prepared to break the silence, but that made it easier to hear Carlos and his crew rolling toward the Majestic.

Jordan's eyes met his. "We can figure out the bats later. Help me get everyone all settled into rooms first." She dusted off her shirt and smoothed her hair back over her shoulder.

Clay heard her say cheerfully, "Welcome to the Majestic Prospect Lodge. You're my very first guests!" when the group drove up.

Wes came alongside him. "She might have a head for this business."

Her father nodded. "She's grown so much from the girl who hid when the emotions got too intense. I don't know if she knows it, but it's clear from this trip to Prospect that the Hearst backbone runs true in every one of my kids. This place brings it out in her. It did at sixteen, too. Thought she'd never speak to me again when I left her with Sadie that summer." He met Clay's stare. "Not sure we've ever been the same since, either, but Jordan is different here. Better."

Clay ran a hand along his jaw, tired and a bit stunned at the way the day had turned out. A real emotional whirlwind that ended with a sheer drop into bat territory, but both Patrick and Wes were right. None of it showed on Jordan's face as she introduced herself to Carlos and his crew. Somehow, Jordan needed to understand she had what it took to connect with guests and make this lodge business a success.

And if flying rodents cleared the way to making that happen, then so be it.

CHAPTER FOURTEEN

ON TUESDAY MORNING, Clay opened his eyes after the best night of sleep he'd had in weeks, thanks to his quiet room at the Majestic. All of the time and energy Jordan had put in over the past few weeks meant his room was clean, the bed was fresh and none of his brothers were snoring or half a second from kicking him in the head on the way to the kitchen. He would give the place five stars, for sure.

He'd bet Carlos and the team would do the same. Then he remembered he hadn't had a chance to talk to Jordan alone after Carlos and his crew had arrived. She had never powered down from host-supreme mode until everyone was settled in their rooms, and neither one of them had the energy to discuss what would come next.

After a hot shower with impressive water pressure, a nice shave and dressing himself with the clothes he'd hung in his own dedicated closet, Clay went to find Jordan.

He tapped on the door to Sadie's apartment and it swung open.

Her father was seated at the island with a coffee cup. "She's down at the dock." He pointed at two empty mugs. "I expected you'd be along, so will you fill these and take one down to her? Keep the other one for yourself."

Clay nodded and moved to the coffee maker. "How is she holding up?"

"She's very quiet. With my girls, that makes me nervous."

When Clay saw Jordan, wrapped up in a quilt and seated in their usual spot at the end of the dock in front of the marina, he was relieved. Whatever finding bats did to her plans, she was still here in town.

"Good morning," he said quietly in case she hadn't heard him tromping over the rocks. "I have coffee."

He studied her face when she turned and he immediately understood that her night had not been as peaceful as his.

"Four and a half stars. That's the review I'm leaving after one night." He sipped his coffee and bumped her shoulder. "Out of five.

Imagine what you could do with a bit of cash and some help."

"Imagine what that rating would be if you hadn't been sleeping on the floor for a week." Jordan clinked her mug against his. "But thank you. I'm glad the accommodations are satisfactory. The bats were a special touch that I threw in at the last minute, a nice effect for the season."

Clay sighed. "Nothing can be easy. You've been on a sweet roll to this point, but it had to end sometime."

This early, before the sun reached the spot where it fully cleared the mountains surrounding Key Lake, the shadows were still deep, but the water was peaceful, mirrorlike as it reflected the sky. This place had a million different beautiful views. Their place on this dock was the best seat in the house.

"Wes will get a professional out here to take care of the intruders, Jordan. You can count on him." Clay straightened his leg out. "Carlos is already loading up the trucks to finish the roof at the Rocking A today. It may be another long one, but tomorrow, we'll get him up there to see what needs to be done after the bats are gone." Clay was already rearranging his schedule on the ranch house so that he could be here when Carlos did his inspection. He wasn't keen on climbing inside to see bats or what they left behind because the only thing that might be worse than mice was mice with wings, but he wanted to get all the information. He'd never worked with another guy as thorough as Carlos, so he trusted the man's opinion completely.

"After all the work I've done to make the lodge show as beautifully as she could," Jordan said slowly, "a bat air display derails the whole thing. The Humphreys did not appear to be as comfortable with wildlife as you or I. They are true-blue city folk, not mountaineers." She bumped his shoulder and chuckled. "What are the chances they'll make an offer now?"

"You don't want them to, anyway. Why would you let that bother you?" Clay studied her face for clues to understand where she was going.

"I wanted my sisters to have a real choice. A decision between the easy option and the perfect buyers versus giving me the keys." She rubbed her forehead. "The Summer of Exile, where you and I fatefully met, I was really angry with my father. You know that. You heard about it. Before you kissed me."

He raised his eyebrows at that. "Or you kissed me, but okay. Continue with the story."

"I was so angry at him for taking my decisions away. I didn't want to move to LA and I certainly didn't want to be in Prospect, away from my sisters, for the summer. I made this silly vow not to let anyone else make my decisions for me ever again."

Clay propped his arms behind him and leaned back. "Doesn't seem silly to me. I get that."

"So…" Jordan inhaled slowly. "I'll have to let go of this plotting out choices for Sarah and Brooke and even you. Why do I think more clearly when you're around?"

The sweet satisfaction that settled over Clay might have been even sweeter if Jordan didn't sound so disgruntled when she said it.

He moved slowly to press his lips against hers. Her blossoming smile relieved some of the anxiety he felt about the distance between them. Then he heard the truck start in the distance.

"I need to go catch a ride or I'll have to walk to the Rocking A." Clay stood and held her hand as long as he dared. "Call me if you need me." He almost believed she would do that today. Things had shifted between them.

She nodded. "Tell your brother he needs to break the bat news to my sister. He's the money guy on this one."

Clay laughed. "I'll do it." He turned to trot up the path when she called out to him.

"Hey, Clay!"

He paused.

"I like it that you're here with me." Her smile was beautiful. "I can't wait to see you tonight."

"When you get sweet like this, I go speechless," he said.

"I know. It's really cute, right?" She was laughing as he ran up the hill.

Carlos was leaning against his truck, tapping at his watch. "Daylight's burning, boss."

"Sorry. I'm ready." He waved at the other truck and slid into the passenger seat.

As Carlos pulled out of the parking lot, Clay said, "You did excellent work yesterday. I can't imagine how we would have ever finished without you."

Carlos scoffed. "This? Easy job. Even had extra help, more crew than usual." He whistled as he stopped at the highway and then drove on when the road was clear. Carlos was a man who was excited to go to work at early o'clock.

"What's the trick to getting those extra hands motivated? Because they were always sneaking away from the job when I was in charge." Clay pulled out his phone as it vibrated in his pocket. "Oh, it's Chaney."

It was awfully early for a business call.

"Hey, what's up?" he said as he answered. There had to be an emergency of some sort.

"Glad I caught you." Chaney's voice was tight with annoyance. "The Russos showed up yesterday, threatening to find more interested partners if we can't make this happen."

Clay studied the yard as Carlos pulled around the Rocking A ranch house. The place was a mess.

"Clay, we need to talk. I'm voting we don't sign, but I'd like to discuss why and what comes next with you." The tension between them surprised him. Was this a conversation about more than the Pagosa Springs golf course? Had he pushed his business partner too far by leaving everything in her hands so he could come back to Prospect?

He owed it to Chaney to have a long talk with her in person, not over the phone, before he decided on a new direction.

He was going to be driving to Colorado Springs today.

"Okay, I'll hit the road ASAP. I should be there by midmorning. I'll meet you out at Fountain Estates."

When he ended the call, Clay squeezed his eyes shut. The day had started out with real promise, but now he was going to dive back into his other mess.

But here, there was his family and the case-worker's scheduled visit. With the updated schedule, they'd pulled back from the cliff.

And the Majestic and Jordan…

All of that would be happening in Prospect while he was in Colorado Springs, putting his business first over her needs.

"I've learned some tricks to managing difficult people," Carlos said as he turned off the ignition.

Clay frowned at him before he realized Carlos was answering his question about how to manage the Armstrong brothers. If he had to guess, Carlos couldn't be any older than thirty, but he ran his business and his crew like he'd been doing it forever.

"Can you share? I'm going to need the help." Especially since he would be managing his brothers remotely from Colorado Springs while he settled this thing with Chaney.

"Confidence." Carlos shook his head. "Mutual respect. You get what you give."

Clay watched Grant greeting Carlos's crew. "And that always works?"

Carlos nodded. "Yep. I'm good at what I do. Treating people right gets you everywhere."

It was a good tip. It wasn't about being the loudest or biggest or meanest boss. Carlos was good at his job and that was enough to lead his crew. "I wouldn't be able to give orders to my own relatives, either, but your brothers heard that I was coming in to save the day. You are paying for my expertise here. Of course they listen. It's not that they don't respect you but the fact that the one they respect holds me up as an expert…" He grinned. "Who would argue with that guy?"

Clay laughed. He wasn't sure it was exactly that simple but there had to be some truth to it.

Clay slid out of the truck and scanned the

yard. "You have anybody who can run your crew on the flip we've got coming up? The one Chaney had to move to get you here?"

"Uh, me?" Confusion wrinkled Carlos's forehead. "Where will I be?"

Clay wasn't sure how it would all work out, but in his gut, he knew he was on the right track. "You ever thought about taking another job, Carlos? Instead of running your own company, you take on projects for me, for us. The title would be site supervisor. Full time with a salary." Clay stared up at the roofline. "Someone who can lead jobs when I'm not around?" He and Chaney needed the help. They had to find a way to make time for this business they loved and their families. "I'll pay you to stay here for the rest of the week, run this job. I've got to go to Colorado Springs, and I can't let any of the balls in the air drop. That means finishing this roof and the bat situation over at the Majestic. Completing the exterior here and the interior renovations, including plumbing for the pot filler that we have to add and a soaking tub, but I can catch you up on all that."

Carlos crossed his arms over his chest as

he evaluated the offer. "And then when this is done?"

"I want a full-time site supervisor who can help keep our projects on budget and on time, while Chaney and I handle the staffing and sourcing, and all that."

Carlos caught his gaze. "I won't do payroll. I hate doing payroll. Like, hate it."

Clay was pretty sympathetic to that complaint, but he'd do payroll if that's what it took to hire someone he knew he could trust. "You won't be doing payroll."

"And all my guys?" Carlos asked. "Took me a long time to find them. I'd be a fool to let them go. You would, too."

"We'll keep them busy," Clay said and wondered if he was going to be able to hold to that promise. "And if we can't, you and I will re-examine our agreement."

A broad grin covered Carlos's face as he offered his hand for Clay to shake. "A trial period, then. Let's go."

The relief was overwhelming as Clay shook his hand.

Carlos yelled, "Oy, TJ, we need to talk about your future, man."

Wes walked up as Carlos trotted away.

"Early start again. Bringing him in was the best decision we've made all along on this project."

"*We?* You may be right, big brother." There was a glimmer of hope that he would navigate this mess of projects without sinking any of the ships on the water. "I'm going to Colorado Springs to handle a problem there, but Carlos will be staying on to complete the renovations. You all seem to work better for him, anyway. Nobody sneaks away for 'important business.'"

"We'll find a way to afford it," Wes immediately said. "Yes, this will work for all of us."

Clay grimaced. "Thank you for not bringing up my promise to see this through. I…" He felt rotten to leave but it was the only option now.

"You're still seeing it through. Never mind about regrets now. You have a solution to the problem, and we'll make the deadline with Carlos. With you in charge? It would have been a razor-thin finish."

Was he going to argue that? His pride wanted to but the realistic part of him knew it was a weak side.

"He's on deck to help with whatever we

need with the Majestic, too. Jordan may never speak to me again for leaving in the middle of…" There was too much, so he held his hands out.

"You'll figure that out, too," Wes said firmly. "I expect you'll struggle, but this Hearst and Armstrong matchup, these relationships, were built in the stars or there's something or someone else weaving us together."

"There is no ghost, Wes. It was bats. You were there." Clay laughed.

"Couldn't it be both?" Wes was whistling as he left and went over to speak to Carlos.

Clay knew he had to get on the road. There would be so much to do when he made it to Fountain Estates, but he didn't want to leave. Going back to work had never been a problem, but Jordan…

"Hey, Jordan said you have to talk to Sarah about the bats and the money," Clay called out to his brother's retreating figure.

Wes gave him a thumbs-up. "Already taken care of, little brother."

Wes was reliable. Clay was reliable. They all could be depended on.

Breaking the news to Jordan was the only hurdle that remained. He stared at his phone and watched the time ticking away. He called and propped one hand on his hip as he paced in a circle.

"Hey, forget something?" she asked as she answered, pleasure in her voice.

"No, but I've got a small emergency in Colorado Springs, so I'll be heading back there earlier than I intended."

When she didn't respond, he said, "Wes is already on top of the bat wranglers. I promoted Carlos, so he will be here to finish up the house and the roof at the Majestic, longer if necessary."

"Are you not coming back?" she asked calmly.

So calmly that Clay frowned hard at his phone in disbelief. "Jordan, of course I'm coming back. I'll resolve the problem and do some work, but I'll be back in Prospect by the weekend."

"Oh," she said. "Okay. Okay! I was afraid you had come to your senses. No way anyone should be giving out stars for the accommodations here yet. Let me put in a continental breakfast at least."

That was a Jordan response, through and through.

The humor was a shield that kept her safe from hurt, but it hadn't done anything to protect him.

"You thought that's how I would leave you? A phone call saying, 'Oopsie, plans changed.'" Irritation bubbled up. "When I get back, let's have a conversation about what promises mean and then we can make some. To each other."

The tense silence on the line had him rethinking his plans for the day, but eventually Jordan whispered, "I'm ready when you are, cowboy." And then she ended the call.

Clay wasn't sure how to make it clear that the inevitable had already happened for him. He'd fallen for Jordan Hearst, for better or worse. On the drive to Colorado Springs, his attention bounced back and forth, from Chaney and his career in the big city, to Jordan and Prospect and the next chapter of his life.

When he slid out of the truck at Fountain Estates, he was annoyed and worried and determined to set the whole world straight and fast.

Chaney was waiting for Clay outside the last lot to be finished. She was talking to the cement guys where they were pouring what would be a decorative patio around a beautiful pool. After the supervisor nodded and walked off, she said, "You made good time."

He nodded. "Show me around." He pointed toward the house. His plans for this subdivision had included "affordable luxuries" like high-end finishes, media rooms, wine cellars and butler's pantries, depending on the options chosen, but all in a smaller square footage than other manor homes.

He had always loved this step, when the interiors were finished except for the minor fine details because it was clear this house was going to be a comfortable home.

"Do we get your seal of approval?" Chaney asked once they climbed the steps into the small, cramped trailer that operated as their business office on every site.

"Absolutely," Clay replied and found his favorite mug in the tiny dish drainer next to the sink, right where he'd left it. She pulled out the coffeepot and filled his cup to the brim. He and Chaney had a rhythm because they'd worked together for so long. Some of his worry faded when they settled right into it.

"I know we've been dreaming of a project like this," Chaney said as she turned her laptop to face him, "but these guys don't have enough history to show they can develop a project this size. I didn't turn up any smoking guns, lawsuits for unpaid bills or anything. I didn't find much at all, which is also a red flag." She bit her lip as she waited for him to scan the short listing of filings in the Russo name.

Clay sipped his coffee and relaxed in his seat. "The suits were a warning, weren't they? Flashy. Not like us." She was dressed in flannel and jeans. They might have been twins.

Chaney let out a laugh. "I've been losing sleep over walking away from this, Clay, because of my gut feeling. Please gnash your teeth over the loss of revenue or something to justify that." She settled back into the ragged office chair she moved from trailer to trailer, job site to job site, as they grew their business.

For so long, it had been just the two of them. It made sense they were both exhausted.

"Remember when we started this by flipping those tiny gross apartments? What was that place called?" Clay asked.

"You mean when we were living off of oatmeal and peanut butter we bought in bulk because every penny was wrapped up in the current flip? It's been ten years and my husband still refuses to eat a PB&J for lunch." Chaney wrinkled her nose. "That was the Chateau Something-or-Other. I never heard a man scream in real life until that day."

"Listen, I didn't know rats were terrifying until that day, but I will scream every single time one runs across my foot." He grinned at her as she laughed. "Hey, I am not ashamed." This was part of their thing, their history, the pieces that connected them and strengthened the friendship that the business was founded on. She knew he was terrified of rodents and thought less of him for it, but it never stopped her from standing by his side.

"We set out to make something we'd both be proud of and we've done that. Your husband misses you. My family needs me. This won't be the last time one or the other of us has to step away for a minute. Is it time to take another look at where we're going?" Clay asked.

"This new direction you are suddenly interested in pursuing wouldn't be about a woman, would it?" Chaney pursed her lips. "One who happens to be in Prospect? Carlos mentioned

how warm and welcoming the lovely proprietor of the Majestic was, and how important
to you it was that her roof was repaired as
quickly as possible."

"Is it a problem if it is?" he asked.

Chaney scoffed. "No way. It's about time,
partner. You've gotten old and boring. You
no longer live for the adventure of economy
apartments and drive-through cuisine. Sad."

He wanted a solid comeback but then he
realized she was right. His priorities had
changed. It had happened. "I hired Carlos to
be our site manager. He's going to finish up
for me in Prospect. While he's there, let's figure out what our next project is to keep Carlos and the crew busy."

Worry immediately crossed her face. He
understood that. They were stretched thin
financially already. This would be another
burden.

"Listen, if this doesn't work for you, it's
okay. We can…" Clay wasn't sure how to fill
in the blank.

She rolled her eyes. "Break up this partnership? Not likely. You need me too much."

"I cannot argue with that," he said and
meant it.

"This is our territory, the one we agreed on in the beginning." She stood to point at the map of Colorado and a rectangle they'd drawn in with a red marker. "Pagosa Springs is outside the boundaries. We never should have considered it in the first place." She tapped a small square west of Highway 85, closer to Denver. "So, here's my idea, land we'll pour every bit of profit from this development into to buy, plan, and build ourselves. We've got flips to keep the crew busy in the meantime."

"That's a lot of risk." Clay watched her pace. Neither of them were unaware of the risk of gambling their own money again.

"It is. That's what we said when we took this on and look at how well it's turning out." Chaney grinned. "At least it will be nice to be closer to home."

He frowned. "Where is home now?"

She grimaced. "Good question. I have all my mail held at a post office in Denver. Does that count? Kai has been daydreaming about a garden off and on for months. Maybe we should find a place with more outdoor space than a balcony." Chaney held up a finger. "Let me pull up our strategic plan. If we replace 'world domination' with 'time with family and a garden for my husband,' then it's easier to imagine the next five years."

Of course she was already plotting five years ahead. Clay was just glad she was still his partner. Chaney loved strategic planning, so he got up to pour more coffee. They would both need it.

One quick check of his phone showed that he'd missed no calls. Talking with Jordan was his next priority, but he wanted to be with her to do it. In the back of his mind, he had been mulling over what she had said about choosing to reopen the Majestic. She'd wanted her sisters to choose her over another good option, not accept her as the default. Being able to choose was so important to Jordan that she wanted the same for other people.

When he got back to Prospect, Clay would let her know that he wasn't making his decisions alone anymore. Whatever he did next would involve her.

And he wouldn't have it any other way.

CHAPTER FIFTEEN

AFTER CLAY CALLED to tell her his plans had changed and he was going back to Colorado Springs, Jordan sat on the dock and tried to come to terms with her disappointment. She didn't want to face anyone yet. Losing his support left her shaky, until she realized how silly she was being.

Clay might not be sitting next to her.

His room at the Majestic would be empty for a few nights.

But Jordan was certain she could still count on his support.

Even if their conversation had been short and succinct, Clay Armstrong had made sure his brothers, his parents and his…Carlos were all on deck to step up. No one would be able to replace him, but his team was strong.

Then she realized Clay had made one of her biggest concerns disappear. He'd put his own needs first when he absolutely should have.

What a relief. Jordan was excited to see the sun rising. It had been a long night, but everything was getting clearer. He'd been the example she needed. Jordan was going to put herself first, just as she'd promised herself at sixteen.

She picked up her phone to text Clay. He'd be on the road, but she wanted him to know that his "inevitable" was growing more inevitable for them by the minute. After puzzling how she'd explain that in a text, Jordan realized deep thoughts like that were better communicated in person.

Besides that, she had guests staying in the Majestic. They might not be able to enjoy the full amenities, such as the lodge had once offered, but putting out clean towels and making the beds was completely within her skillset. Her father had proven to be helpful around the place, so it was easy to keep them both occupied.

And it was the simple first step to being the Majestic's full-time, permanent manager.

Her idea to recruit her dad was scrapped when she made it up the path from the marina and saw that his SUV was no longer parked next to her car. Apparently, he'd left? Jordan was still searching for an answer when she found the note propped against her laptop on the kitchen island. "Gone to Prospect. Be back with lunch."

The promise of lunch lifted her spirits, but the funny porcupine he'd doodled along the edge of the paper made her happy. This porcupine was obviously a silver miner. He was wearing a helmet and had some kind of tool hanging over his shoulder. Jordan wanted to call it a pickax but she wasn't certain why. Mr. Porcupine was whistling cute, bouncing musical notes, so he was definitely on his way home from work.

In Denver, both of her parents had been artsy. Her mother had had a studio at their house where she'd dabbled in so many different media, whatever struck her fancy. When she'd died, Jordan had hidden away there because that was how she wanted to remember Beth Hearst; she'd always been so happy in her studio.

Until her father had confessed to painting Sadie's mountain landscape, Jordan hadn't noticed he'd stopped painting. There hadn't been any funny doodles since, either.

Her mother's death had changed everything. Of course it had. Sarah had become the mother and their guide. She and Brooke had become mortal foes except under strain and duress that required them to team up. Jordan had struggled to contain the hurt and anger and made bad decisions.

And she and her father… They'd never fully closed the distance between them. This time in Prospect could be the first step.

The package Sarah had sent along from Sadie's lawyer was on the island next to her computer. If Sadie had done the same thing for all three Hearst sisters, there was going to be a thumb drive with a video inside.

Jordan rubbed the ache in her chest as she tried to convince herself that crying as she watched would be expected. No one would blame her for the emotional storm then, and she'd almost learned to trust that tears didn't last forever. This could be her only chance to watch it alone.

"Don't be a coward, Jordan." She opened the package, took the card out and set it down to stick the thumb drive in her laptop. As the computer was uploading the file, she settled onto one of the stools. The file icon appeared as she jumped down to run into the bathroom to grab toilet tissue. There was no sense in being unprepared for tears.

Then she clicked it to play.

Sadie's beautiful face filled the screen and Jordan's eyes immediately welled. Jordan knew the pain would soften with time, but it was still sharp.

"Well, now, if it ain't my favorite trouble-maker." Sadie's dark eyes twinkled as she pointed at the screen. Despite the hospital bed, her unnaturally dark hair and bright red lipstick made it seem impossible to imagine that Sadie Hearst had ever been sick a day in her life. She never aged, thanks to careful salon choices and frequent visits. That might have been required for a woman who spent her life on television, but Sadie would have done the same if she'd stayed a lodge owner in Prospect. Her spirit had never aged. She was making sure the outside matched the in-side.

"I bet your little heart is broken." Sadie frowned. "And mine is, too, Jordie. Know this, I ain't even gone and I already miss you. You three are all my favorites, but there's some-thing about you, the one who'd stare right at me with the devil in her eyes. You kept me sharp, my girl, and there ain't too many who can say that."

Jordan wiped her running nose. How embarrassing.

"When my handy lawyer made a suggestion that I tape these goodbyes…" Sadie tapped her lips with bright red fingernails. "I said to myself, 'This man hopes you're going to tell these girls what to do with the lodge so they don't pester him with questions.' Ha! You, me and Howie Marshall all know that he gets paid a fine retainer to answer all those questions, so I say treat him like one of them search engines. Time, weather, the definition of *tomfoolery*, all are within his purview." She cupped her hand over her mouth as if she had a secret. "Don't you tell a living soul this, Jordie, but I don't know the answer to the question. You are as shocked as I am, I'll vow, because neither one of us has ever seen that happen, me without the answers. I couldn't decide for myself. I certainly can't decide for you three." She sipped the glass on the hospital tray in front of her. "Remember when you yelled at me that day your daddy dropped you off and sprayed gravel to get back home? You were in my spare bedroom, the one I grew up in and might have yelled in more than once. It wasn't fair that you didn't get a choice in your life."

Sadie waved her fist. "You were right. It wasn't fair. Your mama died and your daddy struggled. He still struggles, honestly, and all three of you had to do things that weren't fair. This lodge can't be one of those things. So, quit your worrying about me and what I'd do. I bet you found half a dozen signs to support both sides. Forget that. You do what you want."

Jordan rubbed her forehead. It was like she was sitting across the table, and Jordan hated that she'd been so predictable.

"If you sell that place, do something wonderful and know that I'm beaming down at you." Sadie shook her head. "Well, I might be a tad embarrassed by whatever you get up to, but I'll get over it. And if you stay right there in Prospect, and fall in again with the rascally cowboy who got you so worked up at sixteen, well…" Sadie chuckled. "I want to say I told you so. But you, you weren't ready for happily-ever-after then. Fate or destiny robbing you of one or two exciting broken hearts by shoving that happily-ever-after at you in the marina that way? Unfair. Jordan Hearst was meant to make mistakes. They make the victories so much sweeter, my girl."

Sadie's wicked grin flashed. "But if that cowboy lays another kiss on you that shakes you to your soul, don't you run away this time. You grab his ears and you don't let go, you hear? Promise me, Jordie, because that don't happen every day."

Her lips were twitching. "This message is only to say this choice is all yours, Jordan." Some of the amusement faded. "I know you three, and I am telling you that your heart has to take the lead on the Majestic. Sarah and Brooke are depending on you here. Take the step you can see and let the worries fall away."

Sadie rolled her eyes at whoever was holding the camera. "I know! I know we talked about file sizes and all that mumbo jumbo. Hold the camera straight and let the professional work." She huffed out a breath. "Jordan. I love you. I'm proud of you and the decisions you've made. Your heart won't let you fail." She pointed a finger. "But I am there with you wherever you go, and don't you forget it. Love you. I also know you didn't even read that funny card I got you to dry up those tears. Do it now."

The video ended with Sadie's lovely face frozen on the screen.

Jordan sniffled as she reached for the card. For every birthday and Christmas gift, Sadie had insisted Jordan read aloud any cards before tearing open the wrapping paper, so they would all know who the gift was from. Jordan had always been too impatient, so it made sense Sadie would give it one more shot.

She paused when the faint scent of vanilla surrounded her.

Jordan lifted the card and was instantly reminded of Sadie's hugs, the way her kitchen always smelled.

The faint touches that teased her here and there at the Majestic even after all this time.

"Sadie?" Jordan said before she could rationalize the urge away. Ghosts weren't real. Clay and the group had discovered the logical reason for the weird noises in the restaurant's kitchen, even if the source of this scent was still a mystery.

It was a good thing no one was watching her talk to a ghost that definitely did not exist.

When she pulled the card out, there was a

picture of a donkey in a straw hat. Hay was dangling out of his grinning mouth. "Why do donkeys talk with their mouths full?" Jordan read and wanted so badly to groan because she knew there'd be a pun inside, but there was no one around to hear, so she flipped open the card. "Because they have bad stable manners." She closed her eyes as it landed. Her hunch was right, a terrible pun had been inside, but it was also so typically Sadie that it was bittersweet. Sadie had signed the card, "Love you, Jordie. Don't be a donkey's hind parts. Take the first step."

The amazing thing about Sadie Hearst was that she could say the hard things in a way that made Jordan hear them and take them in. There were no signs. Sadie hadn't left clues behind for Jordan to decipher.

And Sadie's sunshine cleared all the fog away.

Jordan wasn't going to wait on the Humphreys to make an offer. She wasn't going to let Sarah take the lead and smooth things over with Brooke. It was time for her to be brave, summon her courage, be like her great-aunt Sadie.

First, Jordan would take care of her guests. She was going to need the practice.

Second, she would draw up a list of things she could do immediately to get the lodge open and earning some revenue, even if it was a bare bones operation. They would make slow, steady improvements over time.

Third, she would tell her sisters officially that the Majestic was back in business.

Jordan made decisions. She didn't let others choose for her, not anymore.

She grabbed the CD player that had saved her life the Summer of Exile, clipped it to her jeans, slipped on the headphones and hit Play, so George Strait could keep her company while she worked.

Methodically, Jordan picked up dirty towels and replaced them with clean ones, straightened up bathrooms and made the beds for all five of the roofing crew. She stopped abruptly at Clay's door. She slowly opened it to see that he'd already made the bed himself before bringing her coffee at the dock. His clothes were neatly hung in the closet. She missed him, but he was coming back.

Jordan marched out and pulled his door closed behind her as she got a text. When she yanked her phone out of her pocket, the excitement she felt over a message from Clay transitioned when she realized it was a text from Wes. He'd copied Jordan, her sisters, Clay and a number she didn't recognize.

Talked with the insurance company. They will cover a substantial portion of the remediation efforts and some repairs required, but I'll meet with the adjustor over there this afternoon who can tell me more. Got a company lined up to come in tomorrow to start working on the bat removal.

He'd put a bat emoji at the end to keep the message light. Jordan appreciated that.

I'll set up a phone call for the day after and we can discuss the money required for this and the roof repair estimate Carlos will draw up tomorrow or the next day.

Sarah immediately texted back, Thank you, honey.

Jordan laughed when Clay added, Yes, sweetie, you're the best.

Brooke sent, Good job, bro.

Jordan wanted something clever, but the longer she waited, the cleverer it had to be. Eventually, she settled on, I knew we could count on you, with the vampire emoji. She would only torment herself the longer she waited to talk with Sarah and Brooke, so she added, Sister call in 3, 2,…

And waited for her phone to ring.

Sarah was the first on the video chat. As she added Brooke, she said, "Not sure the Armstrongs are ready for us, but a group text is a nice way to ease them in."

When Brooke had joined them and they were all able to see each other, Brooke said, "Jordan, bats?" She wailed and pressed her hands to her cheeks. "Move out of there. Go back to town. Don't become a bat victim."

Laughing with her sisters felt so good that she knew she was on the right track. "I mean, I've been here a month or so without running into a bat ever, so they might feel the same way about me."

"Was it terrible, the way the people from Chicago left?" Sarah asked. "Wes thought it was over the top, their reaction."

Jordan sat on the stool again. "The way Jen Humphrey covered her head as if the bats were dive-bombing her like Hitchcock's birds was interesting, but at the time, all I could see was our best hope running away."

"You're over that now." Brooke wasn't asking a question.

"I am. It's time to reopen the Majestic." Jordan held up the list she'd started. "I have my plan of attack, all currently 'no money required' until the bat situation is settled. We have guests staying here. I can get you comment cards if that will convince you that I can do this, but the first thing I want to do is show you what I've accomplished with my own two hands and help from Clay."

The urge to keep talking, to avoid any questions or concerns was hard to defeat, but Jordan settled back to wait for Sarah and Brooke to say something.

"We can figure this out, a way that it fits all of us," Sarah replied slowly. If the three of them were together, instead of staring at a screen, both she and Sarah would be fully focused on Brooke.

"Baby sister needs to be coddled again, I see." Brooke inhaled slowly and Jordan realized she was sitting in a coffee shop. "I'm thrilled I took a break to answer this call. I have a job, you know. It's part-time and it's making fancy coffee, but I had to start somewhere while I figured out the rest of my life."

Sarah raised her eyebrows. "You? Are working in the service industry?"

Jordan laughed at the way Brooke squawked. It was amusing to imagine her greeting customers, as she had one of those faces that made every thought in her head clear for all to see.

"For now," Brooke said ominously. "The guy who hired me seems to hope I have a big future in this industry." Her grimace was hilarious. "Somebody needs to set him straight. I'm the woman for the job."

When the chuckles died down, Brooke said, "We're keeping the Majestic. I'm happy about that."

"But you were sure if I did this and it didn't work out, I'd bail and leave Sarah to pick up the pieces. Isn't that what you said the first time we talked about the possibility of my wild notion?" Jordan asked. It hadn't even hurt to hear it because Brooke's concern was valid. Jordan had a history of leaving, but there was something about the Majestic that made it easy to believe that all that leaving had been because she needed the right place at the right time, and now she'd finally found it.

"I spend too much time worrying about the future. Don't be like me." Brooke fluffed her ponytail. "You'll never hear me say that again."

"Life in Prospect is a whole lot cheaper than life in New York, Brooke. We'll divide the funds that we've been holding from the sale of the pastureland to the Rocking A, so that you get a payout now. We don't know yet when the rest of Sadie's estate will be settled." Sarah had assumed her managerial tone. Business had gotten real. "I know someone has been interested in her LA house, but my crystal ball is on the fritz. Hard to predict the future."

"Paul continues to be the south end of a northbound mule about our divorce settlement. I'm making rent from the savings I had, but selling coffee won't keep me going for long. I may have to come up with a solution faster than I hoped." Brooke sighed. "But not yet. Everything is okay for now. Do not kidnap Jordan and jump on a plane yet."

Sarah held up her hand. "I promise to let

you know before I kidnap Jordan for plane travel."

"So, let's take a tour of the polished Majestic," Brooke said. "It has been so long, I can barely pull up memories."

Jordan hopped down and listened to her sisters complain as she juggled her phone. "I'm in Sadie's apartment, which is clean and ready for visitors whenever either of you needs a place to stay. Eventually, we have to do some updates, get new, more comfortable living room furniture, decor, things like that, but it's not a priority." She slowly panned the kitchen and the bedrooms so they could see how the surfaces gleamed. "The lodge's guests have clean mattresses, bedding and towels. Eventually the bathrooms will need renovation and the floors should be refinished, but for people who want to primarily fish on the lake…" Jordan stood in the hallway and swung Clay's door open to show them a guest room. Then she turned the camera around.

"Whole lot of plaid flannel in that closet, Jordie," Brooke said. "You also have a cowboy on the premises?"

Jordan headed for the lobby. "Not now. That

particular cowboy had to go back to Colorado Springs for a spell."

Silence filled the space on the call until she returned to the screen. Both of her sisters had moved closer, so she was getting a good view of both of their noses. "That's all I know about that. Clay is coming back, but he has a successful business hours away so he couldn't stay."

Her sisters sighed in unison, but Jordan ignored it.

She'd stepped into the lobby. Jordan was proud of herself and what she'd accomplished. It was still so sparely furnished, but it was clean. Neat. And it reminded her of the way Sadie had loved it.

"Oh, yeah, there's the rug," Sarah said excitedly. "I knew there was orange and yellow going on in there." The windows were filled with bright sunshine and the leaves on the trees were hanging on for a little longer.

"Wow, you have been working hard," Sarah said. Jordan was pleased at the awe in her sister's voice. Impressing Sarah meant something.

"I haven't done much in the restaurant because I'm out of my league in there." Jordan knew if she reopened the lodge to paying visitors, she'd need some kind of solution for food.

She stared at the space and mulled over the possibilities, and realized she could handle a breakfast bar without much struggle. Lunch and dinner would be in town for now, but she might be able to stock snacks for sale at the counter.

That led her to the marina...

"Whatever you're trying to answer in your head right now," Sarah said, "it's too far down the road. Come back right here."

Brooke wrinkled her nose. "You had the weird grimace you get when you try to do math, Jordie."

Jordan snorted. "Fine. That's as far as I've made it. I'm going to get Dad to help me hang Sadie's painting behind the desk today. I've been dying to see it up there where it belongs ever since Sarah brought it from LA."

Both of her sisters nodded.

"Do it." Brooke was determined. "If I get evicted, I might be moving in sooner than expected. Breaking and entering into my ex-husband's fancy new place is my last resort, but you two will provide the alibi I need." She waved. "My boss. He's telling me break time is over. Gotta go."

After Brooke hung up, Sarah said, "She sounds better, doesn't she?"

"Yeah, thank goodness. I wasn't sure she was sleeping at all the last time we talked," Jordan said.

"I'm hoping to be back in Prospect before Thanksgiving. Let's celebrate the holiday there," Sarah said.

"Dad will approve of that suggestion, for sure." Jordan moved over to the window that overlooked the parking lot. Her father's car was there. He had returned from Prospect.

"How is the visit going?" Sarah asked.

"He's been helpful. No big emotional discussions, but a pair of hands for whatever job I ask him to tackle." Then she turned the camera so Sarah could see him. "He's out there painting."

When Sarah didn't say anything, Jordan turned the camera back around to see her sister's face. "Did you know he painted Sadie's landscape? It was a thank-you for..." So many things. "I guess for everything. He said it hurt to do. He hasn't painted since."

Sarah said quietly, "I should have paid closer attention."

Jordan smiled at her sister. "We all should have, or he could have talked to us about why he wasn't painting and we could have grieved together, instead of—" she motioned between them "—becoming who we are today."

"I'm glad he's painting," Sarah said. "And I'm glad you're reopening the lodge."

Jordan nodded. "I'm glad I have a smart older sister who has a lawyer for a boyfriend who can help us wade through the financial and ownership questions that are going to come up. You talk to him about that."

Sarah beamed. "If I have to."

"Right. Like you need any reason to talk to your 'honey.'" Jordan channeled her annoying younger sister tone to tease Sarah because it was fun.

Sarah tipped her head back. "Do you want me to torment you with questions about Clay?"

Jordan quickly replied, "I do not. I don't have any answers. Instead, I'm going to go make Dad talk to me."

"Good plan. I have a budget spreadsheet to finish so we can decide how to pay for your pet bats."

Jordan groaned as Sarah hung up. Then she moved to the double doors. She wanted to speak to her father.

His sheepish expression as she stepped up next to him caught her off guard. "Everyone gets a fifteen minute break before they have to return to laundry, Dad."

"Fine. That's all I need to find out I forgot how to paint," he said. "I was never good at landscapes, anyway." He offered her the brush as he always had when she was a little girl. "See that tree? Paint it in."

Jordan was certain any talent she had would have made itself known before now, but she could try if it would make him happy. She studied the dark trunk of the tree and its slant out toward the sunshine and lake before dipping her brush in the paint. She carefully dragged the brush down, doing her best to follow the lines.

"Very good. We can both practice, improve our landscapes," her father said cheerfully.

Jordan was not fooled. Painting was not her talent.

"Seems like Sadie and a couple from Chicago with a fear of bats would disagree about whether you're good with landscapes, but everyone would say I am not." Jordan wasn't a painter but she understood fear. She squeezed his shoulder. "A little bit of practice. It'll come back to you." He'd always promised her all she needed was practice, even when she crashed his boat into the marina's dock. "Got a lot of rooms that need artwork. I cannot pay with money, but it will guarantee exposure. To people who like fish, so practice painting a bass or a pike. Trout? I'm listing fish I've heard of here."

He chuckled. "You're doing fine. How long have I got? Until the Majestic reopens under Hearst management?"

"Sarah says Western Days is our goal, but I'm gonna open the doors as quickly as I can to get the revenue started. Brooke may need it." She smiled. "I'll make sure I have a room open for you at Thanksgiving." Jordan wished she'd brought her own chair over. The lake was still but the sun was bright and the brilliant reds and golds lining the bank were spectacular. This was a scene that deserved to be remembered when the snow came.

Her father glanced up. "Not even Halloween and you're making plans for Thanksgiving? I like it."

Something about the word *Halloween* triggered an idea. "Are you interested in entering the high school's costume contest with me? I have the perfect outfit in mind to let everyone know the Majestic is coming back."

Her father seemed to hesitate, but he agreed.

Ready to dig into the storage closet again, Jordan bent down to press her lips to his cheek. "Thank you, Dad."

"You're making me nervous about this costume. Am I going to be a walking trout?" he asked, chuckling.

"Would you do that for me?" Jordan asked. That was real sacrifice.

Her father wrapped his hand around hers. "I would do anything for you, Jordie, even break my own heart by bringing you here and driving away."

Jordan knelt in the grass next to him. "I'm sorry I was so angry. I have been so angry for a long time and it wasn't fair, not to you or Sarah." She tilted her head to the side. "But Brooke..."

Her father laughed.

"Cats and dogs the two of you and exactly like Sadie in different ways. It's a miracle I got you both to adulthood without your mother." He leaned closer. "You don't owe anyone an apology. You were right. Nothing was fair about losing her. Sadie saved us then and she might be saving us again."

Jordan hugged him. "Thank you for coming back to Prospect, Daddy. I didn't know I needed you here, but it made all the difference in the world."

"I agree. I've discovered a few things myself." He pointed at the canvas in front of him. "I like painting landscapes even if I need practice. I don't miss LA at all." He exhaled slowly. "And Prospect's craft store, Handmade, is amazing, but the paint department needs expansion. One size of canvas and a starter set of acrylic paints do not make an inspiring art section."

Jordan rested her head against his arm like she had when they had fished together. "You'll have to pack up some supplies and leave them here the next time you come, so you will always have what you need when you visit."

Her father tapped the paintbrush before setting it on the plastic plate he was using as a palette. "Or..."

Jordan turned to face him.

"I could take Prue Armstrong up on her offer to help out with the store, expand that paint section," he added as he studied her face. "I'll need plenty of time and inspiration if I'm going to provide artwork for the rooms of the new Majestic Prospect Lodge."

Jordan leaned back on her heels as she considered that. "You're moving here?" The joy that bubbled up inside surprised her.

"Not *here* here," he said as he pointed at the lodge behind them. "We need more distance than that, but finding a place to rent in Prospect seems right. Prue knows a guy who can help."

Jordan laughed. "Wes is going to be so busy with all this Hearst business." Then she hugged her father tightly. Sadie was giving every single one of them a second chance.

"So count me in for Thanksgiving and for Halloween contests." He squeezed her arm. "No smelling like a fish, but anything else is on the costume table."

Excited about all the plans forming, Jordan hurried inside, a vision in her head of the two of them walking together through the crowd in Prospect. She had a lot to get done before Saturday night. Jordan pulled her phone out of her pocket. No message from Clay.

"He's busy, Jordan." She chewed her lip as she considered her options. The cool thing to do would be to...do nothing.

But she'd never been cool and neither had he, so she typed, Hey, cowboy, hope you get home soon. Before she could second, third or fourth guess herself, she hit Send, shoved her phone in her pocket and went to find hidden treasure.

CHAPTER SIXTEEN

CLAY WAS TIRED but jittery with anticipation when he drove into Prospect on Saturday night. It had been four days of playing catch-up in Colorado Springs. His and Chaney's first order of business had been to plot out their next business steps and cram a third desk into the trailer for Carlos. Clay had done payroll, signed invoices, met with their accountant too many times.

He and Chaney had also celebrated handing over the keys for three brand-new, sparkling properties that day, with her husband Kai manning the barbecue for the whole crew. The food had been good and the company even better, but then he'd said his goodbyes, thrown his portfolio, laptop and stacks of files onto the truck's passenger seat and taken off for his hometown. Carlos would finish up the flips and the lots in Fountain Estates under

Chaney's supervision, then everyone would enjoy a week off.

The last time he'd made the drive to Prospect, he'd had nothing but problems to solve. Tonight, the solutions were falling into place like dominoes, one after the other, leaving him with only one knot to untangle.

As he passed the straw bales and friendly scarecrows that decorated Bell House, he noticed a trail of kids in costumes trickling out of the Mercantile. Lucky and Dante Garcia were dressed as hot dogs; each was carrying one of the twins, one dressed as a bottle of ketchup and the other mustard.

Clay had never been much into the costume contest, but it was easy to imagine being roped into participating by Jordan. It might even be fun the way the Garcias were doing it.

At some point, his mother had convinced one of his brothers to make her a display of jack-o-lantern wood cutouts to line the street in front of the store. This year they were all painted white and had light gleaming from their eyes.

His mother used to hang bat cutouts in the windows, too. They were missing this year.

Was that a concession to the Hearst sisters and their recent discovery?

If he had to guess, Jordan was somewhere in the crush of people gathering in the park behind the Mercantile. He'd spent a lot of time in the wide-open grassy field growing up. Every celebration was centered on Sullivan Park.

He noted the Halloween banners and decorations marking the park entrance, and the sign pointing to the high school's costume competition happening soon.

Clay tipped his cowboy hat up as he studied the milling crowd, searching for Jordan. It was nice to see the people gathered around the line of tents at the north end. He'd missed the chili judging, but the high school kids were doing steady business selling bowls to the people lined up there.

Wes maneuvered his way free of the crowd with a big bowl clenched in his hands.

Clay grabbed it before Wes spotted him and took a bite. "Thanks, big brother."

Wes's glare was hotter than the jalapenos dotting the chili in Clay's bowl. "I thought I felt a certain wind blow into town. Come on. Everyone's over here."

Clay ate half the chili in the time it took to wind through the crowd to where his parents were seated. They had front-row spots for the costume contest. When Clay leaned down to hug his mother, Wes yanked the bowl out of his hands and grumbled when he saw how little was left.

"I wasn't sure you'd make it back in time. You missed the kids, but the adults will be promenading any minute. Then the pets." His mother clasped her hands. "That's the big finale every year."

Clay flopped down in the grass at her feet, too tired to stand until the finale was over and he could search the crowd for Jordan. His mother put a hand on his shoulder. "You seem tense. How was the drive?"

He was so anxious to get back to the Majestic, the warm shower, the comfortable bed and Jordan nearby, he hadn't paused his journey for a break. Not even a short one. "I'm fine, Mom. Better now that I'm back here with…you all."

"All right, friends, we've got one final round before we get to the stars of the show." Matt stood at the judges' table.

"Is he wearing a costume?" Clay leaned

over to ask Wes under his breath to ensure his mother didn't hear them interrupting her baby boy.

"Yep," Wes said as he scraped the sides of his empty chili bowl. "Take a closer look."

Clay studied the black fabric that draped over Matt's shoulders. When his brother extended his arm to announce the first contestant, Clay could see Matt had wings. "Is he a bat?"

Wes nodded.

"Too soon," Clay muttered but swallowed the chuckle that welled up.

Clay picked at the grass under his legs as he watched Rose Bell walk down the center of the large field in front of the judges. She was wearing a jersey, shoulder pads and a helmet marked with the faces of her favorite Broncos. She was followed by three famous princesses, Abraham Lincoln in a tall black hat, an astronaut, a bumblebee, Dr. Singh wearing face paint, big floppy shoes and a clown nose, Faye dressed as a banana and…

When Jordan and her father stopped in front of the judges, Clay sat up straight. Patrick Hearst was decked out in a bucket hat with a hundred lures dotting it, a bright blue fishing vest over a Denver Broncos sweat-shirt and overly large waders. He had a fishing pole propped on one shoulder, and he was dragging a small cardboard boat, decorated from one end to the other, anchored to his foot with each step.

Jordan might as well have been sixteen again. She was wearing the T-shirt everyone who had worked at the marina had worn as a uniform so many summers back. It was white with bold, sweeping black letters advertising the Majestic Prospect Lodge. She had a red gingham apron wrapped around her waist, just as Sadie had always worn, and a braid dangled over each shoulder. Her bright red lips curved in a beautiful smile.

Jordan and her father were taking this opportunity to tell Prospect that the Majestic was coming back.

Matt held both of his arms out to make sure the bat effect was clear. "Now, then, if it's not one of the new owners of the beloved Majestic, Jordan Hearst. She's the spitting image of our own Colorado Cookie Queen, and we are pleased to welcome the Hearsts back to town." The crowd clapped and cheered. Jordan squeezed her dad's arm. She was thrilled to be there and Clay was so proud of her.

After the judges conferred and somehow named the bumblebee the winner of the contest rather than Jordan and her dad, the decked-out duo headed their way.

Jordan paused in front of him. "Hey."

"I like the costume. You should have won." Before he could find a better response, Matt was announcing the lineup of pets who were ready for their fifteen minutes of Halloween fame.

Jordan sat in front of him, as if that was always her spot, and leaned back against his chest. Clay decided he could relax a minute, enjoy the evening. He wrapped his arms around her and soaked in the way she laughed at the trio of Chihuahuas dressed like great white sharks, with ominous fins and tiny faces surrounded by pointed teeth. A basset hound lumbered behind the barking shiver of sharks, enjoying the attention he got dressed as a sub sandwich, complete with lettuce spilling over his tail. Clay wasn't exactly sure what kind of dogs came next, large hound mixes, but one was Elvis, and the other two wore jerseys like Rose's.

Jordan tilted her head back. "I'm glad you made it in time for the fun."

He studied her face. "I wanted to get back to you. It's been a long week."

"Did you see your brother's costume?" Jordan shook her head.

"I did. He's a menace, but don't let my mother know I said that."

Matt announced the winner, Elvis the hound dog, and the crowd started to disperse slowly.

"Jordan, I'm planning a big breakfast over at the Rocking A as soon as Clay clears the kitchen for entertaining," his mother said. "If you can get away from the lodge, I do hope you'll join us."

Clay wasn't prepared when his mother shot him a pointed stare. "I hope we'll be seeing a lot of Jordan, Clay."

He ducked his head as she hugged his neck. His father clapped him on the shoulder and offered his mother his arm.

Everyone paused when they noticed the way Patrick Hearst and Rose Bell were chatting, heads close together as if they were sharing secrets.

Then his mother slowly smiled. "Jordan, dear…" She motioned Jordan closer. "Has your father talked to you about our plans to expand the paint and art materials at Handmade?"

Clay watched Jordan cross her arms over her chest and lean closer to his mother. "He has."

"And is your father single?" his mother drawled.

"He is." Jordan grinned. "Should I make him put up a dating app profile to see if he and Rose are a match?"

As his mother studied Rose and Patrick, with her lips pursed and her eyes cataloging details, Clay considered warning Patrick.

His mother said quietly, "Doesn't look like that will be necessary." Rose and Patrick had swapped phones and were entering numbers.

When Patrick turned back to the group to find they were all watching, he said, "I'll meet you at the car, Jordan. I'm going to walk Rose back to Bell House. We're discussing the Broncos' new quarterback."

Jordan held her car key out to her father. "Clay, would you escort me home?"

Clay shook her father's hand and nodded. "Yes, I would love that."

Prue patted Jordan's hand. "We'll talk." Then she and Walt followed Rose and Patrick down the street. Jordan turned to him.

"Do you remember what you told me about this?" she asked and tapped the brim of his cowboy hat.

He nodded. "Special occasions, like business deals and important first dates."

"Which one is this?" Jordan asked.

Clay wrapped his arms around her to tug her closer. "Last first date of my life. Pretty special."

Jordan frowned. "Who is the lucky girl?"

"Will you join me at the Prospect Picture Show next weekend?" he drawled.

"I will. Wear the hat," Jordan replied.

ON THE WAY back to the Majestic, Clay drove with his left hand and held her hand with the other. "Last time you were in my truck, you would have jumped out at the first wrong word. Remember that?"

"Always ready to run," Jordan agreed.

"I like this better." He squeezed her fingers.

"Me, too." They bumped along in the truck, him trying to sneak peeks at her, and her smiling back at him.

When they made it to the lodge, she asked, "Are you up for a walk down to the dock? It won't be warm enough much longer to stay out and watch the stars." She'd been thinking of how she wanted to stake her claim on Clay Armstrong for days now. This was her chance.

"Love to." He followed her up to Sadie's quarters and waited for her to unlock the door. Inside, she grabbed the large basket she'd discovered in the lodge's magic storage room. Before she could click on the flashlight she'd stacked on top, Clay took the basket from her. "You lead the way with the flashlight. I've got the rest."

Since that fit perfectly with her plans, Jordan followed his directions happily. "In the springtime, I'm going to put a firepit over there." She pointed and realized there was almost no way he could see her finger in the shadows, but it didn't matter much. She was making plans for months ahead. He needed to know that.

"You're going to build a firepit." There was no question in his voice, but Jordan was suspicious. "I've been watching videos on the internet. It doesn't seem that hard."

When they made it to the dock, she shined the light in his face and watched him blink. "You don't think I can?"

He set the basket down and pressed his lips to hers. "I know we can. That's all that matters."

Jordan pressed her lips tight as she considered that and realized it was the perfect answer. Why was her nose burning as if tears were on the way?

"We were going to talk about promises, right?" she asked. "You were going to promise me you wouldn't leave without saying goodbye. That's only fair."

Jordan took the two quilts from the basket and pressed them into his arms before removing the fat pillar candles she'd discovered at Homestead Market. She placed them around the end of the dock and lit them, pleased at how they glowed in the dark night without obscuring the brilliant stars overhead.

He moved closer to her and said, "That's your promise to me. *You* won't leave without saying goodbye."

"Right. And I'm still standing by it." Jordan shook the first quilt out and draped it over his shoulders.

Clay wrapped his arms around her. "My promise is I am always coming back to you."

Jordan clutched his shirt. "You're moving to Prospect?"

"Yes, if that's what works best for us, for now, I'm definitely spending more time here and looking forward to it." He tilted his head to the side. "My business partner and I have a new setup, a different strategy for future growth for our company, but that's not what I meant."

Jordan waited.

"You can be here or in LA or Denver or New York." Clay tugged his hat off, so Jordan could read his eyes clearly. "I'm always coming back to you, Jordan. It's not the place that matters. It's you. I can figure out everything else."

He settled down next to one of the dock posts and pulled her into his lap so that they were both staring out over the dark lake. Jordan spread the second quilt over them and leaned against his chest. "That's a brave promise." Jordan tangled her fingers through his and held him tight. "Do you remember telling me Prue and Walt wouldn't let you fail?"

He nodded.

"You make me feel the same way. I can't imagine ever walking away from that again," Jordan whispered, the big emotions overwhelming her but his hands, his arms, their embrace, held her safely until she realized and accepted that everything was right in her world.

"Do you have cookies in this basket?" Clay asked. "Because…"

Jordan could smell vanilla, too. But she wasn't interested in discussing the reality of ghosts.

"I made one more promise." Jordan leaned into him. "To my great-aunt Sadie."

Clay pressed his forehead to hers. "What was that?"

"If the cowboy who shook me up at sixteen ever kissed me again," Jordan whispered against his lips, "I would grab his ears and not let go."

Clay was chuckling when Jordan ran her fingers through his hair and urged his head down for another kiss. For the first time, Jordan knew what she wanted: Clay Armstrong, and a home she made for herself, where she would always belong.

And thanks to her great-aunt Sadie and Clay, she knew how to build it right here at the Majestic.

* * * * *

For more great romances from author Cheryl Harper and Harlequin Heartwarming, visit www.Harlequin.com today!